THE SECRET

of the

GREEN ANOLE

JAKE SHUFORD

D1739177

Publishing Services provided by Paper Raven Books
Printed in the United States of America
First Printing, 2020

ISBN: 9798690455323

ACKNOWLEDGEMENTS

My sincerest gratitude to Louise Shuford Rak, Harrison King, and Ryan Clifford Messinger for taking the time to read a very rough first draft and giving me the insight and encouragement I needed to continue down this journey.

Thank you to Tobey Designs, who delved into my mind and created the amazing artwork for this novel. Your illustrations truly bring the pages to life and I can't wait to collaborate again.

Kevin Anderson and Associates, the editing company who took my work to the next level. Thank you so much for putting up with my countless emails and phone calls. Your professional advice is what I needed to turn my rough draft into something special.

To my wonderful family, whose constant motivation inspired me to keep pressing the ink to the page. Thank you for everything!

DEDICATION

I dedicate this book to my family and friends, for the line separating them is blurred.

To my dad, for gifting me with the competitive spirit and instilling in me what it means to work hard.

And to my mom, to whom I don't say this often enough….. "I LOVE YOU!"

TABLE OF CONTENTS

PROLOGUE

"*H*ave a nice night, Brandy! Any fun plans for the weekend?" the hospital's front-desk clerk asked while tipping his winter hat.

Brandy clocked out from her final hours of the week and released a sigh. "Nursing sure as hell takes it out of me. I'm going home, lighting a fire, then properly ignoring everyone until Monday morning."

Outside, snow was falling in heavy clumps and moonlight reflected off the flakes within the clouds, casting a gray glow over Denver. Ice crunched under Brandy's boots as she trudged along the sidewalk toward her car, her breath turning to white frost when she exhaled.

Since she'd arrived a few minutes late to work, Brandy had to park farther away than she usually did. Now, when she approached the end of the block, she had to squint to see the cross signs, her eyes watering from the frigid mountain air whipping across them. Snow had crusted over the tops of the street signs, so the letters depicting 9th and COLORADO were barely visible.

Brandy took a right and headed down 9th Street, feeling the wind pick up. She tightened her winter jacket and zipped it all the way up so that her chin was covered. She passed an empty alleyway, abandoned but for the hospital trash waiting to be disposed of. When she peered down the alleyway, all she saw was darkness. The wind funneled down the empty passage, and the deserted street seemed to gulp the disappearing white snowflakes whole. Brandy shuddered, unsure whether it was from the cold or the fear of the empty unknown.

She flipped her hoodie up and continued tramping through the winter elements. Her parked car on the opposite side of the street came into view, and she stopped to fumble for her keys inside her pocket. When her fingers felt the familiar plastic and metal, she whipped the keys out of her pocket only to watch them disappear in the accumulating snow below.

"Shit!" Agitated at her clumsiness, Brandy knelt down and started to dig where she thought the keys had fallen.

All Brandy heard was the wind's howl, growing louder until the alleyway behind her gobbled it up and spat it out at the buildings across the street. Then, the familiar crunching of ice under boots resounded from down the block.

Brandy swung around and saw a hooded figure peering out of the alleyway; only a head was visible, as the rest of the body was still obscured by the wall. Terror seeped into Brandy's bones, but the hooded figure didn't move—it just stood there, observing her.

"Can I help you?" Brandy yelled, trying to force her words past the brisk wind.

The hooded figure didn't answer. Instead, it glided from out of the shadows and onto the sidewalk before taking curious steps toward her.

Brandy looked down as she frantically continued digging for her keys. At last, she pulled the keys out of the snow and rapidly pushed the unlock button on the key fob, her car's headlights flashing in response. She got back to her feet and sprinted toward her car, hearing the ice shattering under her boots with every step.

Then she glanced over her shoulder. The

mysterious hooded figure was running after her, the splintering of ice from beneath its Timberlands cackling into the air in a duet of breaking ice and sleet.

Nervous sweat rolled down Brandy's back as the sound of the person giving chase grew louder. She kept running. Finally, she got to her vehicle and threw her hand on the car door; her fingers reached for the handle, but the reflection in her window caused her to freeze: the cloaked person was standing right behind her.

Brandy felt a sting on the side of her neck and the cold immediately faded away as a synthetic warmth enveloped her. She pawed feebly at the car door, the muscles in her arms forgetting how to work, until she fell back into the snow no longer capable of feeling its iciness.

Her wide eyes stared blankly into the twilight sky as the hooded person dragged her into the alley where its blackness swallowed them both whole.

ISAAC

CHAPTER 1

———— ◆ ————

THE INTERVIEW

*A*t first, there was nothing.

Then Earth, Wind & Fire's guitar entry, followed by their famous horn introduction, blasted out of Isaac's headphones. The trees drooped from the heaviness of snow, but Isaac's feet skipped to the funky beat of "Shining Star" and carved fresh footprints in the powder.

Isaac was still not used to the temperamental Colorado weather. On snowy days like today—when the frosty wind helped comb his well-groomed hair and the cold made him button his flannel all the way up—Alabama felt a long way off.

Like most millennials, Isaac was glued to his

phone. His periwinkle eyes first absorbed the national news reports, as he slowed to a walk. Then, after checking the sports scores posted at the top of the screen, Isaac scrolled down to the local news, turning down the volume of the brass horns as he scanned the missing person report. He would typically skip this section, and in fact generally avoided negative news stories, but recently there had been more disappearances in nearby areas.

Isaac paused and shut the music completely off while he read about the nurses who had gone missing in recent years. One woman was last seen at a hospital only a few blocks down the street, close to the hospital where he worked. He thought about how it must feel to be kidnapped, and an eerie chill crept up his spine. Aware that he couldn't be late for his appointment, he glanced at the digital time on his phone screen and saw he was making good time; he turned the volume back up and continued walking, the music controlling his limbs as he tangoed down the snowy path.

Fifteen minutes early, Isaac walked into the coffee shop and found an empty table. Sitting down ungracefully in one of the open chairs, he shuffled for his resume and placed it on the table before him. The scent of lavender and chai wafted into the air and up his nostrils, offering his mouth a preview of what was to come. The smell of freshly ground cocoa beans with a trace of pumpkin permeated throughout the room, and the hissing of milk being steamed made Isaac's stomach roar. A woman walked past him holding a hot cake, the smell of the icing causing Isaac to remember the coffee-shop trips he'd taken with his dad when he was a kid.

As he waited, thoughts of his preadolescent years churned in his mind. While growing up, Isaac had believed that if he made impressive grades in school, graduated from a prestigious college, and found a good job, the rest of his life's puzzle pieces would automatically fall into place. He couldn't have been more wrong.

Once Isaac received his bachelor's degree, he started to realize how little of the real world he actually knew. Trying to find a decent job in a saturated market with little to no experience had proven nearly impossible. His dad had supported him throughout school, but the money stopped when Isaac threw his graduation cap into the air. The memory of the hat drifting down to the ground and landing in the dirt at his feet whirled now in Isaac's mind as he sat in Starbucks waiting for his interview to begin.

Isaac logged into his Wells Fargo app and, upon seeing such a paltry number in his lonesome checking account, sighed audibly. He loved being a registered nurse, but living in the heart of Denver was sucking his resources dry.

The entrance bell jingled and was followed by a fresh breeze, prompting patrons to clutch their warm mugs. The man who entered stood for a moment inspecting the people at their tables until his eyes fell on Isaac. In recognition, the man grinned and rubbed his hands together before taking a few steps forward, carefully avoiding the coffee addicts' foot traffic.

"Isaac?" the man asked, raising an eyebrow as he thrust out his hand for a shake.

Isaac studied the man, trying to match his face with the image of the man he had seen online. "Yes sir, you must be Dr. Tim Hill. I appreciate you taking time out of your Saturday morning to meet me here. It means a lot. Can I buy you a coffee?"

Dr. Hill appeared nervous as he looked around the shop, before taking the chair across from Isaac.

"No, but thank you! I'm usually a coffee drinker, but recently I've been taking a tolerance break. Drinking a whole pot to myself doesn't give me the effects it used to! Plus, I'm saving the environment. Less peeing means less wasted water from flushing toilets, amirite?" He chuckled at his own words, then clasped his hands and set them neatly on the table in front of him. "All righty then, shall we get started?"

Isaac nodded. The caffeine-fueled anticipation had caused his hands to feel clammy. "I know I submitted my resume online, but here it is again if you need to reference it."

Dr. Hill glanced briefly at the resume, then picked it up, rolled it into a ball, and shouted "Kobe!" before draining it into the trash can.

Isaac noticed the words *Always One* on Tim Hill's wedding ring when he brought his hands back to rest on the table.

"Why are you here, Isaac?" Tim asked, snatching Isaac's attention away from the ring.

"I need a second stream of income to pay the bills, sir. I saw your posting on Craigslist for work on weekends and potentially more, and it fits my work schedule perfectly. My main job is Monday through Friday, so it shouldn't interfere with . . ."

Dr. Hill waved his hands to silence Isaac. "I saw on your resume you took business classes in college, so I'm assuming you're a businessman. Sell yourself to me, Isaac. Go."

The abrasiveness of the question caused instant alarm in Isaac, but whereas most people would freeze in the scenario, Isaac thrived. Working all day in an operating room had taught him to remain calm in even the most alarming situations.

Isaac took a deep breath, then regurgitated the lines that had been so successful for him in the past. "I'm the hardest worker you'll ever meet, sir. I don't have a wife or a girlfriend or kids to distract me, and my family lives far enough away that I hardly see them. Plus, my references are all top-notch doctors who will vouch for my rigorous work ethic."

Dr. Hill scratched his stubbled beard, seemingly mulling over Isaac's words. "Why would I hire someone who doesn't communicate with their family often or have a significant other? How does that make you a superior candidate?" he asked, tilting his head in response.

Recognizing the challenge, Isaac set his own hands firmly on the table, his knuckles turning white.

"Because I will be one hundred percent dedicated to you and your family, and make sure I exceed all of your expectations."

Dr. Hill sighed and looked down at his own folded hands. Long, dramatic seconds passed, then he looked up and grinned widely. "I've got one final question for you, Isaac. Do you happen to know your blood type?"

CHAPTER 2

❖

THE HILLS' HOUSE

"*L*ast surgery of the week," the surgeon announced, while tying his mask securely over his face. "Let's make it count."

The patient lay in a supine position on the table; every part of his body except the site of operation, his left ankle, was draped in blue surgical cloth.

"Isaac, can you pull up his X-rays on the screen?"

"On it." Isaac stood up from his stool and headed to the computer. After logging into his hospital admin account, he pulled up the X-rays.

The surgeon squinted his eyes as he looked at the computer monitor. "Yep, pretty sure this is just a fibula fracture. His syndesmosis looks fine. Thanks."

Isaac logged out of his account, watching the black-and-white images disappear. "What's a syndesmosis?"

The doctor made an eight-inch incision along the outside of the patient's shinbone. As he scraped away excess tissue and flesh until his blade touched the broken fibula, he explained, "The syndesmosis is a slightly mobile joint between two bones, in this case the tibia and fibula. Connective tissue resides between the two bones, helping them move together as a unit. In every ankle fracture surgery, you should check the syndesmosis to make sure the joint isn't also sprained."

The surgeon placed a retractor on the outside of the incision to spread the skin apart; the broken fibula was brought into plain view. "Nice, perfect transverse break. Easy to fix. I need the lobster claw, please."

"Here you go," the surgical tech said as he handed over a small pincer-looking instrument from the instruments displayed on his back table.

The surgeon placed the lobster claw right where the bone was broken in half to hold the two pieces together and free up his hands. Once the two pieces were secured, he held a ruler up to the fracture and measured the break. "Let me see a seven-hole straight plate. This patient has a nickel allergy, so I'll need the titanium one."

The tech moved the stainless-steel instruments and implants to the side and grabbed the titanium ones. After digging through numerous surgical tools, he finally retrieved the seven-hole plate and handed it to the surgeon.

The surgeon positioned the plate on the patient's fibula, shifting it until it fit over the fracture site. "Excellent. Guide, then drill, please."

The surgical tech pulled out the drill guide and handed it to the doctor, who screwed it onto the plate's first hole. Next, the surgeon slid the drill down the guide and turned it on, the flutes tearing though bone and creating a small pilot hole. When the drill and guide came out, a depth gauge was inserted into the hole to measure its length.

"Hmm. Looks like it's thirty-two millimeters," the surgeon said.

The tech pulled out the appropriate-size titanium screw, placed it on the driver, and handed it to the surgeon. "Here you go."

Isaac heard the crunching of bone as the screw locked the plate in place. "Just want to clarify, we used a size thirty-two, correct?"

"Yes."

Isaac scribbled the screw size on the patient's implant log for his medical records.

"Guide, then drill again," the surgeon said, his hand already awaiting the instruments.

The doctor, the tech, and Isaac repeated the process six more times, until all seven holes had screws affixing the plate against bone and locking the two broken fibula pieces together. "All done. Let's close him up!"

The tech handed the surgeon the staple gun and the incision was closed, and the plate and screws sealed sterilely in their new home. "Good work, everyone. Isaac, do you have anything planned for the weekend?"

"No, sir," Isaac lied.

Saturday morning, Isaac bounced his fingers off the steering wheel in rhythm with the song on the radio as his car tires ground over the gravel driveway. As he made his way through Green Mountain Village up to Tim Hill's house, Isaac eyed the trees lining the driveway. When the mansion finally came into view, he parked his black Toyota Tacoma and got out, his breath frosty and his eyes wide as they gazed on the magnificence of the home before him.

Two massive stone gargoyles welcomed him as he approached the behemoth of a house that sat on acres of wildwood alongside the village. Dark ivy crept up the statues and ensnared the beasts. When Isaac approached them, the gargoyles' concrete eyes seemed to follow his every step, giving him the impression they were guarding some secret.

The style of the house was contemporary, but a dullness secreted out of its many-windowed walls. Through the glass, Isaac could see the contortions of pearly white staircases, which looked like they acted as dual backbones for the ten-thousand-square-foot house.

Isaac hopped up the winding stairs toward the entrance, avoiding the snowy mud puddles trying desperately to stick to his shoes. He didn't know if he should fear or admire the house, which felt like a gigantic entity: a beast within the woods.

Twin columns spiraled up to the roof and held the house together like Atlas did the world. A mouth hung from the center of the door, a metal knocker jutting out of the wolf's snarling metallic jaw. Isaac took a deep breath and put his hand on the cold metal, unsure of what to expect on the door's other side.

After lifting the knocker from the wolf's mouth and letting it fall, Isaac was startled by the loud bang it let loose—a sound that resounded throughout the woods and filled the frigid air with a vibration that surely notified every organism of his arrival.

When Dr. Hill opened the door, the whole house gasped. A dominating presence almost throbbed through the trees of the surrounding Colorado woods. But when Isaac looked up, or rather down, at Tim, he saw nothing but a quirky short man with an off-angle smile.

"Isaac!" Dr. Hill said, his face lighting up. "Welcome to my humble abode. Please, come in!" He twisted around and marched back into the house. With the air thinning around him, Isaac watched his new boss walk away.

Isaac returned the smile and stepped inside. "The pleasure is mine, Dr. Hill."

Tim's cheeks were rosy from blushing. "Please, call me Tim. None of that Dr. Hill bullshit in this house, understand?"

At this, Tim licked his hand and smoothed back the tufts of brown hair lining the perimeter of his head so as to conceal the hairless center.

Isaac shook Tim's non-licked hand, which felt clammy, then, after an awkwardly long period of time, slippery from the moisture.

"Love the wolf-head knocker," Isaac said when Tim finally let go.

"Oh, it's my favorite," Tim boasted. "Now, hold tight for a minute while I gather the rest of the pack."

As Isaac waited, he observed the artistic details of the house. Seemingly priceless pieces of art hung on the walls, reminding Isaac of the richness of a great European cathedral. Statues of armed gladiators and knights guarded the entrances to multiple hallways that snaked deeper into the house. The ceilings were adorned with hand-painted murals of angels and demons fighting a war over the kingdoms of heaven. Vases on small decorative tables stood in every corner, the flowers drinking in the natural sunlight flowing through the enormous windows.

Isaac looked across the living room and saw a wondrous adjoining kitchen, its magnificence shadowing a door in the wall opposite the front entrance.

The sounds of footsteps echoed down one of the hallways until, one by one, Tim and the rest of the Hill family marched into the room. There were four in total: Dr. Hill and his wife, and a boy and girl.

Tim took a step forward and cleared his throat. "This is my wife, Hanna. She was a waitress, until the arthritis in her knees flared up." He put his arm around his wife and smooched her on the cheek. "Add in kids using her as a jungle gym," he said, winking at Isaac, "and the result is a lot of pain."

"What an entrance, Tim . . ." Hanna teased. "But nice to meet you, Isaac, and thank you so much for your help. You're such a dear! I can be a bit slow in moving around, so I appreciate you taking on the job." She used a small wooden cane to help her stand straight, the veins in her hands squirming underneath her skin.

Isaac could tell Hanna had been beautiful in her youth. She would also have been taller than Tim, though her present hunched-over frame and the cane torquing under her weight made this difficult to believe.

The sound of Tim's voice whipped Isaac away from forming conclusions about Hanna. "Next is my son, Twain. He's ten but reads more books than the rest of us combined."

"Hi," Twain muttered in a voice almost too hushed to hear. Twain took after his father in height and appeared shorter than other kids of his age. Square hipster glasses sat on the bridge of his nose and covered most his face, and a black eye patch was positioned over his left eye. After introducing himself—and unlike his father, from whom confidence oozed—Twain silently filed back in line with the rest of his family, apparently grateful his time in the spotlight was over.

"And the most-beautiful-daughter award goes to Sammi!" Tim announced, pushing the girl out in front.

Sammi looked how Isaac imagined Hanna must have when she was younger. Sammi was fifteen years old, but her ego seemed to expect adult treatment. Unlike her mother's weary gray, Sammi's hair was long and blond and draped over her shoulders like a feathery waterfall. Every few seconds, Sammi whipped out a small mirror, which caught the light and blinded Isaac, and ran her opposite hand through her hair to make sure her beauty wasn't fading.

"Dad, I'm your *only* daughter. I have to be the most beautiful! Do you know that I'm the most gorgeous woman in the entire neighborhood, Daddy?" Sammi said as she stepped out from the line and curtsied.

"Just don't forget who you got it from," Tim replied, his face filling with admiration before turning to Isaac. "And I'm the chieftain of this tribe of misfits," Tim Hill said, puffing out his chest and putting pressure on the buttons of the flannel shirt already visibly stretching across his belly.

The entire family was goofy, each with their own quirkiness. Tim was still pretending he was chief, slapping his hand over his mouth and making strange noises while Sammi repeatedly asked her mother if she looked good in her pajamas. Twain stood uncomfortably distanced from the rest of the family, observing them with his one good eye.

"All righty, Isaac, you ready for a tour?" Tim asked, interrupting the one-eyed ocular scan his suspicious son was currently conducting on their guest.

Hanna rolled her eyes. "You always have to give the tour, don't you?"

"Well, I'd let you do it, but we pay Isaac by the hour and you aren't as fast as you used to be, my honey bunches of oats." Both kids laughed as Tim walked over and kissed his wife again. "You know I'm kidding," he said, smirking. "You're doing much better now."

"Thanks to you," Hanna replied, rubbing the tip of her nose against his.

Sammi looked the other way. "Ew, gross!"

Tim led everyone into the kitchen, where a large marble island sat in the middle of the room. Intricate metal artwork hung from the ceiling where pots and pans were magnetized to the metal and suspended in the air. An artisan-carved mahogany table filled the rest of the space, its wooden gleam reflecting the sunlight that streamed in through the windows. Isaac pictured late-night beer bottles littering the island, which drew in everything with its gravitational pull.

Isaac picked up on the statue theme when they passed another one that guarded the corridor leading to the master bedroom. The armored knight's gear sparkled from the luminescent window above, which illuminated the entire hallway. When they arrived at the master bedroom door, Tim rubbed his hands together eagerly. When he opened the door, Isaac's jaw dropped. It was a room, but it wasn't a room at all. Isaac took a deep breath and smelled lavender and other scents of the evergreens. Vines and flower petals dangled from the ceiling and the sounds of the rainforest echoed through the air. It was as if they had left Colorado and entered a woody overgrowth, a master bedroom at its center.

Columns at each corner of the bed reached the ceiling, with twisting snakes and serpentine vines slithering up them. The bathroom included a clawfoot tub the size of a Jacuzzi and a frameless shower made of stone. The shower was equipped with a twin-head faucet that rained down jungle-like storms.

Tim continued to loop around the house, showing off his man-cave basement that was perfect for watching sports, workout room equipped with surround-sound Sonos speakers, and second floor that featured three bedrooms: one for Twain, one for Sammi, and the third that acted as Tim's office. The perfect house for the perfect family.

Isaac's favorite feature was the art appropriately positioned in every room. Paintings of gazelles and zebras lined the hallways and pranced from room to room. Wall-sized frames of waterfalls and snow-capped mountains hung in the kitchen. Tim walked up to every piece of art and shared its story; whether it was Vincent van Gogh's *Starry Night* or da Vinci's *Mona Lisa*, everything was mentally filed and ready to be recalled and regurgitated by Tim at a moment's notice.

Tim did general surgery, which meant he operated on anything related to the abdomen, throat, esophagus, and digestive tract. Isaac believed it was his nursing experience that scored him this gig. During the tour, Tim kept rattling off anatomy trivia questions, probing Isaac's mind.

"Name the four rotator cuff muscles!" Tim yelled as he turned the corner and headed back into the kitchen.

Isaac chuckled. "Supraspinatus, infraspinatus, teres minor, subscapularis."

"Bingo! For your correct answer, you win . . . *lunch*!"

Isaac loved Tim's enthusiasm, how it kept him on his toes and made time fly. Tim beckoned Isaac and the rest of the family to sit on the bench at the kitchen table as Hanna prepared sandwiches. Tim got up to help her serve the toasted turkey sandwiches with melted pepper jack cheese and avocado. He grasped the plates like Frisbees and hurled them at each of the five designated place mats, with a sixth plate skipping across the table and resting on its own.

Isaac looked at the sixth plate, confused. "Who's the sixth?"

"Ha! I can do surgery but can't count, I guess," Tim said cheerily before picking up the extra plate and carrying it away.

Isaac squirted mayonnaise on the sandwich. Seeds from the whole wheat crunched under his gnashing teeth, popping as their guts spewed down his throat. When Isaac noticed Tim staring at him, he stopped chewing.

"Do you know why humans live longer than cats and dogs, or why horses live longer than squirrels?" Tim asked as he gazed at Isaac, his head cocked to the side.

Bits of bread and seed shot out of Isaac's mouth as he simultaneously coughed and laughed, surprised by the question. "Um, no sir. I don't."

"Don't call me sir," Tim muttered, before switching from a stern to an affable expression. "It's because of metabolism. The faster one's metabolism, the faster one dies. It makes sense, right? The harder the body has to work to digest food, the shorter the life span, because more energy is expended. So, don't eat your lunch too quickly—gotta conserve your precious energy."

At this, Tim winked at Isaac then took a big bite of his own sandwich, chewing it slowly.

After lunch, Tim and Isaac shuffled back into the living room where the tour had started. The rest of the family stood awkwardly in the corner, except for Sammi, who continued to stare into her mirror.

Tim suddenly grabbed Isaac's shoulder and pinched it in the way of an elder. "Do you know why I hired you, Isaac? Why I need you here during this important time in my life?"

Isaac shook his head, in truth wondering the same thing.

"I need someone I can trust to take care of my family while I work. You see, I have this important procedure coming up that I need to focus my time on. I'll be in my office nonstop for the next few weeks to figure out how to make this surgery work, and I need someone to help my family out around the house."

Tim nodded in Hanna's direction. "My wife is quite capable of helping me, but ever since . . ." Tim leaned in close to Isaac, speaking in a hushed voice. "Ever since the accident with Twain, she needs to be with him to help him cope. So, I need you to pick up her duties, such as cooking dinner and doing the dishes and making sure all my artwork is clean."

Isaac let Tim's words fumble around in his mind, as he tried to make sense of the situation.

Before Isaac could answer, Tim continued, "Does that sound all right to you, Isaac? Speak now or forever hold your peace." Tim guffawed at his own joke, his molar fillings gleaming in the sunlight.

Isaac placed a reassuring hand on Tim's shoulder, mimicking the doctor. "Of course. I should be able to handle anything, and I am happy to help you and your family until you find a solution for your work dilemma." Isaac paused and debated asking his question. "What *is* this procedural problem you are tackling, if you don't mind me asking?"

"Ha. That's the medical professional in you talking, and I love it! However, don't worry about it. It is something me, myself, and I alone must solve, but I appreciate the interest," Tim said, ushering

Isaac out of the house as the rest of the family said their goodbyes.

The metal handle in the wolf's mouth clanged against the door as it shut, making the animal howl. The mountain wind coming from the bellows of the Rockies swooshed through the trees and whistled a winter tune.

Isaac breathed in the fresh air and took a few steps toward his truck just as the front door swung back open and Tim's red face peered out. "Oh! Almost forgot. Be back here at 10 a.m. next Saturday. We all look forward to you coming back!" A grin flashed across his face, but as quickly as it had appeared it was gone.

Isaac wheeled around and walked down the long, tree-lined driveway. Leaves were rustling around his boots until, without warning, the air stilled and the hairs on the back of Isaac's neck suddenly shot up—summoning an uncanny chill.

Isaac felt a presence, watching him.

Unsure of what he expected to find when he turned around, all that awaited him was in fact the huge glass house lit up in contrast to the dull surrounding woods. The great wooden front door was closed; the metal wolves seemed asleep. Isaac was just about to turn back and trudge toward his car when he noticed Twain up in his room, looking out the window and directly down at Isaac with his one good eye.

Unnerved, Isaac trekked to his car and drove off, the hairs on the back of his neck erect all of the way home.

CHAPTER 3

◆

NO CUSSING

Isaac rolled the next patient into the operating room. Once the patient was asleep, he grabbed his medical records and waited for the rest of the staff to situate themselves.

"Shut it! The nurse is trying to start the timeout!" the anesthesiologist yelled over the blasting music.

Isaac reached up and turned down the volume on the speaker, halting the rhythmic hip hop beats. "Today, we have Justin Mayfield, born June 20, 1963. He's here for a right knee scope, autograft anterior cruciate ligament reconstruction, and possible medial and lateral meniscus repair. He has no known allergies. Doctor has marked the correct leg?"

The surgeon stood intently under the surgical spotlights, listening to Isaac read the patient's medical documents. "Yes, right leg is marked and ready to go."

Isaac nodded, then looked at the anesthesiologist. "Ancef dosage?"

"Two Gs," he replied before watching Isaac write his response on the whiteboard beside the surgical counts.

"Counts are correct, his right leg is marked, let's get this party started." Isaac turned the volume back up to the speaker, Tupac's lyrics serving as effective medicine for their ears.

Since the patient elected to have an autograft ACL, the surgeon would need to harvest what would be the patient's new ligament. The surgeon sat on the stool and rolled it close to the patient's right leg, which was dangling off the bed. He made a small incision on the outer perimeter toward the top of the shinbone, sticking a small clamp inside the wound to spread the flesh further apart. "This is where the hamstring attachment point is on the tibia." He directed his question toward Isaac. "Can you name the hammies we will harvest?"

Medical thoughts rattled through Isaac's mind as he pondered the question. "I know there are four in total. But I think we normally just use the gracilis and semitendinosus, right?"

"Good." The surgeon used his blade to release the most distant aspect of the two tendons from the shinbone. "Tendon stripper, please."

The surgical tech stared at the numerous instruments resting on his table, searching for the long rod with a sharp circular top. "Got it, here you go."

The surgeon pulled the two tendons through the sharp, O-shaped end of the harvesting instrument, sliding it up the patient's inner leg toward the hip. Once he got adequate length, he twisted the harvester, using its leading edge to slice the two tendons high up in the thigh, then used his other hand to pull them out of the leg.

The gracilis and semi-T tissue shined under the bright lights. Blood trickled out of the puncture hole and gravity sucked it down until it pooled on the floor, waiting to be sucked up by the plastic vacuum connected to the Neptune machine.

The surgeon handed the tendons to his assistant, who took them to the back table and attached them to the graft workstation. While the doctor sewed the harvest incision, his assistant prepped the graft, weaving sutures through the tails of the tendons to hold them in place. Afterward, he grabbed a looped suture with a button connected to the top. He passed one tail from the gracilis and the semi-T through the looped suture and folded them evenly over it.

"Meniscus looks great, actually," the surgeon said, the tiny arthroscopic camera staring at the joint space between the femur and the tibia. "I'm ready to drill our new ACL tunnels."

The assistant walked back over and stood next to the surgeon and the patient's leg to hold the camera and free up the surgeon's hands.

"Tibia first, right?" the tech asked, holding the assembled tibial drill guide.

"Yep." The surgeon took the guide from the tech and stuck the marking hook through a new incision, watching it appear on the screen. When he liked his angle and projection, he drilled a small pin from the outside of the leg inward, until the tip of the pin hit the tip of the marking hook on top of the tibia. "That's perfect. What did we get for a graft size?"

"It's a nine," his assistant responded.

"I'll take the size-nine barrel reamer, please."

The tech handed him the large, fluted drill and the doctor slid the drill over the pin, using the reamer's cannulation to his advantage.

Tissue and bone spat across the room as the drill ate away at the shinbone, creating a perfect tunnel that ended at the tip of the marking hook. Satisfied, he pulled out the tibial guide, drill, and pin and placed them on the back table.

"Femur guide," he said, holding his hand back out to the tech and keeping his eyes glued to the screen.

The tech quickly assembled the femur guide and handed it to the surgeon, who positioned it in the correct anatomical location on the outside edge of the femur. Using an innovative retro-style drill, he and his assistant created the femoral tunnel.

Satisfied with his two drill holes, the surgeon slid a long shuttling suture down both holes and grabbed it from outside the tunnel on the patient's tibia.

"I'm ready for the graft."

The assistant retrieved the prepped gracilis and semi-T tendons connected to the looped suture and button and tied it to the long shuttle suture traveling through both tunnels. With one hand, the surgeon shuttled the long suture up while guiding the button and the new graft inside the tibial hole. Eventually, the button and new graft appeared on the screen and the doctor gently tugged until the button lay firmly on top of the femur, locking the new graft in place on the femur side.

"I'll take a ten-by-thirty screw."

Isaac opened the white box and handed the tech the screw. The tech then loaded the screw on the driver and passed it to the surgeon. The surgeon took a deep breath and with one hand pinched the remainder of the two tendons sticking out of the tibial hole to hold tension and with his other inserted the screw and locked the new ACL in place on the tibia.

The surgeon performed a Lachman test on the patient's leg to test the new ACL. "Oh, yeah, that feels good." Testing the tightness, he stuck the camera back inside the knee joint and probed the new ACL. "Nice and tight. I love it!"

"That's what she said," Isaac exclaimed to resounding laughter.

Saturday, Isaac threw his car into four-wheel drive to power through the slippery mud up the Hills' driveway. His tires churned and burrowed into the gravel, spitting out dirty ice before lurching onward. When Isaac peered through the windshield, dark and heavy clouds loomed above and warned him of some storm to come.

He drove through the main gate and parked his car, walking past the twin gargoyles and arriving at the wolf-head door. A few months had passed since his first visit, and he finally felt comfortable enough to let himself in. The wolf howled and the door swung open, and the house's interior warmth melted the cold bite.

Twain and Sammi were chasing each other around the living room; Sammi's hair was waving behind her as she dashed after her younger brother. Following his routine greeting of the kids, Isaac headed back to the laundry room that sat adjacent to the master bedroom. He started to pull warm clothes out of the dryer and fold them before placing them in neat piles on top of the dryer.

Green colors on the right and reds on the left. Anything blue can be folded and placed top middle. Isaac's mind was focused on the task at hand until voices interrupted his train of thought.

"We should get out of the house today, Tim. Just me and you. I want some us time," Hanna whined, the master-bedroom walls unable to prevent her voice from entering the laundry room.

"Why?" a seemingly distracted Tim asked.

"We have been cooped up in here and I, quite frankly, am bored. Let's go skiing. We bought season passes, we might as well use them."

"But what about your knees, Han?"

Hanna's voice dropped to a whisper. "My knees feel great, Tim. Ever since you gave me that serum, they've felt better than ever! And you know I only stay on the greens, anyway. Nothing too hard for this ole gal."

Isaac felt guilty for listening in, but soon enough he found himself pressing his ear to the wall. The conversation seemed to have ended, but right before Isaac gave up Tim's voice once again became audible.

"I *need* to keep studying and learning so I can do this procedure coming up. It's stressing me out, Hanna! Do you have any idea what it feels like to have another person's life in your hands? One false move, one slip of the hand, and I cost someone the ability to return to normal. Imagine if you couldn't go get pedicures anymore."

Isaac imagined Hanna crossing her legs with a sassy attitude. "Seems like someone doesn't want to get laid tonight," she scoffed.

Tim's voice pitched with amusement. "Is that a threat, babe? Because it's not funny."

"Oh really?" Isaac heard Hanna say playfully. "Well, if you aren't back in this room and ready to ski in ten seconds, enjoy being a virgin for the rest of this week."

Silence trailed Hanna's words, then Isaac heard rustling footsteps.

Tim ran into the laundry room. "Oh! Hi, Isaac! You surprised me. Didn't know you had arrived. Have you seen my ski socks?"

"Yes sirree, I've got them right here. Not inside out and paired with the correct matching sock," he replied, trying his hardest not to burst out laughing. "Good choice, going skiing today. I heard the *weather* will be really nice out," Isaac said, winking at Tim as he handed him the socks.

Tim blushed and muttered some mumbo jumbo, then grabbed the socks and took off down the hallway and back to his room.

"Nine! Ten!" Hanna's voice trailed.

Isaac heard Tim yell, "I'm here! I'm ready to go. Honey, will you go get the car started?"

"On it. What a great team we make, dear."

After Isaac heard what sounded like a hand spanking an ass, Hanna raced down the hallway. She stopped in the laundry room to say hello to Isaac and inform him of their plans, an adolescent bounce in her knees as she darted into the living room.

After Tim and Hanna left, Isaac remained in the laundry room for a few more minutes to finish folding the clothes. "Wicked Game" poured out of the portable speaker, Chris Isaak's smooth voice and guitar accompaniment helping the clothes fold themselves. Isaac tried to match the song's high-pitched chorus until shouting from the living room interrupted him. The stone floor muffled his footsteps as he walked briskly toward the noise.

What he found was Twain, red-faced and fuming, and Sammi making expressions into her mirror.

"Hey! What's all the fuss about?" Isaac asked, agitated about his ruined duet.

Sammi glanced up from her mirror and shrugged. "I don't know," she said, nodding toward Twain. "How about you ask Sir Cries-a-Lot?"

"Why, I oughtta!" Twain said as he waved a clenched fist in the air.

Isaac strode across the room and placed a hand on Twain's shoulder. "Hey, look at me, Twain. What did she do?"

"She won't let me look at the damn mirror!" Twain yelled, reaching his hand out in an attempt to snatch it from Sammi.

"C'mon, language, bud," Isaac muttered, trying to act the adult.

But Twain's fuse had run out. "Oh! So, a tragic freak accident can happen to me that makes me chronically anxious, but I can't say cusswords? Fuck! Shit! Balls!"

"Balls is *not* a cussword, dumbass," a giggling Sammi responded.

"Hey, no cusswords, please, Sammi. I know your parents are gone, but let's try to have some decency here. I don't want Tim to think I taught y'all those words."

Sammi rolled her eyes. "*Please.* Tim is the least harmful person in the entire galaxy. He thinks we are his fellowship, off to conquer some stupid ring. Total nerd alert."

Shocked at her Tolkien knowledge, Isaac looked at Sammi in bewilderment. He fumbled for words until the question he was dying to ask came out. "Who's your favorite character? Wait, no." Isaac slapped himself, halting his descent down the rabbit hole. "Never mind, don't answer that. Please, no more bad words or I will have to tell Legolas of your actions!"

Sammi and Twain looked at each other, then burst out laughing.

After their team approach to deter Isaac's lameness, Sammi and Twain's laughing fit ceased. Sammi went back to gazing in her mirror, and Twain kept staring blankly at Isaac. A stillness filled the room except for the TV news channel talking about the missing person report, until Isaac broke it. "Twain, do you mind if I ask what happened to your eye? I know it's a personal question . . . but I guess I'm curious."

Twain glanced down at his feet, and for once even Sammi was actually looking up from her mirror and at Twain, an eyebrow raised in curiosity.

Isaac tried again, this time coming from a different angle. "Do you know what I do for a living, Twain? I'm a nurse."

Sammi ducked behind her mirror, trying to control her laughter.

Isaac rolled his eyes and continued. "I'm in surgeries all day and assist the surgeons when they operate. I help with fake arms and legs and sometimes even eyes."

As soon as Isaac mentioned the word "eye," a vacuum filled the room. Twain's cheeks turned an embarrassed pink and his shoulders hunched heavily.

Isaac was about to change the subject back to *The Lord of the Rings* when Twain finally looked up and muttered, "I thought only girls are nurses . . ."

Sammi held out a fist and Twain bumped his knuckles against hers. "Nice burn, little bro."

Heat flashed through Isaac's head and seared his ears at Twain's comment. "What! No. Medicine is universal!"

"Jeez, you sound just like Dad! *Major* nerd alert!" Sammi snickered before pouting her lips and making eye contact with her reflection of herself.

"Okay, Miss Priss. What is it you aspire to be when you grow up?" Isaac challenged.

Twain stood up quickly, a red glare in his one good eye. "Isn't it obvious? She wants to be a model."

Sammi jumped up, swishing her hair while exclaiming, "Not just any model, *the* model. I want to be the most beautiful person in the entire world."

She then thrust her hips out and walked gracefully around the room, wowing an invisible crowd.

Isaac glanced at Twain and they both cackled, finally sharing a moment.

CHAPTER 4

THE SHED, PART 1

The temperature dropped below thirty-two degrees in just a few hours, turning the falling rain into crystallized snow. The wind caught the descending flakes and pummeled them against the glass, plastering the windows with frozen soot. Sammi was upstairs in her room, probably staring into her elephant-sized wall mirror and pretending to be a model, while Twain was lying on the living-room couch reading a book.

Isaac loved the snow: how it felt when it touched his skin, how it looked when it lay like a soft fleece blanket on the ground and tree limbs—the snow tucking in Mother Nature for a quiet sleep.

The fireplace crackled in the living room, informing Isaac that it was time to put on another log. He went outside to the shed where Tim kept the stacked wood. The grass had turned to mud, and Isaac's footsteps squished with every step, leaving imprints in the soft ground behind him. He stood in front of the pile and stacked the logs, one by one, in his arms until he could carry no more. A sense of unease flowed through him once again: the feeling that someone was watching him and eyeing his every move. But when he looked up at the house, there was nothing unusual to be seen.

Isaac shook off the feeling and prepared to head back inside when he noticed footsteps leading into the shed itself, which struck him as odd because the ground had only recently become wet and he didn't remember seeing Tim leave his study.

After wiping his feet on the doormat, Isaac headed into the living room, where the warmth welcomed his return. Twain glanced up briefly from his book, then looked back down as Isaac trudged over to the dulling fire careful not to drop pieces of wood along the way. The fire hissed when the new log was placed on top, causing the embers to burn hot and immediately fill the room with new heat.

Isaac glanced down at his watch to see that he still had a lot of time to kill until he could return home. Sammi would remain upstairs in her room, so she was easy. Twain, however, didn't like being in his room unless he was sleeping. He was always up and about in the house, though never without the constant shield of his leather eye patch.

All was silent in the living room except for the popping of the wood. Isaac mulled over how to pass the time when he decided this was the perfect opportunity to break the ice with Twain. If he was going to continue working here with these kids, he decided he should make it as pleasant as possible.

The fire hissed again as angry embers flurried out of the hearth and charred the marble floor. Isaac's eyes followed the black soot until his gaze came to rest on Twain's book: *Frankenstein*.

"You're a little too young to be reading that, don't you think?" Isaac probed, trying to jump-start a conversation.

At first, Twain didn't seem to hear, but soon Isaac could tell the boy's brain was churning for a witty comeback.

"Old enough to need, old enough to read," Twain said, without glancing up.

But Isaac dug deeper. "And what is it that you need?"

Several moments passed until Twain looked up again and slammed the book shut. He sighed and shook his head, his unpatched eye watching the snow accumulate outside. "Don't make me say it," he said, barely louder than a whisper.

Isaac pondered what to say next, wanting to ensure it was appropriate. "Losing an eye isn't the end of the world, Twain. I don't think any differently of you."

A game-show buzzer mimicking the sound of an incorrect response rang in Isaac's mind, as the veins in Twain's neck bulged in response to his obvious unease.

"Well, I don't care what you think, Isaac! You just have no idea, do you? Great job, making money. You are whole. You couldn't even fathom the horrors I have been through."

"I try to—"

But, with tears dripping from his single eye, Twain cut Isaac off before he could finish: "Yes, you try to understand, and I respect you for that. However, you just don't get it and you never will!"

Persevering, Isaac nudged the conversation again. "If it's looks you are concerned about, there are prosthetic eyes that look very realistic. I doubt people would be able to tell a difference."

Twain swung his legs off the couch and stood facing Isaac, his cherry-red cheeks filled with hot anger. "I don't want anything fake! I want something real."

Isaac shook his head, saddened at the thought of the turmoil Twain had endured. "That technique isn't viable yet, but maybe sometime in the next decade someone will figure it out. The optic nerve is extremely delicate, no one has been able to figure out a way to reconstruct it."

Suddenly, the hairs on the back of Twain's neck pricked and a cold sweat doused him. He looked down at the cover of his book and sneered before tossing it on the floor, the hardback smacking loudly against the marble. Twain muttered something indistinct, then stomped out of the living room.

Isaac looked at the clock on the wall; it wasn't even close to Twain's bedtime.

The sound of footsteps woke Isaac, who was dozing on the couch. His eyelids allowed a sliver of fading light to creep in, until they adjusted enough to be fully open. The wall clock read 4:30 p.m., and the door leading to the backyard was cracked open. Isaac looked out the window and noticed that the door to the shed was also open. Seconds later, a silhouette appeared inside the shed. Tim walked out and shut the shed door, securing the padlock behind him.

Tim carefully jumped across the yard to avoid the muddy areas, until he reached the house and entered the kitchen.

Isaac stretched his limbs and said, "Hiya, Tim. How's your day going?"

Startled, Tim jumped at the sound of Isaac's voice. His face was sallow and his hands were covered in red clay. "Oh! Hi Isaac! Didn't know you were there." He placed his hands awkwardly behind his back and walked to the kitchen sink. "Day going well?"

Isaac yawned, then hopped to his feet and strode over to where Tim was vigorously washing his fingers. Reddish-brown water splashed in the sink basin and soap bubbles floated in the air, as Tim shook his hands dry. "Day's going great! Were you doing yard work? I can help, ya know."

Tim grabbed a paper towel and gingerly wiped his hands. "Yep, that's exactly it. Just doing yard work and cleaning the shackled bodies down in the shed." He tossed the dirty paper towel into the trash and winked at Isaac. "Why don't you head on home a little early today. You've worked hard this week."

As quickly as Tim had washed his hands, he was back upstairs in his study and Isaac found himself alone with his thoughts.

CHAPTER 5

THE PECULIAR PICTURE

Isaac always listened to music when he cleaned. The songs, a simple cure to washing dishes and clothes, influenced his body to move rhythmically.

Tim was in his study, trying to fit together the pieces of his mysterious puzzle, while the rest of the family, minus Hanna, were downstairs enjoying glasses of juice. The kids had never heard of The Eagles before, and when "Hotel California" played on Isaac's iPhone speaker, they watched his hips groove. His dance moves were so "amazing" that Twain and Sammi were guffawing with laughter, so much so that Twain spilled his cranberry juice all over the pristine marble floor.

Twain stared at the purple pool widening on the floor, the color draining from his face. "Oh no!"

Sammi covered her brother's mouth with her hand. "Shh! If you yell, Dad will come down and see the mess you've made! He might even snatch out your other eye in anger!"

Twain—defeated—nodded and kept quiet.

Isaac clapped his hands to the beat of the song. "Guys, it's time!" His voice rose with excitement as the band members harmonized. "I'm about to teach you a secret to life. Y'all ready?"

Sammi and Twain looked at each other in amusement, then gave unsure nods.

Isaac stepped into his mental spotlight. "Right, if we can get down to some tunes, then this mess will disappear faster than Houdini."

He pulled out his phone and connected the Sonos app to the Bluetooth speakers scattered around the room.

"What's Houdini?" both kids asked.

Isaac's jaw dropped and his eyes bulged. "What! Never mind. I'll make this mess disappear faster than the Nimbus 2000!"

Sammi giggled at the Harry Potter reference, and even Twain looked delighted.

Isaac one point, kids zero, Isaac thought before clearing his throat in preparation for his announcement. "All right. Eyes on me . . ."

Sammi looked nervously at Twain, who looked down at the purple puddle of juice still spreading across the kitchen floor.

"I'm sorry, Twain, I didn't mean to . . ."

Sammi stepped in and put an arm around her brother, glaring at Isaac. "There's a mop upstairs in the pantry. Can you get it? I'll stop the spread with some paper towels."

Irritated, Isaac walked through the kitchen to the living room and went up the staircase, his hand gliding across the smooth railing as he hopped up the stairs two at a time until reaching the top. His feet were on autopilot as they steered him toward the large pantry doors and past Twain's bedroom on the left, which was almost immediately followed by a quaint bathroom. Past the bathroom was Tim's office.

Isaac passed the study, noticing the dip in temperature he felt whenever he was near the room. His mind fluttered back to the only time Tim had allowed him to enter the space. It had happened during Isaac's first day on the job.

* * *

Tim had just finished introducing Isaac to his family and was giving him the house tour. They had looped around and arrived at the top of the stairwell, the hallway leading from it long and carpeted, which made being barefoot a blessing. They had passed Twain's room and the half bath, and then reached a white-painted metal door equipped with insulation around the edges.

"This door here," Tim said, tapping the metal door with his knuckles, "is why I hired you, Isaac. Do you know the key ingredient to creating genius ideas? Peace and quiet. I swear, you can figure out anything with a little peace and quiet."

Isaac studied the door. "Yes, sir."

"I want this door to remain closed at all times, unless you need me for an emergency. Capeesh?"

Isaac nodded in agreement, instantly curious about what was behind the door.

Tim placed a hand on the door but paused before he opened it. "This room is my sanctuary, Isaac. It is purer than a virgin, and I need it to stay that way."

"What's a virgin?" Twain, his voice meek compared to his father's, yelled from downstairs.

The sound of scurrying footsteps rang out downstairs as Hanna overheard Twain and tried to quickly change the subject.

Tim shook his head in bemusement while swinging open the office door. "Gotta love my family."

The room was well-lit for there being no windows and was also quite large. There was hardly any furniture, except for a small wooden desk in the far-left corner. Several electrical cords, looking to connect with something, dangled from the middle of the ceiling. False sky panels filled the remainder of the ceiling and produced a blinding light. The floor was marble, similar to the one downstairs, and also boasted a spectacular gleam. There were no decorations on the bland white walls that absorbed some of the light coming from the ceiling.

"Welcome to my study," Tim said, walking to the center of the room and holding out his arms as a gesture that Isaac may enter.

"It's definitely . . . interesting," Isaac replied, trying to suppress his disappointment at the bland and boring room.

How can he find peace and quiet in a room that screams silence? Isaac thought.

"I know it's pretty empty, but that's the way I like it. An empty room for an empty mind. The perfect amount of space to fill with creative ideas. After today, no one is allowed in here unless there's an emergency," Tim said, raising an eyebrow in emphasis.

Isaac glanced around, drinking in every detail— or lack thereof—his curiosity draining. "No one can come in here?"

"No one but my partner, Dr. Shung. If he ever decides to come back, that is . . ."

"What is this surgery you are working on?" Isaac said, snapping Tim out of his rumination.

Tim winked and continued to pace around the room. "Since you asked twice, I'm trying to find the secret of the green anole lizard. You see, these lizards have fabulous regenerative properties that I'm trying to identify for use in medicine."

"Is that the lizard that can regrow its tail after an attack?" Isaac asked, his interest increasing.

Tim beamed, the tops of his cheeks turning a Christmastime red. "Indeed, it is!"

"We have plenty of those crawling around in Alabama," Isaac said, thinking how he could use this study for future assignments. "Would love to help, any way I can."

"Trust me, kid, you are more helpful than you think."

With that, Tim shuttled Isaac out of the room and closed the door behind them. Isaac expected to hear the sound of a lock clicking in place, but he realized the door could only be locked from the outside.

* * *

Isaac pushed the thought of Tim's study out of his mind as he ambled past the office and toward the pantry. He swung open the door and observed the room's inner contents, searching for the mop. Between a pair of shelves was a cabinet as tall as Isaac, the perfect place to stow a mop. The cabinet door creaked, and the mop almost toppled on top of him before Isaac caught the handle with both hands.

Grinning at his athletic skill, Isaac bent to one knee and hoisted the bucket from the floor into the air, only to reveal what looked like an old photo that had been trapped under the mop bucket.

Isaac plucked the picture from the floor and blew off particle clouds of dust that lazily drifted to the floor. The first thing he recognized was Tim, prematurely balding and leaning against a golf club. Holding Tim's arm was Hanna, with Sammi and Twain positioned in front of her. But something was off. The two kids under Hanna's arms didn't look anything like Sammi and Twain.

The little girl was pretty but had red curly hair and horrible burns running up her arms and down her legs. When Isaac studied the boy, it felt like his heart stopped. It was Twain, but not the Twain who was downstairs.

In the photo, Twain wasn't wearing an eye patch— for there was no need. Both of his eyes were visible, and both looked healthy. Twain's smile stretched from ear to ear, an expression Isaac had never before witnessed from him.

Then, the rest of the puzzle pieces began to fit together.

Even with the burns, the little girl was Sammi; there was no doubt. While the top of her head reminded Isaac of the 1982 flick *Annie*, the girl had the same green eyes and bone structure as the Sammi downstairs, the same sassy attitude flashing out of the picture.

Isaac thumbed the photo. Of all the photo's mysteries, the one that most intrigued Isaac centered on Twain. People are usually most interested in things that are lost, and rarely wonder about how things are found. If mystery fuels the desire to learn, Isaac was an empty tank waiting to be filled.

Before he had time to put the photo back, he heard Sammi yell from below: "Isaac! Get down here, quick! It's about to hit the carpet!"

Isaac jumped at the sound of Sammi's voice. The *thump thump* from his racing heart drowned out all other noises as he tucked the photo away and grabbed the mop and bucket. When he turned to leave the pantry room, however, Isaac was alarmed to see Twain standing at the doorway, puzzlement etched into his face.

CHAPTER 6

THE STING

The rain sloshed and the familiar battle of tires against wet gravel resounded all the way up to the house. *Braaattt, braaattt, braaattt!* Isaac parked his truck in his usual spot underneath the trees and flipped his car keys ninety degrees, silencing the Thievery Corporation radio.

When he stepped out into the wetness, his hood flopped in the wind and gusts whipped across his body. If there was any city in the world that could be classified as bipolar, it was Denver. One day it could be sixty-five degrees and sunny, and the next there would be a blizzard.

It was only midmorning, but gloom had already spread across the sky, defeating the sun in today's battle of light versus darkness. Isaac put his soaked hand on the wolf-head knocker, matching his pounding with the booming from the thunder above.

Isaac let himself inside and shook the water droplets off his head, then hung his rain jacket on the mantle next to the front door. The house was quiet, with only Twain in the living room reading *Frankenstein* by the fire.

"You almost done with that book?" Isaac asked as he removed his shoes and walked toward the flames to warm himself.

Twain looked up and eyed Isaac, exasperated, as if he hadn't slept in days. Isaac wondered if the eye beneath the patch matched the ruggedness of the other.

Twain answered sheepishly, "Almost, I'm at the good part now."

Isaac raised an eyebrow. "And what exactly is the good part?"

"He's about to create the monster!" Twain said. His excitable tone matched the burning logs' high-pitched crackling.

Isaac sat cross-legged on the marble floor beside the furnace, his body consuming the warmth as the flames ate away at the moisture clinging to his skin. The whole room glowed an ominous orange, making silhouettes dance harmoniously on the walls.

Besides the moving shadows, no one else seemed to be around. "Where is everyone?" Isaac asked. "Are your parents skiing again? I bet Sammi is looking at her mirror . . ."

For a moment, only the popping embers responded, but finally Twain put his book down. "Want to play my favorite game?"

"Depends. What's your favorite game? If it's quidditch, then you know I'm in." Isaac pretended to hop on an invisible broom and ride it around the house.

Twain half-laughed, simultaneously scratching at the eye patch and giggling. "No, it's hide-and-seek! I bet you'll never find me."

Isaac halted. "Is that a challenge, young one?"

This time, Twain had a big grin on his face, as wide as the one in the photo Isaac had found in the upstairs pantry. Twain hopped up from the couch and clapped his hands, the first time the similarities between father and son were apparent to Isaac.

"Okay, close your eyes and count to ten!"

"One!" Isaac counted. "Two!" Making tiny slits

between his fingers, Isaac wanted to see where Twain ran off to.

Twain wasn't falling for it, though; he marched right up to Isaac and put his hands on his hips. "No peeking!" he scolded.

Isaac closed the slits between his fingers and darkness barricaded his vision. He started the count over and heard Twain scurry across the room, his bare feet slapping down on the stone floor, before suddenly changing pitch and fading when he hit the carpeted stairs.

"Nine. Ten! Ready or not, here I come!"

To increase the suspense, Isaac started the quest downstairs by searching behind the couch and under the dining-room table, then looping back to the main room where he searched the closet of winter jackets. No Twain to be found.

The rain was falling harder and drowning out his footsteps as Isaac trudged up the stairs. Intense wind tested the durability of the glass, which clattered like a rattlesnake's tail.

It was no secret that Twain's favorite place to hide was under his bed, because the *Toy Story* comforter hung far enough down to where no one could see him. Since the bed was pushed up against the wall, the comforter created a cozy cocoon that hid Twain from the horrors of the world.

Isaac pushed open the door to Twain's room but was met with a cold silence, the only sound coming from the curtain flapping at the open window. All was quiet, until the monotony of the rain filled the room.

"*Twain, I know you're in here,*" Isaac whispered, a sly smile creeping across his face. Adrenaline pumped through his veins: the hunt was almost over, and the scent of his prey thrilled his nostrils.

A muffled giggle crept out from under the bed, the whining wind incapable of stifling it completely.

Isaac knew that Twain didn't want to be found right away. Twain loved when people checked other places in the room to increase the suspense. Isaac first checked behind the long curtains. Nothing.

"Hmm, no one here," he said in his falsely malevolent tone. "How strange. I could have sworn I heard someone in here. Maybe I'll check the closet!"

Isaac ran to the closet and quickly swung the door open but was met with nothing more than hanging clothes and a floor littered with shoes.

"Interesting, I really thought I heard someone in this room. Maybe I'll leave and go check Sammi's room," Isaac said as he strutted toward the door and put his hand on the doorknob, pretending he was about to exit the room, part of the plan to lure out another sound.

And that's exactly what happened: the slightest chuckle emerged from under the bed.

Lightning flashed across the sky and irradiated the room a momentary bright blue, then faded back to its original dark. Isaac tiptoed across the room until he was standing next to the bed and a stoic Buzz Lightyear.

"What was that! Perhaps someone is hiding under the bed?" Isaac grabbed a handful of the comforter and threw it back over his head. Then, until he was halfway under the bed, he crawled underneath. Thunder and lightning combined their synergy and generated a heavenly explosion.

At first, all Isaac saw was blackness, but then a blue bolt shot across the sky and illuminated the space under the lifted box spring. Isaac winced as the light reflected off the metallic rim of his glasses.

"I found y—"

As Isaac's eyes adjusted once again to the darkness, he realized he wasn't looking at Twain's face. Instead, it was Tim's ice-blue eyes and maniacal smile that greeted him. Before Isaac had time to react, he felt something prick the left side of his neck and the cool flow of an unknown fluid as it entered his veins.

He fell back and screamed in recognition of the inches-long, needle-tipped syringe protruding from the side of his throat. Isaac ripped it out and a tiny flow of blood trickled from the hole in his skin, meaning that the syringe's maple-colored liquid was already inside his body, his bloodstream transporting the strange substance to every part.

"What the hell did you do to me!" Isaac shrieked as the walls and ceiling blurred into one. The whole world started to spin—pink, white, and orange blended, as the thunder and lightning continued to sound overhead and the rain kept its beat against the house's glass walls.

Tim rose slowly from underneath Twain's bed. "Shh, relax, Isaac. The more you panic, the quicker the Valium will spread."

Red became blue, which turned into green, then blended to brown as the whole world swam in front of Isaac. His muscles relaxed and went completely numb; his head rolled on his neck like a loose ball-and-socket joint. Then, he fell limp to the floor.

Isaac felt pressure on his legs and arms, as Tim tied thick rope around him. The veins in Tim's hands bulged when he squeezed his fingers around the binding rope and dragged Isaac across the floor. Isaac tried to kick and fight but found it useless, the diazepam already having done its work of turning his muscles into wet noodles.

Tim pulled Isaac toward the one room shrouded in mystery. He took out his keys and unlocked the door; the bright overheard lights seared Isaac's eyes. In a final attempt, Isaac managed to latch a fingernail on the doorframe, peeling off the paint as Tim heaved him into the room and slammed the door behind them. Inside the study, the brightness didn't bother Isaac—for all he saw was black.

FAITH

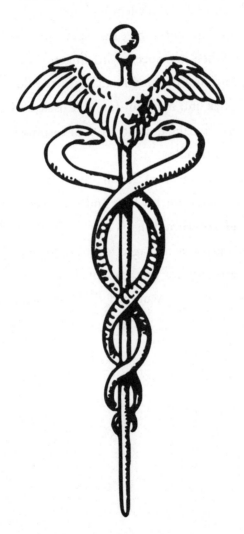

CHAPTER 7

FAITH

"The umbilical cord is wrapped around the baby's neck. We need to open her up!" the doctor yelled, signaling to the rest of his staff that it was time for plan B.

The anesthesiologist walked behind the hospital bed and knelt down beside the small opening that exposed the patient's back. He flicked the syringe and squirted a bit of the medicine to push out the excess air. "Administering spinal block now."

The woman flinched, then felt the lower half of her body go numb. The nurses shaved her belly and quickly configured a drape that wrapped around her abdomen.

The doctor's blue eyes shined above his mask; a scalpel was in his hand. "Let me know if you feel this," he said. The knife hovered over the drape, then disappeared behind it.

The parents didn't think the baby would survive long after her birth in the small Colorado hospital. When she came into the world, she was underweight and didn't make a sound. The parents clung to each other when the doctor told them their baby probably wouldn't make it through the night. The sacrifices of selling unused items, painting the extra bedroom, and picking up extra shifts to earn more money were for nothing if the baby didn't survive.

The doctor's easygoing eyes tried to communicate something that would ease the parents' pain. After a long stretch in which no one could find words, the doctor finally stood up and locked his gaze on the parents, his tranquil eyes turning serious. "You should name her. The Native Americans believe names give power. Maybe it'll work on your daughter."

Both parents nodded in agreement and gazed at the child lying motionless in her mother's arms, the baby's chest barely moving as she fought for every breath.

"You should name her, honey. You're the one who fought through this," the father said, nodding at the child.

"*We* fought through this," the mother responded, fixing her green eyes on the sleeping child.

"Faith. I want to name her Faith."

Faith grew to be beautiful, her long locks of gorgeous blond hair draping below her shoulders and fluttering in the wind. Her green eyes were sharp and could slice through the feelings of any man. Faith's parents always told her she was special and had a purpose in life, and she believed them, which led her to grow up with the ambition to help people.

Right before Faith graduated from high school, her father died of cancer. The interminable disease broke him down and swallowed him whole, ending his life at a tragic time for Faith.

When the doctor had told them the news, Faith's mom had run out of the room in anguish, leaving Faith alone with the nurses. Faith admired the nurses, deciding then and there that she wanted to join their ranks and comfort others as they had her.

Faith's mother was a broken woman after her husband's death, not wanting to leave home or meet anyone new. She started to live in the shadows and no longer showed her face in public; everything seemed to be a constant reminder of her deceased spouse.

Witnessing her father's death and her mother breaking down solidified Faith's idea of applying to nursing school and fulfilling her destiny of helping people. Nurses are among the most underrated people who exist, she recognized, despite being the teachers of the medical industry and putting in the longest and most difficult hours, while barely getting paid for the incomparable difference they make in people's lives.

After graduating high school, Faith was accepted to the University of Anschutz Colorado School of Nursing. But just before college started, Faith's mom was hit by a car and suffered extensive damage to her hypothalamus. She was left in a vegetative state, and the driver of the vehicle was never found.

Faith continued with her studies for a while, using her father's death and her mother's accident as the fuel to keep pressing on, but eventually her ambitions faded away. Faith had to quit her bartending job because her nursing studies were eating away at the precious time she set aside for her mom. Between juggling a job, college, and time with her mother, Faith was overwhelmed and started to feel her drive to make a difference in the world dwindle.

It was during this time that she met Tim Hill.

* * *

Tim Hill was a prestigious surgeon who taught classes at the university; he also believed in giving back to the world. Tim knew all about Faith and her family issues and how she wanted to make a difference; he believed it was his duty to help her reach her goals. When Tim discovered that Faith was dropping out of school due to the financial burden, he decided it was in his destiny to offer her a job.

It was while Faith was diligently taking notes from PowerPoint slides during one of her classes that she met Tim for the first time.

The auditorium lights snapped on and Faith's surprised professor jerked up from her computer, Tim's presence sucking the oxygen from the room and leaving her breathless.

"Okay, everyone," the professor said as she rose from her chair and cleared her throat. "I have a surprise speaker for you all today. This is Dr. Tim Hill, board-certified general surgeon, and he would like to say a few words to all of you. Please put your phones away and listen!"

Tim accepted the microphone and stepped up to the podium, looking eagerly into the crowd with a twinkle in his eyes and a smile curling his lips.

"What do you call a meniscus in a female patient?" his voice boomed through the auditorium speakers.

Everyone remained silent and confused. Was this a joke or an intimidation tactic?

Tim gazed down at the students, hoping someone would raise a hand, though no one did. "A *wo*meniscus! Ha! Get it?" His shoulder blades collapsed inward when he chortled, and a few students, Faith among them, giggled at his corniness.

Tim wiped away a tear of laughter and collected himself. "Now that the ice is officially broken, I want to thank all of you for taking on the rigors and hardships of nursing. Not enough people recognize the bravery it takes to do what you will do." Tim looked down and made direct eye contact with Faith, giving her a wink before continuing. "There are not enough words to express my gratitude to nurses for the assistance they provide me and my patients. Tonight, I'll drink a beer in your honor! I'll remain up here for a few more minutes, if anyone wants to chat."

Tim then placed both index fingers on top of the lectern and drummed. "Aaaaaaand . . . class dismissed!" he yelled to the students' applause. He glanced at Faith one last time before stepping away from the podium.

The majority of the students quickly packed their things and left the auditorium, but Faith decided to stay behind and ask Tim a few questions; it wasn't every day one got the privilege to speak to a renowned surgeon.

Faith waited until the few students were done asking their questions and approached Tim while he collected his bag.

"H—hi. My name is Faith," she said. "Thank you for . . ."

Tim turned toward Faith and gave her a warm smile. "Oh, I know who you are, Faith. I'm so sorry to hear about your mother. How's she doing? Any better?"

"No, sir," Faith said, unable to contain her surprise. "But thank you for your kind words. I really appreciate them."

Tim took a moment, feeling a connection he would struggle to explain. "Here's my card, Faith. Please feel free to contact me whenever you wish. I want the best for you in your studies."

Faith grabbed the card and gripped it tightly, fearing it might disappear if she let it go. This card could be her golden ticket to reclaiming her ambition—her future—and she didn't want to let it slip between her fingers.

Before Tim walked away, Faith asked one final, bold question: "Why are you being so kind to me? You don't even know me."

Tim paused, the oiled gears in his mind working. "I'm always open to helping a student in need," he said as he turned around and flashed a bright grin at Faith.

With that, he left the auditorium and the usual oxygen returned to the air.

CHAPTER 8

SISTERS BEFORE MISTERS

A few weeks had passed since meeting Tim when Faith noticed the flyer:

Help wanted! Please send resume to Dr. Tim Hill at tim.hill@surgical.com for details.

Faith's eyes swelled in delight when she saw it, tacked to her locker alone, and immediately snagged the flyer and tucked it safely in her backpack.

Throughout the rest of that day's classes, Faith daydreamed about getting the job and using the experience to shoot her way to the top of every list for her eventual dream job. She couldn't think of someone better for a referral than *the* Dr. Tim Hill, her cheeks becoming rosy as butterflies fluttered their wings and delightfully tickled the inside of her stomach.

After a long day of classes, Faith headed for the hospital to spend time with her mother. The double entrance doors slid open on her approach. Hospitals provoked fear in many people, but seeing her comatose mother was for Faith a daily routine that helped her grow immune to the horrors. She didn't need to ask what floor her mom was on or how to navigate the confusing hallways; her feet automatically guided her to the correct room.

Faith pressed the elevator button and waited, still dreaming about what working for Dr. Hill might be like. After quitting her bartending job, she was in desperate need of a paying job; anything affiliated with nursing would be a plus.

The elevator dinged and Faith exited on the fourth floor. She walked down the hallway, humming "Amazing Grace," until she reached the door with *418* etched into it.

"Hello, mother!" Faith said cheerfully, barging into the room. The only response she received was the steady tone of the breathing monitor, beeping to signal oxygen being pumped into her mother's lungs. Tubes were going in and coming out, twisting and contorting to avoid other structures, reminding Faith of the ants she used to keep as pets.

As a kid, Faith had received a small colony as a Christmas gift. At first, she was disgusted and grimaced just looking at the creepy-crawlies burrowing in the glass box. But eventually, she grew to respect the tiny beasts.

The glass tank her father gave her that Christmas day lasted a couple of months before the colony grew too big and a housing upgrade was needed. Faith's mom and dad took her to the nearest Hobby Lobby to buy supplies. She needed clear tubes to expand her tank by connecting one colony to another. The more tubes she bought, the healthier and stronger her ants would get. No one was buying more tubes for her mother.

Her mom's room had a nice ambiance, with the last orange shades from the sunset peeping through the window blinds and striping her mother's unconscious body.

Faith approached the chair next to the bed and positioned her laptop on the small desk. She started to edit her resume, updating her experiences and referrals and hoping to make it appear perfect before she sent it off to Tim.

"What do you think, Mom?" Faith said. "Should I add my physics professor as a reference?"

The breathing monitor responded with its usual beeping and caused Faith to smile. "Yeah, I think so, too." She then clicked SEND and her resume was on its way to Tim's inbox.

* * *

To her amazement, Faith got the job and started right away. The new income in her bank account was a pleasant and very necessary sight. The work mainly consisted of Faith doing odd jobs and chores around the house while Tim was at the hospital; when he got home, she would leave to continue her nursing studies.

At the house, Faith cleaned, did laundry, and prepared food; she did anything Tim and Hanna wanted, and she was happy. Since she was an only child and her father was deceased and her mother unresponsive, Faith felt like she had a family.

One day months into the job, she was upstairs with Sammi, with whom she had bonded, brushing the girl's fiery red hair.

"Ouch, Faith! You know my hair doesn't straighten like that," Sammi yelped as Faith ran the comb through her tangles.

Faith grunted as she pulled the comb through Sammi's hair. "I know, but if you don't brush it, it'll clump. Do you want to look like a homeless person?"

Sammi stared at Faith in the mirror she held. "No."

"Then stop struggling and let me do this," Faith said good-naturedly. She had always wanted a sister, and Sammi was now fulfilling that role.

Sammi sighed. "I wish I could look just like you," she said, before turning away from the mirror and swinging her body around to face Faith, grimacing as the scars stretched her skin in every direction. "You're so pretty."

Faith beamed, for she had never felt pretty. "Oh, don't be silly. You're just as beautiful!"

Sammi turned back around, anguish riddling her face. "No, I'm really not."

Faith saw Sammi's eyes glance at the scars covering her body, following their zigzagging trails around her legs and up her torso. "I'm disgusting."

Faith put down the comb and folded an arm around Sammi. "Look at me."

Sammi rolled her eyes and looked away. "Twain's so lucky he's normal. Everyone always talks about how pretty his eyes are."

"Hey. Look at me." Faith steered Sammi's face until they were gazing eye to eye. "You're amazing. Don't let anyone tell you otherwise."

Sammi nodded. "I just wish I was you."

Faith laughed. "Trust me, girl. You don't. Dead father, comatose mother, and no other family. This isn't a contest, I know, but what you have here is special." She grabbed the mirror and placed it facedown on the counter. "You, Sammi girl, are special." She touched the tip of her finger to Sammi's heart. "Remember that."

TIM

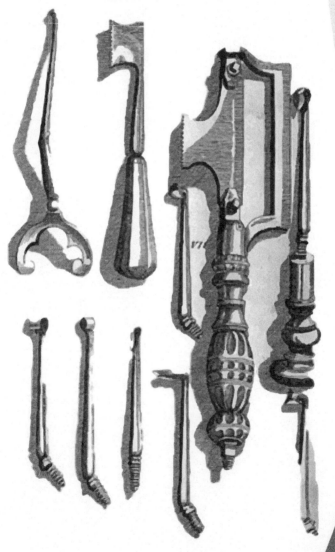

CHAPTER 9

◆

SAMMI'S WISH

"*H*ave a nice nap. We'll see you soon, okay?" Tim said as he watched the patient inhale the gas clouding the mask's interior.

The patient lifted his hand and gave Tim and his surgical team a thumbs-up, before the drugs knocked him out.

"Good, he's out. I'll put in the breathing-assist tube now," the anesthesiologist said. He walked to his desk and opened the top drawer, pulling out a long, clear plastic tube. After opening the patient's mouth wide and inserting the tube down the throat, the patient's throat muscles expanded in acceptance of the plastic. With another tube, the anesthesiologist connected the oxygen tank to the top of the breathing assist to pump fresh air into the patient's lungs. "All done here. Take it away, Dr. Hill."

Tim pointed to the nurse. "Cue the music."

The nurse, a woman in her late sixties, nodded and hit the power button on the speaker, sparking The Beatles' "Get Back."

"Excellent. Who's ready to remove this appendix?" Tim asked rhetorically. "Knife, please."

Tim's team included the anesthesiologist, a nurse, and a surgical tech, each doing their particular job to facilitate the surgery. "Yes sir, got the knife right here," the tech said, brandishing the blade from its plastic holster.

"Don't call me sir," Tim said as he grabbed the instrument.

He placed the tip of the blade right above the patient's belly button, plunging it downward until the tip disappeared in a pool of blood. "Gauze, please."

The tech grabbed a square of white gauze and handed it over.

Tim placed it gingerly on the incision, carefully dabbing the blood until the flow slowed. "Hmm, this guy is a little bigger than the average joe. I'll take the blue cannula. I think it's a tad longer than the other one."

The tech nodded. "It is. The orange one is five centimeters, the blue is seven."

"I'll take that with a side of fries."

The tech smiled under his mask. "Here you go," he said as he handed Tim the sterile blue tube.

Tim placed the tip of the cannula in the incision, pushing until it was halfway down. He then connected the tube to another gas tank for a couple of minutes, the gas expanding the patient's stomach cavity for easier viewing. Once the cavity was inflated, Tim removed the gas tube and inserted the laparoscopic camera inside the cannula, safely introducing the scope into the patient's abdomen. The screen in front of Tim flickered, then burst to life as the scope entered the stomach cavity and illuminated its contents. "See right there," Tim said as he directed the camera to the left. "That's the small intestine. Look how beautiful it is."

"Only you would think intestines are beautiful, Tim," the nurse said, looking away from the monitor.

"Better than looking at all of y'all." Tim grinned and winked at the nurse. "You know I'm kidding."

He swiveled the scope inside the stomach. "And right here we have the large intestine. If we follow it to the lower right portion of the torso, it should lead us to the appendix."

The large intestine filled the screen, its pink tissue pulsating. Stomach juices encased the outer layer of the intestine and reflected the scope's light. Capillaries wrapped themselves around it and fed the tissue nutrients as it worked to pulverize the food.

"Aha, there's our culprit!" A small, shriveled appendix that looked like a piece of dried fruit appeared on the screen. "Yep, definitely needs to come out. I bet that was pretty painful, bud. All right, knife again, please."

Tim made another small incision right above the appendix, the tip of the blade appearing on the screen. He wiped away the gurgling blood from the new incision, then stuck another cannula inside, which would act as a portal from the outside world to the inside. "I need an arthroscopic grasper."

The tech handed him a small instrument with a beak-tipped jaw, perfect for grabbing things.

Tim nodded and shoved the grasper into the second cannula until it appeared on the monitor. He grabbed the inflamed appendix and gave it a small tug, watching as dark blood oozed out. He removed the grasper and placed it back on the table. "Arthroscopic scissors, please."

The tech handed him the small scissors, which Tim inserted through the second cannula. The doctor maneuvered them around the intestine until the base of the appendix sat between the two blades of the scissors. Tim squeezed his hand, watching on the TV monitor as the appendix tissue was excised. More blood leaked out from the base and poured into the stomach cavity. Tim got rid of the scissors and reached back in with the grasper to remove the separated appendix, then dropped the inflamed tissue into the waste container.

Tim heard the nurse and anesthesiologist whispering in the background, seemingly thinking he couldn't hear them. "How does he do it so quickly? He's a machine," the gas doctor said.

"He works so fast, it's like there's two of him," the nurse responded, trying to keep her voice hushed.

Tim smiled at the compliments before moving ahead with the procedure. "I need to close the inner incision before the bleeding makes him swell. Do we have the mini staple gun in the room?"

"Yep. Got it right here," the tech replied, the small gun gleaming under the surgical lights.

Tim placed the mini gun inside the second cannula and fired four staples to close the hole where the appendix had attached to the large intestine, sealing off the oncoming flow of blood.

"Oh, he should feel much better when he wakes up." Tim removed both cannulas and sutured the two skin incision sites. He stood up from his stool and drummed his fingers on the back table. "And . . . that's it! I hope everyone has a great weekend."

Tim untied his bloodstained mask and exited the operating room.

Tim pulled up at home and parked his car before hopping out and listening to his Timberlands smash the frozen ground below. Equally relieved that the weekend had finally arrived, the wolf-head knocker growled when Tim opened the door.

Faith peered out from the kitchen holding a plate and a washcloth. "Hi Tim! I have this last dish to clean, then I'll be out of your hair. Hope you had a good week."

Tim touched the bald spot on top of his head and chuckled. "Faith, my dear. Take your time."

Tim heard the dishwasher door slam shut, then the corresponding beeps that signaled the start of a new wash cycle. Faith strolled into the living room and grabbed her things. "All right, I'm all done. Tell Hanna and the kids I said farewell."

"Bye Faith! Have a nice night," Tim said, waving to her as she hopped in her car and drove off.

"She's nice. I like her," Hanna said, walking into the living room. "She's done a really good job of helping us out, too."

Tim sighed. "I know she has. Unfortunately, it's not your decision . . ."

Hanna nodded and then walked back to their room, her robe dragging on the floor behind her.

Tim massaged his eyes, then went upstairs to check on his daughter. "Can I come in?" he asked, knocking on the door.

"Yes," Sammi responded, opening the door for him, then sitting back on her bed. Her scars formed a racetrack on her skin where only despair could win. Sammi picked up the scissors in one hand and the mirror in her other and resumed cutting her hair; the soft red drifted down onto the bed before Sammi scrunched it all up and tossed it in the trash.

Tim watched her, grimacing every time the blades sliced her hair. He wanted his daughter to be perfect—to feel like she was perfect.

Sammi paused as the last of her hair fell to the floor. "Do you think I'm special, Daddy?"

Tim mulled over the question. Of course, the answer was yes, but he wanted her to feel excited for what was to come. "After this, you absolutely will be, my dear."

Disgusted, Sammi looked at the red locks accumulated in the trash.

Tim strolled over and sat next to her on the bed. Trying to change the subject, he asked, "Well, whatdya think?"

"I like her, Dad. She's kind."

Tim brought his tone down to a whisper. "You know what I mean."

Sammi placed the scissors on top of the bed but continued to grip the mirror firmly in her hand. "She's so beautiful. I think my answer is yes."

Tim raised an eyebrow. "You think?"

Sammi stared into the mirror, observing her disfigurement. "She's the one."

Tim sat still on the bed, rubbing his daughter's back. "I'll go get her, then."

FAITH

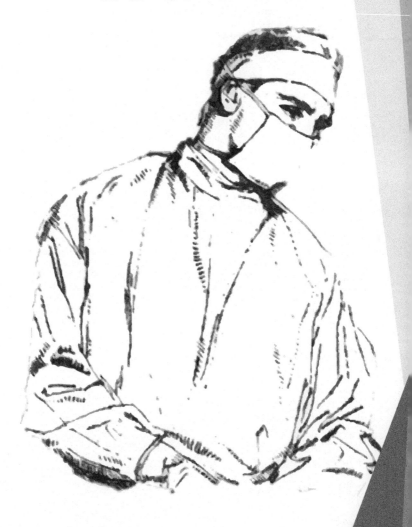

CHAPTER 10

⸻ ◆ ⸻

PINK MIST

*M*inus the dull scorpion sting on the side of her neck, Faith couldn't see or feel anything distinct, only a warmth surrounding her. *Is this what being inside a womb feels like?* she thought.

There was nothing but silence, then a steady beeping penetrated the darkness and stroked her eardrums with auricle vibrations.

Her eyes slowly focused, the darkness transforming into muddy swirls of color. The first thing she saw was a green luminescence emanating from the monitor's screen. The leaf-green lights jumped all over the place until swirls became structural and the dancing green lights turned into numbers: sixty-seven beats per minute.

Faith's eyes scanned the room. She was in a small bunker-type area, but a clean one without a single sign of dirt or rust. The room had a single massive light hanging in the center of the ceiling that beamed brightness into all corners. Small shadows waltzed silently on the walls, trying to warn her of the lurking danger, but she felt oddly calm and couldn't quite remember why she would be in bed right now.

After her ears adjusted to the noise, they picked up the sound of another monitor beeping to her left. She strained her neck muscles to look over and saw another bed with a body atop it covered completely by blankets.

Faith's eyes followed the dancing lights on the screen until she saw clear tubes protruding from the monitor. She traced the tubes around a mounted pole that circled her bed until they came to a sharp end in her left wrist, the needle tip diving into her dermis and secreting an unknown substance.

Tim sat on a stool at the foot of her bed, the scalpel in his hand glowing ominously as it waved through the air. While humming "Wade in the Water" by Eva Cassidy, he brought it down to touch the flesh on Faith's leg and started to systematically saw back and forth, using the sharp blade to carefully slice away patches of skin. Once the skin was separated and removed, Tim pinched the pieces with sterile tweezers and dropped them into a container filled with a yellow liquid.

Faith felt like she was an observer in a studio, watching as an artist creates a masterpiece in his natural environment. Tim appeared peaceful while diligently preparing the skin segments, then dunking them in the yellow pool.

The machine in the corner dinged. Tim stood up, flipped open the lid, and pulled out the inner chamber before untwisting a second lid and pulling out a filled syringe. The bottom portion of the liquid was dark red, diluting in color until the top portion was light yellow. Tim flicked the syringe to further separate the two colors, then squirted only the yellow portion into the basin containing the skin; the rest he ejected in the waste container. He walked back over to the side of Faith's bed and screwed the empty syringe onto her IV, withdrawing another vial's worth of blood. Once filled, he placed the syringe back in the machine's inner chamber and closed the lid before pressing the start button and sitting back on his stool.

His gloved fingers wrapped around the blade handle once again, and the dance of doom restarted.

A sharp pain shot through Faith's left leg, which caused her to flinch and switch her perspective from distanced third to terrified first person.

"Whoops, did you feel that one, dear? I'm so sorry," Tim muttered under his mask. "Let's get you some more regional anesthesia for that leg block."

He stood up and walked over to a cabinet in the far corner of the room, then opened one of the cabinet doors and rifled around inside it. All Faith could hear was the clinking of glass vials as Tim's hands searched for the correct one.

The beeping of her monitor increased in frequency, and Faith started to recognize her circumstances. She couldn't remember how she'd gotten here, but she knew she had to get out—this could be her only opportunity.

Her arms were tied to the bed, but only at the shoulders. While Tim searched for whatever vial he was looking for, Faith tried wiggling back and forth to pry one of her restraints loose.

Her legs burned more as her senses started to return. She choked back a scream by swallowing the built-up terror, aware that she would need to utilize the energy later. It was then that her eyes viewed the surgical blade sitting atop her belly on a sterile blue towel. Tim must have left it there when he went to search the cabinet, she realized. Straining her right arm, her fingers inches away from the blade handle, Faith thought, *Keep going, keep pushing* as she stretched every sinew in her body toward the knife. Tears turned to beads of sweat as she finally felt plastic. She let out a sigh of relief when she grasped the handle and tucked the knife under the blankets at her waist.

Her victory proved short-lived. Tim withdrew more mysterious liquid into a syringe and injected it in the tube entering Faith's vein. The burning sensation in her legs receded as the medicine corroded her nerve endings.

Fear birthed horror as not just pain, but all sensation, drained from her body.

"Tim! Help me, please. Don't do this!"

"Oh, goodness me. I didn't realize you had awakened. Let me take care of that, real quick."

Tim pulled out a gas mask and placed it over Faith's nose and mouth, making sure to cover all of the cracks to achieve optimal suction.

"No! No! *No!*" Faith shrieked, spit launching from her mouth and lining the inner mask as Tim tied it over her face.

"Just breathe, nice and easy," Tim said soothingly.

A pink mist filled the inside of the mask. Faith held her breath for as long as possible, until her lungs screamed and forced her to take in a big gulp of the pink air. Her head vibrated as the medicine infiltrated her body. Her muscles relaxed and her eyelids grew heavy, as if the accumulation of particles was weighing them down. Her last image before slowly slipping into a dark abyss was of Tim pressing the mask firmly over her mouth.

CHAPTER 11

ARCTIC FREEZE

*F*aith regained consciousness a few hours later. She felt nothing: no pain, no sorrow, no fear. A slow thumping gonged behind her eyes and, a few seconds later, her nerves awoke to a searing sensation exploding in her legs. The agony crept up toward her head, which felt like a million needles were piercing her scalp.

At first, she suppressed her screams, but the pain quickly became too much to bear and Faith howled in agony. Her anguish amplified, reverberating in the poorly lit room and rattling the lightbulbs from their sockets. Yells turned into moans, which eventually slipped into sobs of exhaustion. Faith's thoughts flickered to her mom lying comatose in her hospital bed; more than ever before, Faith yearned to be at her mother's side.

Her eyes darted around the room. She recognized that she was alone but didn't know how much longer it would last. If she was going to try and escape, there was no better time than the present.

The room looked almost identical to the one in which she'd accidently regained consciousness in the middle of the procedure. But this room was also different. The bed next to hers was gone, and the air had a musky scent and felt cooler. Faith realized she was below ground.

The four-piece surgical lamp over her bed had only one light turned on and cast a strange glow. Her arms were still bound to the operating table and the IV needle still punctured her vein, feeding the drugs to her capillaries.

Trembling, Faith moved her eyes downward to her legs. She felt sick to her stomach at the thought of what she was about to see.

It wasn't as bloody as she'd expected, but her legs had been completely skinned of their top dermal layer. All of the way up to mid-thigh on both legs, light-pink–colored gauze was wrapped firmly to prevent the oozing pus from dripping onto the bed.

Okay, deep breaths, Faith, she told herself. *Slow your heart rate.*

She shuddered at her attempt to slow her heart rate to a rhythmic pattern. *Start with the basics. Try moving your toes.* She glanced down, grimacing from the pain, but was relieved to see that all toes were present and moving. Next, she noticed a tightness on her head. When she flexed her scalp, she could feel several bandages wrapped like a turban.

When she tried to move her fingers, she felt those of her right hand bump against something hard that was tucked neatly under her buttocks. When she remembered what it was, a sinister smile stretched from ear to ear.

Approximately forty-five minutes later, Faith heard the stutter of footsteps coming down the stairwell above her. A rustling of keys was followed by the lock clicking, the silver knob being twisted, and the door slowly being eased open. Faith was prepared to fight Tim to the death, but she froze when it was Twain who instead walked in.

Twain stepped into the room holding a glass of Gatorade and a small plate of cheese and crackers.

He strolled over to the bedside table and set the plate down. "Dad says you need to eat, if you want to recover."

Eyeing Twain suspiciously, Faith asked, "And why would I want to recover? Just so you can do this to me again?"

Her harsh words cut deeply into Twain, who flinched and withdrew.

Faith broke the silence when she realized he wouldn't. "Well, don't make me beg for it. I'll take some of that Gatorade, please," she said, unable to look the boy in the eyes.

Twain steadily eased his way back to the side of the bed. It took both of his hands to grab the glass and tip it to Faith's lips. She took long gulps of the precious liquid, feeling the electrolytes energizing her body.

When she nodded to Twain that she was done drinking, he quickly receded back into the shadows.

"Dad will be down soon to check on you," Twain murmured, turning his back and heading toward the doorway. Before twisting the knob and exiting the room, he allowed his hand to linger on the knob and a whisper escaped his lips. "I'm sorry for this."

TIM

CHAPTER 12

---◆---

GOOD VERSUS TIM

Tim was upstairs watching a local news channel when Twain emerged from downstairs holding the empty Gatorade glass, his hands and shoulders trembling.

"What's goin' on, bud? You look like you've seen a ghost. There aren't any monsters down in the basement I need to take care of, are there?" Tim said, half grinning at Twain and half listening to the news.

"I feel bad, Daddy. This is wrong. In my Harry Potter books, our actions are things Lord Voldemort and the bad people would do."

Tim grimaced at the accusation. His family was a strong unit, and they would only remain so if everyone stayed on the same page.

"Come here, boy," Tim said as he patted his thigh and beckoned Twain over to sit on his lap.

Twain quietly ambled over to his father who, with outstretched arms, lifted him up and placed him on his lap.

Tim winked at his son and, with his finger pressed to the tip of the boy's nose, said, "You think I'm like Lord Voldemort, now, do you? You know he's the most powerful wizard in all the land?"

"Yes, Dad, he is. But in every book I've read, good conquers evil." Twain looked into his father's eyes, his own blue matching his dad's brilliant hue. "I guess I don't want you to be beaten."

Tim raised his voice. "Now you are saying I am evil? Mwahahaha!" Twain bounced up and down on Tim's lap as he fake-evil laughed.

When his laugh finally subsided, Tim wiped tears from his eyes. "Now, what makes Mister He-Who-Must-Not-Be-Named so bad? Tell me, Twain. What is the difference between good and evil?"

Twain looked up into his father's eyes, his brain shifting into gear. "Because he hurts things?"

"Maybe, son, but just because you hurt someone doesn't make you evil. Let's say a girl from your class really likes you, but you don't like her back in the same way, and this hurts her feelings. Does that make you evil?"

"No, Dad . . ."

"No, it doesn't. What makes you evil is intent. To do harmful things knowing they won't benefit you or anyone else. Hurting someone or something for no reason, doing evil for evil's sake, is what makes someone bad, Twain. I know what I did downstairs to Faith seems horrible, but I'm doing it for the good of your sister. Never forget that." Tim paused before asking, "What if it were you?"

Twain stared blankly at the wall but absorbed every word his father said. It was true. What Tim did was horrible, but it wasn't for nothing. It was for the love of his only daughter, which gave him permission to do what he did, and that was something Twain could accept.

He nodded in agreement, then slipped off his father's lap. "Thank you for that, Dad. I think I understand now. Family first, right?"

Tim beamed down at his son. "Always."

CHAPTER 13

THE DONOR

Tim walked upstairs to check on Sammi, the carpeted stairs dulling the sound of his footsteps but doing nothing to calm his racing heart. Sammi was sleeping peacefully on her bed, her chest rising with her steady breath. Her bald, scabbed head reflected the gentle sunlight coming through the windows, its orange glow matching the color of the shaved hairs in Sammi's trash can.

Tim walked over and stared at her, content with the way things had progressed. He went over to the sink in her bathroom and washed his hands, making sure to eliminate every germ under his cuticles. As he reached for the towel, he saw his reflection and paused, trying to convince himself that what he did was right and that he wasn't evil.

Tim shook the notion from his head and quietly went to work changing Sammi's bandages and cleaning her skin. Memories of a scar-free Sammi flashed through Tim's mind as he dotted the washcloth in antibacterial soap and cleaned her surgical wounds. He wet the cloth again and gently wiped the scalp of her bald head, feeling the tiny lumps under the cloth when he dabbed her newly inserted donor hair follicles. The new follicles looked like young trees on a farm, lined in perfectly symmetrical rows and awaiting their new growth.

Sammi groaned and her eyes flickered open.

"Shh, my dear," Tim cooed in a soothing voice. "Everything is all right. Let me take care of you."

"Where's my mirror, I want to look."

Tim stood up and disposed of the dirty bandages in the trash can. "Not now, baby. Just relax. Your body needs time to heal. You'll look so beautiful after this."

Sammi smiled, then yawned, the drugs still making her sleepy. "Did it work?"

"Only time will tell, sweetie. But I think it did."

Sammi fell back asleep and Tim exited the room, trying his hardest not to make any sound and disturb his sleeping beauty.

He quietly closed the door to Sammi's room, barely hearing the audible *click* of it slipping into its groove. When he turned to see Hanna in the hallway eagerly waiting for him, he let out an exasperated sigh.

As soon as their eyes met, Hanna immediately started asking questions. *How's she doing? Is everything healing? Did it work?* Her eyes were wide with anticipation, famished for answers. Her eagerness made sense to Tim, especially after their first child was born still, but he tried to never bring that up.

Instead, he beamed with pride and replied, "It went splendidly. She's comfortable and there's no sign of infection. Her body seems to be accepting the donor graft and follicles."

Hanna's face lit up for a moment before quickly losing color. "Donor . . ." she whispered, shaking her head. "I wish there was a better way to say that. What do you plan on doing with 'the donor'?"

Tim avoided Hanna's stare. "Whatever is necessary," he whispered as he walked past her and headed toward the basement.

CHAPTER 14

SAMMI GIRL

Tim descended the stairs, watching the lights from the kitchen fade away with each step—a reminder of why he was doing this—but halfway down, he froze. A putrid emotion enveloped him, making his stomach sick and filling his mouth with an awful taste. He took a deep breath and closed his eyes, allowing memories of Sammi to enter his mind and give him the strength he needed to continue onward.

* * *

Sammi was a breech baby: her feet had entered the world first, toes wriggling with the excitement of being born. When the rest of her body finally came, Tim and Hanna were surprised to see she had a full head of curly red hair, as no one in their immediate families was a redhead. "Touched by fire," they would come to say.

Tim cradled their new baby girl, who had already filled the void in his and Hanna's hearts.

"Don't be a ball hog, Tim! Let me hold her, I did all the hard work!" Hanna said with a smirk, grinning in anticipation of holding her newborn. And as soon as Hanna wrapped her arms around Sammi, the baby was wide-eyed and cooing to show affection toward her mother.

The hospital room was dark, but it looked to Tim like Hanna was glowing unlike ever before, emanating a light so warm that he, the doctor, and the nurses who swarmed around her did so like insects to a lamp.

Sammi reached out with her little hands and touched Hanna's face as if it featured Braille, feeling both the smoothness of her skin and memorizing her mother's every orifice and pore. Tim walked over and stuck a single finger out in front of his daughter, toward which she extended her grasping hands.

He was amused by her tiny fingers, barely the size of peanuts. Sammi cooed again, and both Tim and Hanna responded in turn.

When Tim looked up, numerous members of the hospital staff were beaming at him, making him and Hanna feel special, as if this was the only baby ever delivered in this hospital.

Dr. Greene nodded at Tim and tipped an invisible hat. He beckoned the staff outside the room, to give Tim and his wife some time alone with their new daughter.

The hospital door closed, and Tim looked back over at Hanna, whose eyes were halfway shut, heavy with exhaustion.

"You look tired, my dear. Want me to take over baby duty so you can get some rest?"

Hanna looked at her husband dreamily, then glanced back down to the baby in her arms. "No, I'm happy right where I am."

Six amazing years had passed since Sammi was born. Hanna was cooking fried chicken with her daughter wrapped around her legs like a baby chimp. Sammi's curly red hair was bouncing up and down as Hanna carefully moved the chicken from the pan to a plate. When the heat caught an air bubble in the oil, the grease popped and spattered onto Hanna's arm, causing her to shriek in pain and drop the pan. Hot grease was ejected from the pan and flowed down on Sammi's bare skin, encasing her stomach, legs, and lower back with instantly blistering burns.

Sammi screamed, and Hanna ignored her own mild burn as she saw Sammi's back and legs bubbling with lavalike pus that swelled under her tender skin.

"Tim! In the kitchen! *Help!*" Hanna screeched, gingerly picking up her daughter and plopping her in the sink. She turned on the faucet and allowed cold water to run over the blisters and ease Sammi's pain. But no matter how frigid the water, it couldn't stop the burning sensation spreading throughout Sammi's body.

The little girl's arms and legs flailed in agony when Tim ran into the kitchen, his face reddened from the sprint. "What . . . what is going on!" he yelled, his eyes widening in terror when he saw the blisters eating away at Sammi's precious skin, turning it into vanilla pudding.

Tim headed toward the medicine cabinet, the doctor in him taking control. He grabbed a bottle of aloe vera and a wad of nonstick gauze, then hustled to the freezer and grabbed an ice pack.

When he reached the sink, Tim gently patted Hanna on her back—her hands trembling as icy shock coursed through her veins—saying, "It'll be okay." He twisted the knob controlling the water coming out of the faucet to shut it off. "It wasn't your fault."

Hanna collapsed to her knees, wrapping her arms around her shins and burying her face in her legs. "But Tim! It *was* my fault."

Tim looked at his wife crumpled on the floor and felt anger flash through him. "Hanna, get up. I need your help!" He glanced back over at Sammi, who had quieted. She seemed normal for a moment, then her eyes rolled back in her skull and she started to seize. "Hanna! Get up! She's going into shock. I need you to get some paper towels, now!"

Hanna jumped up and grabbed the paper towels, her eyes bulging and pleading for Tim to give her direction.

"Good, now carefully pat her dry so we can put on some ice and ointment. Do not rub her skin or it'll pop the blisters."

Hanna nodded and did as she was told, carefully patting the water droplets until Sammi was completely dry.

"Great. Now help me put on the aloe, it should ease the pain for now. After it's on, we can cover it with this gauze, then use the ice pack."

Tim held his seizing daughter still until Hanna finished putting on the ointment and gauze. "Keys are on the hook by the door, quick, go get the car started. I'll put this ice pack on her, then meet you there."

Hanna left to get the car started, hearing Sammi's arms and legs pounding against the kitchen floor. Tim gently picked up his daughter up and carried her to the car. "Shh, I know it hurts, baby girl, be strong. You'll be feeling good in no time."

The only response came from Sammi's uncontrollably flailing limbs.

Tim thought that when the seizing stopped, she would be better; he was wrong. Shrieking replaced the shaking, and he wondered if infection had already consumed Sammi's white blood cells. Brown pus seeped through the bandages and dripped onto the leather in the car's back seat. When they were safely inside, Hanna slammed the gas pedal and the car tires screeched, burning away the rubber like the grease had her daughter's flesh.

They arrived at the hospital and Tim quickly got out of the car and scooped Sammi into his arms. He could feel her skin sliding underneath the bandages. When Hanna returned with a wheelchair, he placed Sammi on the seat, half of her skin ripping off her legs and sticking to his arms where he'd just held her. Tim grimaced and shook his daughter's dead skin off his arm, then wheeled her into the hospital lobby.

The double doors slid open and an all-too-familiar clerk welcomed them. "Hi, Dr. Hill," the receptionist said with a cheery smile. "What brings you in this time of . . . Oh my gosh! Is she all right?"

White foam was gurgling out of Sammi's mouth and sliding down her chin.

Tim yelled, "Check us in and call up to the burns unit, immediately! Tell them it's me and we're on the way up."

The receptionist nodded, worry casting a shadow on his face as Tim and Hanna ran past him to the elevator.

They arrived on the second floor and the burns doctor was waiting. He showed them to their room

121

and had them change Sammi into a paper-thin gown so the specialist could examine her.

The specialist came back into the room holding two Vicodin in the palm of one hand and a paper cup filled with water in the other. "For the pain," he said to Tim as he handed him the small white pills.

Tim took the pills and the water and held them out in front of his daughter. "Here, put these in your mouth and use the water to help swallow. Don't chew."

Even though Sammi was conscious, her brain couldn't register what her father had just said. All of her nerve endings had been seared and were now disconnected from her neural network, which confused her preadolescent mind.

The doctor noticed that Sammi was unable to swallow the pills, so he yelled to his staff, "Someone, bring me more Vicodin, in liquid form." He glanced toward Tim. "Sorry, but we'll have to do this intravenously."

A nurse ran back into the room and handed the doctor a plastic bag filled with liquid meds. A clear tube, ending with a needle, dangled from it. The sharp tip pierced Sammi's pink, unprotected flesh and the liquid flooded in.

Thanks to modern medicine, in a matter of minutes the powerful drugs took effect and knocked Sammi out into a painless slumber—for the time being.

Six hours later, when Sammi awoke, her fried nerve endings were still keeping the pain at bay.

Tim was grateful to see his daughter open her eyes. Since she was so young, the doctor didn't want to give Sammi any more painkillers.

Sammi's eyes glimmered with curiosity when she saw the two ibuprofen pills the doctor had handed to Tim. She took them both from her father and gave them a sniff. "What are these, Daddy?"

"They're a special kind of candy that will make you feel a little bit better. Go ahead and take them."

Sammi tried to move her head backward and forward without aggravating the burns on her back. She plopped the two ibuprofen in the back of her throat, then sipped the water. Closing her eyes, she gulped hard and swallowed them both.

"Well done, sweetie. Now be a good girl and allow the doctor to check out your burns. It may sting a little bit, but he will make you better." Tim looked over at the doctor before he spoke his last words. "I promise."

The doctor nodded, recognizing the vibe he was getting from Tim. "All righty now, Sammi girl," he said as he moved toward Sammi. "I'm going to need you to tell me where you hurt the most. Can you do that for me?"

Sammi stared at him questioningly, then glanced at her father. When she saw Tim nod his head, she lifted the back of her gown and said, "It hurts most right *here*." She then lifted the front of her gown and showed her calves and thighs. "And also *here*."

"All right, let me take a look at ya," the doctor said as he flashed a small flashlight at the places she mentioned. The affable expression on his face shifted, and he turned to look at Tim and Hanna. "What happened?" he asked, suddenly serious.

Hanna looked away, which forced Tim to answer. "Hot grease spill," he mumbled.

The doctor winced. "Ouch. I bet that hurt, little girl. But let me tell you, you've got to be the bravest person I have ever seen to deal with something like this the way you are."

Sammi managed to muster a smile. "Thanks! I always knew I was stronger than the other boys and girls."

The doctor chuckled and rubbed the cherry-red curls on Sammi's head. "I'm going to get some bandages and medicine," he said. "Tim, will you accompany me, please?"

Tim closed the door behind them when they left the room, fully aware that he was about to get some bad news. The doctor pinched the bridge of his nose to relieve some stress. "I'm going to be real with you, Tim. Those burns are third-degree, if not worse. I'll give you some antibiotics to prevent infection, but nothing I have will prevent the scarring."

Tim sighed. "Okay, that's not too bad. I was expecting way worse."

The doctor half-smiled at Tim's reply. "It's not the burns I'm worried about, Tim. It's the scars. Burns like those will leave your daughter horribly disfigured. If it was me, I wouldn't care, but a five-year-old girl growing up covered in—"

Tim raised his hand, interrupting the doctor midsentence. "You've made your point." He paced back and forth on the spot, one hand on his chin as he thought of possible solutions. "Is there anything we can do? Any special ointments or . . . surgery?"

"Well, there is skin grafting, where we would take skin from another part of her body that's less noticeable or potentially take from a cadaver donor, but neither result is great."

Tim shook his head, seeds of worry sprouting in his mind as he imagined Sammi in high school with all of the other boys and girls pointing at her scars and making fun of her. "Cure one scar by creating another? No, that won't work. There's got to be another solution. Anything?"

The doctor eyed Tim cautiously, weighing up whether he should say what was on his mind. Rumors of Tim's past had always circled within the hospital, and he didn't want him getting any ideas.

Tim sensed the man's discomfort and took another approach. "Imagine if this was your daughter. What would you do?"

This hit its mark, as Tim saw the doctor mentally run through the scenario. "It's possible you could try synthetic skin, but the results haven't been great."

Tim's ears perked up, unsure if the reason was because of the possibility that an alternative solution could save his daughter years of embarrassment or the fact that the method was unorthodox. *You aren't that man anymore, Tim. You promised Hanna you wouldn't go down that path again*, Tim recited in his mind.

But he succumbed to his curiosity and asked, "Tell me more about this artificial skin. What's it made of?"

The doctor crossed his arms and debated whether he should continue. "Tim, from one medical professional to another, the synthetic skin is not yet a viable option. But if you must know, it's a collagen scaffold that helps skin regenerate."

"Interesting." Tim pushed his glasses firmly back up the bridge of his nose. "So, it's like a healthy petri dish for skin growth?"

"Precisely. But like teleportation, it won't work. I think, for your daughter, ointment and rest are best. She will have to learn to live with the scars. I know as a father that's hard to hear, but when life throws you a curveball you still gotta swing."

Without making eye contact, Tim muttered, "Ointment it is," then swung around and headed back to Sammi's room.

The following year, before Sammi started first grade, Tim and Hanna had a second child, a boy.

This time Sammi joined her parents in the hospital to greet her new brother. "He's so tiny, Mommy! What're we going to call him?" she asked, the restrictive scars forcing her to lean awkwardly over the side of the bed to get a better view.

Tim and Hanna exchanged looks, and Tim said, "You want to do the honors, Han?"

Sammi's eyes were greedy for answers. "Wait! Can I name him? Please, please, *please*," she begged. She hopped up on the bed next to her mom, stuck a finger out, and lightly touched her baby brother's nose. "From now on, your name is Princess Buttercup, and you will do everything I command."

Tim smiled and lifted Sammi in his arms. "We aren't naming him Princess Buttercup, and you can't boss him around like you do your dolls, Sammi," he said, before placing her back down on the ground.

Sammi shrugged and folded her scarred arms, then scrunched up her face into a frown. "Hmph, fine, Daddy. What are we going to call him, then?"

Tim glanced at Hanna and raised an eyebrow. Hanna stared deep into their son's eyes, still unsure of what she wanted to name him. The longer she gazed into his blue irises, the harder her brain churned for an answer. Finally, one came, and she said, "Welcome to the world, Twain."

A few weeks later, Sammi kissed Twain on the

top of his bald head and threw her backpack straps around her shoulders. "See you around, kiddo."

Twain looked up at his sister and squealed with delight when she rubbed his head, making gurgling noises. A snot bubble formed on his nostril and when it popped Twain rolled around and shrieked with laughter, seemingly for his own entertainment.

"Ew, boys are so gross. Princess Buttercup would never do anything like that," Sammi said as she scooted away from Twain to avoid his phlegm-drenched face.

"You did the same things, ya know?" Tim said when he walked into the living room holding Sammi's lunch bag. "Except you were even grosser! Constantly farting and pooping yourself. You were a nightmare, compared to Twain."

The color drained from Sammi's face as she pictured herself making all those messes. "I'm so sorry, Daddy. I didn't know . . ."

Tim got to his knees and opened his arms wide. "I'm just teasing, sweetheart. You were an angel. Now, come give me a hug before your first day of school!"

Sammi grinned and showed off the gaps where her front two teeth used to be. She spread her arms wide and, slowed down as usual by her limp, swan dived toward her father. Even though her prescribed ointment had prevented infection, it hadn't been able to heal her scars. The disfigured fascia tightened the skin on her back and legs, causing her to hobble, but that didn't stop Sammi. She threw her arms around her father's neck so as to be picked up and twirled through the air.

"Oh, my turn!" Hanna said when she entered the room. Sammi shuffled over to her mom and gave her a hug. Hanna picked up the car keys and swung them around her finger. "You ready to rock 'n' roll, Sammi girl?"

Sammi beamed and once again showed off her dark absence of front teeth. "Always."

* * *

Tim blinked away a tear and continued along his path, memories unfreezing him from the stair he was glued to.

CHAPTER 15

TIM, THE FIXER-UPPER

*T*im felt his foot hit concrete and knew he had reached the bottom. The basement consisted of low ceilings and winding corridors: a labyrinth invisible to the outside world. The passageways forked, and dead ends were prevalent enough to confuse even the brightest of minds—but not Tim.

He had made this trek several times in the last few years of his life, mentally mapping out every nook and cranny and memorizing the halls like he'd done with his vocabulary when he was in med school. *Walk to the end of the hall and take a left followed by a quick right. Keep following this path until you reach another fork in the path and then veer left.* At the end was a door that led to a place only Tim could enter, where he could be himself and remain hidden from the outside world.

He no longer needed to think about the directions; his feet guided him as if they knew where he needed to go and what he wanted to do there. The soft *pat-pat* sound of his feet on the concrete followed him along the hallways. The absence of windows required Tim to carry a small candle in order to light the other candles hanging from the walls as he proceeded. The wicks hissed when they caught aflame, almost screaming at Tim for rousing them from their slumber. The light produced dark shadows that wavered on the walls and distorted the hallways like a room in a fun house, but Tim didn't mind. This was his safe place.

After navigating the dungeon maze, Tim finally saw the door at the end of the hall—his personal light at the end of the tunnel. He took a deep breath, then exhaled, making sure to breathe out every last bit of air in his lungs. He paused as he felt Faith's presence ooze through the door. "Habanera" by Georges Bizet played in his mind as he tried to figure out what he was going to say when he walked in.

Tim placed his hand on the doorknob, then quickly recoiled it as if the metal was scorching hot. Guilt settled into his bones like cement, hardening and filling the empty spaces that should be occupied by love and happiness. *I can't do this*, Tim thought.

He didn't expect anyone to respond, for he always burdened himself by concealing his thoughts. Fresh tears gathered, then slid down his cheeks, crashing on the dusty floor and binding with dirt and moisture.

Then that's when he heard it: *You can fix this.*

The words bounced around in his skull, gaining in volume with every smack against his temporal lobes and reminding him of the last time someone said those very same words.

* * *

Hanna had just arrived home from dropping off Sammi at her first day of school when Tim packed his briefcase and headed out the door for work, thankful his wife was there to take care of their newborn son.

Mondays were a clinic day for Tim, meaning all he had to do was check on a few patients and see how everyone was doing after their recent surgeries. It was his favorite day of the week: no surgical procedures, just meeting new people who didn't feel well and observing the ones he was helping heal.

Usually on clinic days, Tim would stop by a coffee shop on his way to the office and buy everyone lattes, cappuccinos, and doughnuts, along with some other breakfast items. And that's exactly what he did this morning. He figured he could get away with being a few minutes late, if he brought everyone food and coffee.

When he departed the Starbucks parking lot, the scent of ground espresso beans and fried dough filled his car. Tim took a deep breath, inhaling all of the marvelous smells. "Mmm, smells like God," he said to himself while adjusting the rearview mirror.

He parked in his usual spot at the hospital, grabbed the drinks and food, and slammed the door closed with his foot as he walked into the clinic.

Tim found it interesting how smell worked. Scientists always talked about the speed of sound or light, but no one seemed interested in the speed of smell. As soon as the wonderful aroma reached Tim's coworkers' noses, one by one they sprang up, starting with those closest to him when he entered the office.

"Thanks, T-Bone!" the first one said, stuffing his mouth with a doughnut and grabbing a latte.

"You're the man, Tim!"

"Thanks, Dr. Hill!"

Tim greeted all of them with smiles, while hiding the brown bag filled with the special items behind his back. Tim always thought that his nurses, and nurses in general, were the kindest people around. They literally cleaned puke, shit, and blood while barely making what most people considered a median-level income. Nurses worked because of their passion and earnest belief that what they were doing made the planet a better place; Tim wanted to reward them with buttered biscuits and egg sandwiches.

He walked into the pre-op area and nurses in blue scrubs, bright-eyed and eagerly awaiting their food, ran over in greeting.

"Thank you for everything you do, ladies," Tim said. "Couldn't do it without you." He started to hand out the food, feeling a little like a mama bird feeding her chicks.

Tim next headed over to his office, nodding to his secretary when he passed her. Once he was comfortable, he gave her the green light to start sending his patients back.

The first one came in clutching her stomach, her face a light shade of green and her breathing labored. Tim examined her and decided it was best to put her on some antibiotics and nature's best remedy: rest. Tim asserted that most of his patients just needed a little time to relax and let their bodies heal naturally; he tried to avoid antibiotics and painkillers unless they were absolutely necessary.

The next patient that walked in was a seventeen-year-old male who appeared to be what some might consider a "skater bro." He wore skintight black jeans with holes at the knees. Even though it was warm inside Tim's office, the boy had his hoodie up so that only his perfectly swooshed hair protruded out the front. Tim didn't want to stereotype, but he was always careful with people like this young man. They usually came in faking a cough and saying that they couldn't sleep, before requesting a powerful sedative.

Tim eyed the boy skeptically before asking him what seemed to be the problem. The boy, clearly having memorized the script one of his friends had provided him, recited: "My throat hurts." At this, he put his arm over his mouth and faked a cough. "And I'm having a hard time falling asleep."

Tim chuckled and pulled out a small flashlight. "All righty then. Come over here and let's take a look." He pressed the button and the light flashed on. "Open wide."

The boy's jaw spread open, his breath reeking of marijuana and cigarettes. Tim shined the light inside but saw nothing out of the ordinary. "Oh dear," he remarked.

The boy looked taken aback, since he hadn't expected anything would actually be wrong with him. "Wh . . . what do you see, doc?" he asked sheepishly.

"Two cavities, my man. I think you need to go see a dentist. As for the sore throat, you can mix warm water with salt and gargle it. The salt will clear out any bacteria that's causing the pain."

The boy frowned in defeat, then scurried out of the room. A few minutes later, Tim heard him skateboarding outside the office window. "Called it," he muttered to himself before summoning the next patient.

When lunchtime came, Tim had to answer the unexpected phone call from his wife with a mouth full of peanut butter sandwich. "Well, hello there, lovely lady," he began. "How are—"

But Hanna interrupted him: "Tim, can you please come home? It's urgent."

Tim tried to force down the peanut butter that was clogging his esophagus.

"Tim? Are you there?"

"Yes, yes, I'm here." He coughed to clear his throat. "What's the matter?"

"It's Sammi, just please come home as soon as you can."

Tim sat still for a few seconds, his appetite entirely gone. He stood up and grabbed his coat off the rack, then headed out the door. "Cancel the rest of my appointments today, and give them my sincerest apologies," he called to his secretary. "An emergency has come up."

His secretary looked concerned, but she was far too polite to ask any questions. Tim ran out the door and was greeted unkindly by a freezing wind, as if the world was trying to tell him that something was wrong. The engine revved when he stuck the key in and floored the car out of the lot, running through stop signs and red lights in order to get home to his family as quickly as humanly possible. Hanna's uncertain tone had caused a cold anxiety to seep into his chest, freezing his innards and making him feel sick. A shiver ran through his back and he jerked the steering wheel, almost driving on the sidewalk.

The glass house was in sight, and soon he was pulling into the driveway and skidding to a stop as the gravel slid underneath the car's tires. The wind roared and whipped the few hairs left on his head around in circles and almost blew his glasses off his nose.

When Tim opened the door, he was welcomed by a wailing Sammi and a disgruntled Hanna, whose face was puffed up with anger and sadness: a dangerous concoction. Tim ran over and put his arm around his daughter, but she pulled away and buried her face deeper in her mom's shirt, unable to look him in the eyes.

"What happened?" Tim asked.

Hanna shook her head, signaling that this was not the right time to talk.

Sammi let go of her mom and glowered at the two of them. "How could y'all do this to me?" she screamed, her tears running like a creek after a rainstorm.

Tim tried to reach out to her, but she pulled back again and this time her lips curled into a snarl. "You knew this would happen, but you didn't do a thing about it! I thought you were supposed to fix people, Tim."

Hanna gasped. "Sammi! Don't talk to your father like that!"

"I wish I was dead," Sammi said, turning on a dime and sprinting upstairs to her room, slamming the door shut behind her.

Tim was still kneeling on the ground, rooted to the spot. He was shocked. Sammi had never called him Tim before or anything other than Dad, for that matter.

He looked quizzically at Hanna. "What did I do? What happened?"

Hanna strode over to the chair and sat down, crossing her legs and resting her head on her hands. "A couple hours after you left, I got a call from the principal." Hanna moved her hand up to her eyes and wiped away the leaking sadness. "Sammi was already bawling by then, Tim."

"Hanna, I can't help unless you tell me what the fuck happened," Tim said, clearly aggravated that everyone was upset and he didn't know why.

"Her scars, Tim. It was her scars. Apparently, many of her classmates made fun of her." Hanna reached for a Kleenex and blew her nose. "They called her horrible names: ugly and nasty Sammi. Some even called her Frankenstein and monster." She stomped her foot. "They abused our daughter!"

Tim's blood boiled and he was surprised, when he looked down at his arms, to see that his skin wasn't bubbling. "I'll fucking . . ."

Hanna sat motionless in the chair, continuing to look at her feet. "I'm sorry, Tim." When she glanced up, her eyes met his and when she stood up, Tim could see her whole body was trembling. "It's all my fault," she said. "If I hadn't spilled . . ."

"No. It was a freak accident. Get those horrible thoughts out of your head, Hanna."

But when his wife looked up, Tim barely recognized her. Hanna's once-beautiful green eyes were cloudy; even though she was standing next to him, she seemed distant. Her usual warmth and goofiness had evaporated and left behind a dryness Tim had never encountered.

"Is this how you felt after our first child died?" she asked, her voice emotionless.

Her question pierced Tim like an icy dagger. "What do you mean?" he said. "That wasn't anyone's fault. Hanna, get these evil ideas out of your head. Please! For God's sake."

Hanna cackled coldly. "God? I thought *you* were God once, able to fix everything. But you can't fix anything, can you? You couldn't help our stillborn child, and now you can't help your only daughter."

The disturbance Tim felt at what his wife was saying caught him utterly by surprise. "How could you say such a thing? I only wanted to help. I only *want* to help."

He took a step toward Hanna, reaching his hand out to grasp hers, but she whipped it away and collapsed to her knees.

Tim knelt down beside her and turned her face, watching the hate and sorrow consume it and leave behind only a trace of the person he loved. "What do you want me to do?"

The question hung in the empty room. Hanna stopped crying and turned her head, a twisted grin shaping her lips. "What you were born to do, Tim," she said. "I know I made you promise all those years ago, but family first." She latched her hands on his face, squeezing it tightly. "Go upstairs and *fix* this," she hissed. "Make our family whole again."

The wind continued to roar outside as Tim deliberately placed each foot on the next stair as he thought about what he was going to say. Losing a son who had never been alive was bad enough, but a daughter who was alive and wished to be dead was unbearable.

Branches scraped against the house like nails on a chalkboard, but Tim continued his ascent. The stairs seemed to stretch in perpetuity, as if the devil added two steps every time Tim conquered one. Finally, however, he reached the top. The hallway was eerily still; Tim had entered the eye of the storm. He wanted to run back downstairs and pretend none of this had happened, but his inner will moved his legs until he found himself at his daughter's door. He raised a hand to knock, then dropped it to his side. After drawing a deep breath, he once again raised his hand.

Tap-tap

No noise sounded from behind the door. Tim was about to turn around and head back downstairs when he heard the wood floor panels in Sammi's room creak.

"May I come in?" he asked.

Nothing. Tim's ears had become accustomed to noise by spending his days in the operating room using drills and hammers and listening to the constant beeping of monitors; his hearing was sensitive to silence. It had gotten to the point that silence was louder than noise, and the quiet coming from behind Sammi's door was deafening.

"Sammi, may I please come in?" he asked a second time, this time with a tinge of fear in his voice.

Once again, nothing.

Confident that he had heard Sammi stir when the floorboards creaked, Tim firmly twisted the knob and entered. On the far side of the room, Sammi stood wearing only a backless shirt and her underwear. There were two mirrors: a full-size one on wheels and the other in the palm of her hand. The large mirror was positioned behind her, and she was holding the handheld one up in front of her—using the two mirrors to reflect in each other so she could examine herself. When the mirrors lined up exactly, the effect was an infinite number of Sammis, who each held a mirror to reflect a horrible past.

Tim didn't say anything and instead observed the scars snaking up her back and legs. He had never realized just how catastrophic they were. Maybe it was the father in him that had blinded him. He couldn't be sure but seeing how the damage was woven into her flesh unsettled him and made him sick to his stomach.

Even though he had two kids and had been a father for years, parenting still felt new. When he saw his daughter's true disfigurement, he didn't know if he should be honest and tell Sammi the truth about how people would forever treat her differently or lie to her and pretend people wouldn't notice . . . that her defects made her special.

Heads or tails? Tim thought, as he considered the option that would result in a better outcome.

Just then, Sammi reached up and touched her hair, its fire running between her fingers. "What's a ginger?" she said, catching Tim off guard.

"It's . . . uh, another word for someone with red hair."

Sammi dropped her hand, the fingers on her other hand still wrapped around the mirror handle. "Why do they say gingers are gross and have no soul?" Sammi asked, then released a hiccup. "I shower every day and I put on deodorant and perfume and I . . ." The mirror she was holding wobbled as she started to cry. "I just don't understand, Daddy. Did I do something wrong?"

Her crying was like a spreading virus. A sadness Tim had only felt once before knocked on the door to his heart and caused him to weep. "I'm so sorry" was all he could muster, while any courage he'd felt drained from him.

Sammi straightened her posture, stretching the discolored skin across her back. Her hand no longer shook, and her whimpering turned to anger. "But then I look at myself, and I begin to understand," she said as her free hand traced the contours of her scars.

With snot dribbling from his nose, Tim fell to his knees. "No, sweetie. Listen to me. You are so beautiful, and I love you so much."

Sammi spun around to face her father. "I'm a monster!" she shrieked, then raised the mirror high and, in an explosion of glass and animosity, smashed it into the wheeled one.

Goose bumps rose on Tim's arms like hedges on a farm field. "Please, Sammi, what can I do to help?" he pleaded.

A voice from behind startled him.

"You know what to do." Hanna strode over to her daughter, leaving behind bloody footprints from the glass under her feet. When she reached their daughter, she bent down on one impervious knee and touched a hand to her daughter's face. "Do you want Daddy to fix you?" she asked softly. "Do you want him to make your scars go away?"

The twinkling in her eyes long since extinguished, Sammi merely nodded.

Hanna patted her daughter on top of her head. "Good girl."

The light in her own eyes was no longer present when Hanna turned to face Tim. "You said you wanted to fix our son all those years ago, and you failed." Standing up and walking to Tim, who was still on his knees, Hanna then placed a single finger under his chin and lifted his face so that he was looking into her eyes. "But this time you will."

* * *

Back in the basement, Tim opened his eyes and started to pace. He realized his hands were shaking, an undesirable affliction for any surgeon. Beads of sweat trickled down his neck and were sure to stain the collar of his white undershirt. Even his RawChemistry pheromone cologne was quickly defeated by the perspiration's pungent odor. After blowing into his hands and slicking back the few remaining hairs on his head, Tim took a deep breath and twisted the knob on the door to face his most recent experiment.

HANNA

CHAPTER 16

◆

THE MAGICIAN

He's not evil, he's evil, Hanna thought, throwing Sammi's bloody bandages one by one into the trash.

The thought continued to circle in her brain as she trudged down the hallway. She entered their bedroom and sat on the edge of the bed.

When Tim entered the room, she shook off the flimsy self-reassurance that what her husband was doing was justified and enthusiastically jumped up from the bed. "Hiya, honey!"

"Hi, Han. How's our baby girl doing?"

Any internal struggle of right versus wrong all but forgotten, Hanna threw her arms around her husband. "She is amazing, Tim! Our little girl is doing so well!" Even when she unwrapped her arms and stepped back, her face glistened. "You can't even . . . You can't even tell she used to have burns, Tim. Once the new hair grows in, she will look perfect."

Hanna knew that hearing her speak this way made Tim feel powerful: like his work wasn't just some high school science experiment and in fact made a real difference. She wondered if this was how van Gogh felt about *Starry Night* or Pablo Picasso about *The Weeping Woman.* Were they aware of what they'd created, or was it only when people expressed amazement that these visionaries realized the magnificence of their work?

Hanna gazed tearfully at Tim, like he himself was a painting. "You're an artist, Tim. I want you to know that."

Tim laughed at Hanna's comment, for he had never before thought of himself this way. "I guess I am an artist of sorts," he said as he followed his wife's lead and sat on the edge of the bed. "An anatomical artist! How's that for alliteration, babe?"

Chuckling at his creativity, Hanna leaned back until she was fully reclined, her legs hanging off the bed and her toes grazing the floor. She stared at the ceiling for some time, before jolting back upright.

A mysterious interest was rising with ferocity in Hanna. She crossed her arms and, her emerald eyes narrowed, gave Tim a long look. "So, when are you going to tell me your secret? What's the special ingredient to this brilliance?"

Tim responded with a wink. "You know a magician never reveals his secrets."

"Hmph." Hanna stuck up her nose in the air, pretending to act like she didn't care to know, when in reality she was desperate for an answer. "I thought you said we were a team, Tim."

"I'm playing, Han. The simple answer is biological science, science is the key."

"You think I'm dumb?" a clearly offended Hanna spat out. "Give me the complex answer, Tim. This is *our* daughter we're talking about. I have a right to know."

Tim knew he wasn't getting out of this, so he rose from the bed and crossed to the other side of the room. Ever the professor, he pulled the leather chair from his desk and sat down. "All right, the secret is so simple many people overlook it. Typically, when someone gets a severe burn, the skin dies. It's similar to wood. If a deck is made of wood and some of the wood rots, then you take out the old and replace it with new, fresh wood."

Hanna looked annoyed. "I understand that, doc. But what are you doing that's different from other surgeons?"

"If you have one type of wood, let's say oak, lying next to another type of wood, we'll say pine, they will sit right next to each other. But skin is different. Skin has to be accepted by the body, and skin is unique to itself for the most part. Meaning, if I take donor skin from one person and try to attach it to another person, the donor skin won't be accepted. It'll be seen as foreign and the body will attack it, or may accept it, but at the cost of a lot of scars."

Hanna nodded in agreement, as if she understood precisely what Tim was saying. As thoughts started to race through her mind, she asked, "How do scars form?"

"Think of it like this. Let's say you have a raft, and this raft splits right down the middle and is separated into two halves. It wouldn't be wise to rebuild what's broken using the same material; the raft will just break again because nothing has changed since the initial break. So, instead, you go back to the store and buy different, stronger materials to rebuild the broken raft in the hope that the new material will work better than the original. And this new material is probably a different color, which results in scarring."

Recognition filled Hanna's face. "So, when someone's skin gets damaged, the body rebuilds it with different material that causes the discoloration?"

Tim sprung out of his chair. "Precisely, it's called collagen."

"So, you created something that easily binds foreign material to Sammi's body?"

Hanna wasn't sure if she should take it as a compliment when she saw her husband's jaw drop in amazement.

Tim and Hanna had always tried to keep his work separate from their family time, so he was surprised to see her taking such an interest in his medical life. "Why, yes. That is exactly what I have done."

"Well, go on!" Hanna said. "Don't leave me on a cliff. What's the secret!"

The fire hissed again, seemingly aggrieved by Hanna's response. Tim wrapped up part of a newspaper and set it under the logs. In an instant, the paper caught alight and flames licked the ink from the "Missing Girl" headline. When the logs ignited, their orange glow mimicked the sun that had set just a few minutes before.

"Think of it this way, Han," Tim said, looking around the room. "Take this fireplace, for example. Moments ago, the wood was crumbling apart and the fire was diminishing. If I had just kept adding logs, nothing would likely have happened. But by adding the paper, I caused the fire to intensify. Now look at how healthy the fire is."

The flames reflected in Hanna's eyes. Thanks to Tim's explanation, she was mesmerized by its warmth. Her voice was as soft as paper when she said: "The newspaper is a metaphor for your secret."

Tim walked over to his wife and sat beside her on the bed. "Yes, my dear," he replied as he pulled her into an embrace. "And just look at how beautiful it is."

"You never used to tell me things like this, Timmy," Hanna whispered. "I'm glad you are now."

They sat together for a time, gazing at the dancing flames and drinking in the fire's heat.

Not evil, Hanna thought.

FAITH

CHAPTER 17

J. MARION SIMS

An immeasurable length of time had passed since Twain's visit, and Faith was grateful for every second. She finally finished cutting the rope. Thankfully, Tim was alone when he operated on her, since he couldn't have the luxury of a nurse's assistance. If there had been a nurse present, she—or, nowadays, he—would surely have noticed the blade hidden under Faith's waist.

It had taken several minutes for Faith to maneuver the knife from under her buttocks, flipping it 180 degrees so that the blade faced her head and the handle her feet. She wiggled her body like a molting snake, loosening the rope around her shoulders just enough to free her hand a little. Time stopped as she began to clumsily saw at the rope's heavy threads.

When Faith was three-quarters of the way through and starting to believe she might actually escape, the doorknob began to twist.

Shit, her mind screamed. *I'm out of time.*

The stench of his RawChemistry odor stung her nostrils when Tim entered the room. He didn't say a word, but his body language spoke volumes; as he looked at Faith, his eyes watered with happiness. "Thank you," he choked out. "Sammi is healing very well, no sign of infection or—"

"Sammi?" Faith cut him off.

"Ah, of course. How could you possibly know? Sammi was in the bed next to yours. Her body is accepting your donor grafts extremely well. No sign of infection."

Faith glared at Tim, who was clapping his hands in obvious delight, and felt her rage sizzle to the surface. "*Donor* grafts? One has to actually donate something in order for it to be considered a donation, Tim. You straight up stuck a knife in me and sliced off my skin! You're a sick human being! You know that, right? I don't care if you did it to help your daughter, you're sick and twisted."

Tim's lips trembled; whether from anger or sadness, Faith couldn't tell and didn't care. He took a deep breath and gathered his composure, then walked over to the table directly in front of her, slamming his fists on the cold wood. Afterward, the only thing Faith could hear was the dripping of her IV bag.

Drip, drip, drip.

The sound resonated and summoned an uncanny chill.

"We made history, you know," Tim said softly. "The two of us." Despite the words, his tone was monotone. "One day, people will celebrate my achievement and countless lives will be saved."

"How will you do that, Tim?" Faith scoffed. "You can't keep me a secret forever."

Tim continued to talk with his back to Faith, the monstrosity he had created. "Do you know how many Americans were wounded in Iraq and Afghanistan? Over fifty thousand. With this newfound technology . . . just imagine the greatness that can be achieved, not just nationally but globally."

Faith worked quickly, moving the blade back and forth as it gnawed at the threads tethering her to the bed. *Just keep talking*, she thought.

"I know what you are thinking, Faith," Tim said, his voice rising with emotion. "That because of the sacrifice you had to make, this isn't worthwhile. But what achievement comes without sacrifice? How do you think J. Marion Sims became the godfather of gynecology? Human sacrifices had to be made."

Faith prayed he wouldn't turn around.

"From where do you think all these cures and vaccines come? They all exist thanks to experimentation on humans and animals. All great achievements require sacrifice," he said, pausing for effect—for someone, though Faith didn't have the time to consider who.

Although Tim had intended for his last words to be suspended in the air and sink in, the only response he received was silence. "Well, Faith," he asked, "what do you have to say to—"

THWACK!

The collision of the IV pole with the back of Tim's head sent blood spurting at Faith. The shock sent Tim to his knees, where he managed with obvious difficulty to look up at Faith. A trail of blood was pouring down his forehead and zigzagging across his face and, when he tried to speak, only nonsense burbled out.

"Great achievements require sacrifice," Faith yelled, this time slamming the pole into Tim's face and knocking him to the ground.

Although the pain in her legs was excruciating, Faith stepped over Tim's motionless body and made a rush for the door.

CHAPTER 18

———————◆———————

THE VARIABLE

*F*aith nudged open the door to her captivity, the sense of gratitude that washed over her almost as intense as the drugs that had flushed through her system. That is, until the true nature of her disfigurement dawned on her. She took off the bandages wrapped around her head and threw them on the ground before gliding her hands over her hairless scalp and feeling the scraping from countless tiny scabs against her fingers. She lifted her surgical gown above her knees and found pink flesh pulsing along her legs, her dermal layers entirely removed and sewn back on top of each other. Nausea rose at the sight and the recognition that she was Tim's personal voodoo doll. She let go of her gown and refocused on the task at hand.

Several candles lit the hallway, their ominous glowing flames welcoming her to a life outside the room. Her first few steps were shaky, as her leg muscles twitched and attempted to muster the necessary strength to support her own weight. One step became two, which turned into three until Faith was able to run again, the breeze finding her hairless scalp. When she came to the first fork in the path, she slowed her pace. Both paths looked like they led to even more darkness. She blindly chose one, praying it was correct. But Faith's prayers weren't heard, and her chosen path ended. The candles' shadows on the walls leapt with joy at her mistake.

As Faith began to panic, her strength faded and her head spun as her dehydration took hold. She tried to catch her breath and desperately licked the drops of sweat that fell from her forehead. Soon, Tim was going to wake up and find her. Faith knew it was time to escape or die trying.

After making several wrong turns and stopping each time to rest, the realization that she was lost dawned on her and any remaining energy slipped away like sand from between her fingers. *Escape one room only to get lost in another*, she thought as she struggled to find a solution. *If I keep running in circles, I'll exhaust myself and Tim will find me.*

If I remain still to rest, Tim will find me.

If I find a place to hide, Tim will find me.

If I go back to kill Tim, his strength will better mine.

No matter the scenario, they all resulted in the same answer.

Pissed that she couldn't find the variable to change the equation, Faith flailed her arms. The candles erupted in laughter, a harmonizing humiliation from leaping flames. Faith walked over to one of the candles and stared into the flame, puckering her lips and blowing air to extinguish the fire.

"Not so tough now, are you?" she mocked as she watched the smoke float away in the direction of the hallway from where she'd come. At this, Faith realized something: not just the smoke but the flames on all of the mounted candles were blowing in the same direction . . . down the passageway toward the room she had just escaped. Faith had found her solution. The door that now held Tim captive was open and must have been sucking in a draft coming from another source. If she went in the opposite direction from where the flames pointed, she would find her freedom.

Maybe the flames weren't mocking her after all, Faith realized, as she once again started to move.

Eventually, she could make out a dim light at the end of the bleak tunnel. All she had to do now was run.

Before she started to sprint, Faith took a moment to thank the candles. Not a second later, her toenails were scraping the concrete as she exerted all of her energy and lunged for the light. The stairs to the main floor came into view, signaling the front door up ahead and her liberation from the dungeon prison.

That's when Faith heard the voice of the devil himself.

"Hanna! Quick! Grab the gun, she's fucking escaping!" Tim screamed, his voice echoing off the chamber walls and serving as audible fuel for the surging flames.

Run away, they glowed brightly at Faith.

The open wounds on her legs burned when she ascended the first stair; the wind penetrated the cracks, like crevices in a valley, in her hairless scalp. Trails of oozing pus were dripping down her legs and onto the stairs. *Maybe Tim will slip on it*, Faith thought.

Her muscles were jelly and a burning sensation ripped through her thighs, but she grabbed the railing and ascended. Halfway up, the stairwell made two right turns that twisted upward in the opposite direction. Faith could make out the door at the top and a sliver of light that pierced through its open crack. She powered up the last set of stairs when she heard a loud noise at the bottom of the staircase behind her and Tim shrieking in disgust: "What the—. Is this pus?"

As he rose to his feet and wiped his hands on his jeans, Faith felt thumping behind her eyes at the recognition that she had just a few steps left to take.

Instead, she skipped them entirely and thrust her hands on the doorframe to fling open the door. But standing at the entrance was Hanna, awkwardly holding a 12-gauge shotgun.

"Well, hello, dear!" Hanna screamed as she cocked the weapon with a loud *snap*.

When Hanna pulled the trigger, shotgun pellets whizzed past Faith and punctured the wall behind her.

Tim yelped in surprise when the pellets barely missed him as he reached the top, and dust rained down from the holes in the wall.

Faith stumbled through the kitchen and into the family room, where another set of stairs led to the house's second story. As she started to clamber up the staircase, Hanna checked on Tim. "I'm fine!" Faith heard Tim yell. "Now go get her!"

Faith's entire body throbbed when she reached the second floor. Behind her, Hanna and Tim were grunting to catch their breath. Faith darted into the nearest room and quickly locked the door behind her.

The only sound was her heavy breathing, and all she felt was her own body heat. When she turned around, Faith saw a large dresser in the corner. Thanks to the adrenaline that had latched onto her platelets, she was able to haul over the wooden dresser and lean it against the door, barricading herself.

On the opposite side of the room was a small window leading to the roof outside. Faith flipped the lock switch and thrust up the wooden frame to open the window. A howling wind welcomed her, the rain like shotgun pellets hitting the roof.

Tim and Hanna arrived, making their presence known by banging on the door. Acting quickly, Faith put one foot out the window and on the slippery roof and used her arms to brace herself as she thrust all of her weight forward. The banging on the door ceased right when the screaming wind—its dominance overwhelming—took over.

Faith grimaced as the rain beat down on her skin and pounded her skull. She looked down to the ground, its distance from her dizzying. *Too far to jump*, she thought as she closed the window behind her and slid across the roof. One benefit of the vicious storm was that the rest of the family couldn't hear her footsteps across the roof.

Faith's head swiveled to scan the scenery and determine where she should go next. Seeing only paths that looked to lead to a steep and slippery doom, Faith's eyes finally found another window ten or so feet in the distance.

Cautiously placing one blistered leg in front of the other, she nimbly made her way across the shingles. The raindrops continued to fall on her bald head and awakened a feeling she had never known existed. The droplets dripping down her face were likewise arousing the nerves on the surface of her skin.

Faith reached the other window and, hoping it was unlocked, whispered a quick prayer. When she grasped the window frame, she was amazed to feel the frame slide up and warm air grace her face. Closing her eyes, she dived into the dark room and landed on soft carpet. Nevertheless, she grunted from the impact of her landing as the hard floor beneath the carpet reminded her of the injuries she had sustained.

She rose gingerly to her feet and looked around. She couldn't make out much, but she could hear Tim and Hanna still trying to break down the barricaded door down the hall.

A small voice came from the shadows "Wh— who's there?"

Faith turned in the direction of the voice and waited for her eyes to adjust to the blackness.

A twin-sized bed shrouded by an animated *Toy Story* cover so large it hung all the way to the floor emerged in the background. It was then that Faith realized she was in Twain's room.

"Twain, is that you?" she whispered. "Come out from under the bed."

"Faith?" A hand shot out from under the bed and pushed the comforter aside. Twain crawled out. "I heard gunshots. What's happening?"

Twain pushed himself into an upright position and stared at her, his eyes adjusting to the same darkness.

When he was able to make out Faith, or what was left of her, he went pale. She was wearing a bloody surgical gown. Her legs were bare and glistening from the ooze in the dim light. Faith was still holding the small surgical scalpel, but it was her bald, crusty head that terrified Twain the most. Faith's hair always gleamed and flowed from behind her head like a crystal river.

"F—Faith?" Twain asked.

Twain's fear was nothing compared to Faith's when she witnessed the boy's expression of pure horror at the sight of her—his daddy's science experiment.

Twain screamed a piercing shriek fueled by utter terror.

"Mom! Dad! She's in here! *Hel*—" he yelled, until Faith ran over and covered his mouth with her hand. But it was too late. Tim and Hanna had stopped banging on the door of the other room and were now running in the direction of Twain's.

CHAPTER 19

NEWTON'S LAWS OF MOTION

The fight-or-flight phenomenon is a term first coined by physiologist Walter Bradford Cannon. This acute stress response is a direct reaction to a perceived threat or harmful event and causes muscles to become tense and primed for action, which can result in a full-body tremble. Pupils will dilate in order for additional light to filter in, which results in better vision in darkness and is perfect for navigating a hasty escape or fighting off a predator.

Both scenarios were true for Faith. She knew she had to escape or die trying. She could feel the muscles in her body tensing, causing her arms and legs to convulse in anticipation. Her dilated eyes also absorbed the shadowed room's surrounding light and acted as illuminating lighthouses.

She had to act quickly, knowing that Tim and Hanna would barge into Twain's room at any moment to kill her or, worse, keep her alive for harvest.

The sound of the Hills' footsteps increased in volume as they approached the door. Without thinking, Faith dived at and snatched Twain for use as a shield. She pulled out the small scalpel and pressed it to Twain's neck.

At first, the boy didn't move. Then he struggled, his arms flailing like wings and rocking back and forth in an attempt to free himself from Faith's grasp.

"Twain, stop moving," Faith hissed in his ear, "or I swear to God, I will slit your throat. And Daddy won't be able to fix that one."

Twain halted and stopped all movement but continued to whimper. A few seconds later, the bedroom door burst open and white lights penetrated, causing Faith's pupils to constrict. Tim and Hanna rushed forward but skidded to a halt when they saw Faith—and their son being held hostage.

"Take one more step and your son dies!" Faith screamed. Her entire body was trembling with rage and adrenaline, the knife barely flickering off Twain's goose-bumped skin.

Tim froze, his face morphing from an angry purple to ghostly white. After her initial shriek, even Hanna didn't move as everyone assessed the situation.

Time slowed and Faith's former psychology professor's lecture about the fight-or-flight reaction came to her mind. In order to escape this dilemma, she had a choice to make.

She already knew what that choice would be.

Faith felt the edge of the cold blade that was pressed firmly into Twain's neck rise and fall in time with the blood pumping through his carotid artery. She narrowed her eyes and took a step back toward the window. When she did, Tim and Hanna took a step forward.

Twain's room was filled with thunderous noises from rapid heartbeats to the *pitter-patter* of raindrops as they trilled against the roof, orchestrating events yet unknown.

Faith continued to step slowly back from Tim and Hanna, until she felt her rear hit the wall next to the window. Tim snickered and took a careful step forward, knowing Faith couldn't go any farther.

"Nowhere to run, girl," he said in a tone intended to dominate. "Now, hand over our son and let's figure something out."

Not to be intimidated, Faith raised her voice and calmly replied, "Step back or he bleeds."

Tim chuckled and took another step forward. Faith could hear his tongue clicking anxiously in his mouth.

The predator had almost caught his prey. The chase was nearly over.

But this prey wouldn't be giving up.

Faith pressed the knife deeper into Twain's neck, until a light stream of blood trickled from the small puncture.

Twain let out a yelp and, in shock, Tim stepped back.

"Here's what is going to happen," Faith said as she raised her hand and pointed the dripping knife at Tim, then Hanna. "Hanna, my dear," she mocked, "you are going to drop that gun and slide it toward me. Nice and slow. No sudden movements, or I paint these walls with your son's blood."

"*Please!* Don't hurt my boy!" Hanna screamed, her upper lip quivering like a cell phone on vibrate.

Feeling the tables turn and newfound power in her muscles, Faith yelled back, "No one has to get hurt worse, but you will be getting a new paint job if you don't drop the gun and slide it over to me!"

Defeated, Hanna dropped the gun immediately. When Tim stepped over and kicked the gun toward Faith, the sound of metal sliding across carpet was music to her ears.

Christmas has come early, Faith mused as she reached down and grabbed the gun, careful not to release her hold on a squirming Twain. The shotgun felt surprisingly light when she picked it up, even while using only one arm.

Still holding the knife to Twain's throat, she pulled up the shotgun and swung it over Twain's head to rest on his right shoulder. With Twain's shoulder bearing the weight of the barrel, Faith slid her hand down to the trigger and swiveled the gun to aim directly at Tim.

Tim's snicker disappeared and was replaced by a look of pure terror. He played out scenarios of how this could all go down, but none were appealing. He was stuck—and this infuriated him.

This wasn't some medical-school exam he could bullshit his way through, which enraged him but brought back his time in college. One of his favorite professors had taught a class about Sir Isaac Newton. Isaac Newton is renowned for a number of things but is widely acknowledged as the father of physics thanks to his three laws of motion.

Newton's first law of motion states that anything in motion will stay in motion unless an external force stops it. Tim delighted inwardly at the literal nature of Newton's laws. Faith was holding his son captive and pointing a gun at the rest of his family. The scenario would remain in motion unless Tim acted as an external factor that did something to stop it.

Newton's second law of motion is more literal and states that force equals mass times acceleration. Tim's mind immediately drifted to the shotgun in Faith's clutch. The force of the pellets would surely penetrate a human body, causing devastation to bone and massive blood loss and, in all likelihood, death.

However, it was Newton's third law of motion that most interested Tim. The law states that for every action there is an equal and opposite reaction. Some people consider this law fairness; others call it karma. Tim called it Newton's third law and thought that maybe this situation was payback for what he had done to Faith. Maybe, he realized, what Faith was doing to his family would work itself out . . . in an equal and opposite fashion.

Faith continued to point the gun at Tim. "Your asses need to touch the opposite wall now." The Hills obeyed without question. "Now I'm going to shuffle right. You two will do the same. When I step right, you step right. We will move in a circle. Got it?"

They nodded and everyone started to move by taking small steps to the right, their backs against the opposite walls. The howling storm outside kept beat with everyone's shuffling until Faith's back was at Twain's bedroom entrance and Tim and Hanna were standing near the window.

Only the sound of the storm could be heard until Tim spoke: "Now what? How do you think this will end? The nearest public store is miles from here. Do you think your skinless legs will carry you that far?"

"You shut the hell up," Faith bellowed, feeling the power slipping away from her. She had no idea what she was going to do next, but one thing at a time. First, she had to get far away from here.

With the knife still at Twain's throat and the gun cocked and pointed at Tim, Faith took one step out of the room and into the hallway, where the house's internal warmth welcomed her.

"If I hear either of you take a step . . ."

"Yes, we know. New paint job and everyone dies," Tim said, rolling his eyes. Hanna was still holding his arm and shaking uncontrollably.

With a deep breath, Hanna halted her shaking and using a reassuring voice said, "Twain, my son. Just do what Faith wants and I promise you, we will be okay. Be a good boy and listen to Mommy."

"Permission to nod my head," Twain mumbled.

"Granted," Faith answered in monotone.

Tim closed his eyes. He knew what needed to be done to save his son. "Faith," he said. "I can save your mother."

The storm above reached a crescendo, and Faith's eyes locked on Tim. "What are you talking about?" she stammered. "My mom is a vegetable. You said so yourself."

"Give a vegetable sunlight and water and it begins to grow. Think about it. You can be the water, the substance that gives your mom strength. And I can be the sunlight, giving your mom what she needs to survive. I can do for your mother what you did for Sammi."

Faith's eyes softened when she thought about her mother, but then she shook away the tears and felt her senses return. "No, Tim. That is not what my mom would want for me," she said while keeping her eyes glued to Tim and Hanna and continuing to back out of Twain's room. Her backside finally brushed against the opposite hallway wall, her signal to walk to her right and toward the stairwell that led to the living room.

Without warning, a thumping noise echoed throughout the house.

Thump . . . thump . . . thump . . .

The sound was at first soft and inconsistent but gradually grew in intensity.

Faith looked at Tim and Hanna, who still hadn't moved; they seemed equally confused. The noise grew louder, until a bandaged Sammi appeared at the end of the hallway with a baseball bat in her hand where a mirror should have been.

Sammi was hunched over in pain, but that didn't stop her from doing what she did next.

"Let go of my brother!" she shrieked, releasing a bloodcurdling scream and charging at Faith and Twain with both hands holding the bat high. Before

Faith had time to turn and aim at Sammi, the bat had swung and knocked the shotgun loose from her hands, sending it spinning down the hallway.

When the shotgun fell to the floor, only one thought fluttered across Tim's mind: Isaac Newton was right. Everything in motion will stay in motion—until an external force stops it.

CHAPTER 20

THE EXTERNAL FACTOR

When it hit the floor, the shotgun fired and sent pellets piercing into nearby walls. Everyone dropped down and covered their heads to protect against the ricocheting metal beads that sliced through anything that got in the way.

When the dust literally settled and the Hill family realized no one was shot, the true frenzy started.

Faith brandished the scalpel once again and pressed it to Twain's neck. This time, she could feel his carotid artery bouncing the knife up and down like a trampoline. The gun was on the ground a few feet from Faith, puffs of smoke still leaking from the barrel. When she bent down to reach for the gun, however, Twain started screaming and kicking his feet off the walls, throwing her off balance.

With every action, there is an equal and opposite reaction, Tim thought as he approached the gun, recognizing the external factor that could interrupt the motion of Faith's plan. Then several things happened at once. Faith had finally regained control over Twain by wrestling him down and regaining her position behind him with the knife held at his throat. Sammi had toppled over and was lying in the middle of the hallway moaning in pain, her white surgical bandages turning a soft shade of pink with her wounds now reopened. Hanna was still frozen by the window, pale-faced at the debacle unfolding in front of her.

Tim grasped the gun in both hands. As he raised the barrel, he glanced over at Hanna and their eyes locked in a firm gaze. "Hanna, grab Sammi and take her back to her room. Help her to her bed, then come immediately back," he ordered.

Hanna shivered in fear.

Tim raised his voice while cocking the gun and aiming it at Faith. "Hanna, I love you, but goddamn! Grab Sammi and help her to her room!"

Hanna quickly gathered herself and hustled over to her daughter. "Come on, sweetie. Up you go. Let's get you to your room and change you out of those bandages."

Sammi offered one last moan, then wrapped an arm around her mother's neck to boost herself to her feet. "Mommy, I don't feel so good. Will I still be the prettiest after this?"

"Always," Hanna replied firmly, her voice having finally regained its motherly strength.

Tim held the gun securely as he waited. Faith continued to squeeze the scalpel and press the blade against the neck of her human shield.

Surgeons are known for their steady hands: hands that whisk with ease around nerves and arteries. Tim's hands always remained still and calm enough to avoid the dangers possessed of the human body. Even with more than a decade's worth of experience as a top-notch surgeon, Tim couldn't stop the quiver he now felt in them.

With one eye closed and the other open to aim down the sight, he recognized the waver of the barrel and couldn't confidently lock on a single target.

When Tim realized the true extent of his predicament, he lowered the barrel and stared at Faith and his son. "Twain, listen to Daddy, everything will be fine, I promise."

Faith looked back sheepishly. "I don't want to hurt your son, Tim. Put the gun down and throw me a phone. It's over."

"Over? *Ha!* Faith, I'm sorry to say this, but this doesn't have a good ending for you. Think about your options. If you waltz out of my house with my son as your hostage, I call the cops and say a deranged bald woman has kidnapped my son. If you decide to murder him, then I pump your face with shotgun pellets."

"B—but."

"No buts. Faith, my dear, who do you think they will listen to? A prestigious surgeon like myself or a dumb girl with subpar grades whose parents are dead and dying?"

Faith knew Tim was right: she was stuck between a rock and a hard place—in her case, jail versus death.

Hanna sprinted down the hallway to rejoin her husband, her formerly pale face now filled with crimson rage.

Her nostrils flared in anger as her dress swept behind her like a cape, and without saying a word she wrestled the gun out of Tim's hands.

Tim's face filled with shock and confusion. "H—honey? What are you doing?"

Before Tim realized what was happening, the butt of the gun was resting comfortably on his wife's shoulder and the barrel was pointed at Faith and Twain.

"Mom! Please don't! I don't want to die!" Twain wailed.

Faith could feel Twain's sweat-soaked shirt pressed against the front of hers. Beads of moisture emerged from the pores on the back of the boy's neck before they were pulled downward by gravity.

Hanna was silent but for the *pat-pat* of her bare feet on the carpet as she walked steadily toward Faith.

"Let him go," she said, pausing barely ten feet away from them only to let out a warning shot at the ceiling that blew a hole into the attic. Fine particles of wood rained down from above and landed on Faith's bare head, inflaming her empty skin sacs. Hanna cocked the gun again and aimed it back at Faith, this time with purpose in her eyes.

Faith almost felt guilty when Twain started to cry, but she continued to hold him in her grasp.

"Hanna, stop!" Tim cried. "You could accidently shoot Twain! Please! Give me the gun."

"Ah, shut it, Tim. You are better with a knife anyway, doc. No one scares my baby boy and gets away with it," Hanna bellowed, vengeance powering her words. "Maybe, this time, *I can fix this.*"

Tim didn't have a witty comeback, so he stood back with his eyes glued on the situation; riding passenger in such an intense experience was a bizarre feeling for him.

At her husband backing down, Hanna perked up and flashed a smile. "Listen up, buttercup. When I count to three, one of two things will happen. You will either let my son go or this gun will give you a makeover. Which do you prefer, sweetie?" Hanna cooed.

The rain mimicked a percussionist beat on the roof.

Faith didn't have an answer, nor did she want to wait to figure one out.

Hanna stood rigid. "One."

Braat-braaaattt-braaattttt went the rain drummer.

"Two," Hanna said, lengthening the word for dramatic effect.

Tim collapsed to his knees. "Please, Hanna, don't do this," he begged.

Hanna exhaled a deep breath, closing her eyes and hunching her shoulders. For the first time in a long time, the drummer stopped playing.

Then Hanna looked up, her emerald eyes flashing open. "Three!"

BANG!

The muscles of her hand closed the distance between her index finger and the trigger, and metal beads flew out in a puff of smoke expelled from the mouth of the gun.

The blast rang through the whole house and pellets whizzed past Twain, hitting Faith square in the shoulder. The force from the blast sent her backward and knocked her off her feet.

Faith staggered to her knees and glanced at her shoulder. Several bloody holes had united in a red splotch on her gown. As her bleeding continued, Faith's veins released their contents. When this liquid of life failed to form clots, blood drops gained mass and splashed on the carpet in rhythm with the chorus of raindrops coming from outside.

The drummer on the roof finally reached his crescendo.

Splash, splash, splash was all anyone heard until Twain screamed. He was squirming on the carpet, blood pooling where his face had met the floor.

Faith realized she felt faint and recognized that she was no longer holding the scalpel.

Twain looked up slowly at Faith. The knife that was once gripped in her hand was now lodged in his left eye.

Acting on pure instinct, Faith reached out to snatch the knife that was moving in time with Twain's right eye as it made circles in the socket—and waved it at Hanna.

Twain let out a few more wails as his solo now took the stage. One eye was discharging blood and pus, and the other was sleepily looking past Faith. When his screaming ceased, he collapsed headfirst on the floor.

Tim's and Hanna's eyes almost bulged out of their skulls as they witnessed what Faith had done to their son.

"I'll kill you, bitch!" Hanna screamed at Faith as she cocked the gun and sent the used shell case flying across the hall in a jet of smoke.

Tim stood hastily and threw his arm in front of the gun in an attempt to stop his wife from shooting another round into the bloodied girl before them.

"Stop," he said calmly, walking toward Twain and pressing two fingers to his neck. Tim sighed. "He's still alive, probably just fainted from the pain and shock. Hanna, give me the gun then take Twain to my study and get the room ready for surgery."

"But Tim! How will you save him? He's . . ."

Tim waved his hand to signal silence. Without a word, he pointed a finger at Faith and communicated his answer to Hanna.

Hanna nodded and passed him the gun, then walked over to Twain's motionless body and carefully scooped him up.

"I'll see you soon, don't take too long with her," Hanna hissed, motioning her head toward Faith. Twain was unconscious in her arms and dripping a trail of blood down the hall.

Tim, cool and collected, nodded. He knew what needed to be done.

Faith struggled to sit up, her hand slipping in the pool of blood that was gurgling under her palm. She couldn't tell if it was her own blood, or Twain's, or a mix of the two. With the last of her strength, she held the knife in her quaking hand and pointed it at Tim. "Either I kill you or you kill me," she said faintly.

Tim walked over and knelt down beside her. "Oh, my dear Faith. I'm not going to kill you. Oh no, no, no." His tongue clicked behind his teeth. "You are going to live a beautiful, fulfilling life helping kids."

Tim leaned in close to Faith's ear and whispered, "Piece by piece."

Faith froze in recognition, and an unnatural chill crept from the tips of her toes to the top of her inflamed scalp.

With all that remained of her will to live, she pushed Tim back and stood up tall, pointing the sharp blade with his son's blood dripping from its keen edge at him.

Tim smirked and reached for the gun. "Bringing a knife to a gunfight, hmm? Not so smart, but you *did* drop out of school."

Faith chuckled. As her laughter turned hysterical, tears rolled down her cheeks one last time. "I once thought you were different. I thought, no, I *believed* in you."

Tim allowed her words to slice through him and the gun temporarily slouched.

"You were a hero to me!" Faith bellowed. "I looked up to you!"

Tim took his time lowering the gun and then held out his hands. "I can fix this," he said as he inched closer toward Faith. "Let me help you."

Finally at ease with her destiny, Faith smiled and ever so softly muttered her last word: "*Never.*"

Faith pulled the blade back from Tim and toward her own throat. In a single horizontal slash, she parted her skin like Moses did the Red Sea.

HANNA

CHAPTER 21

THE CERCLAGE

"Here. Wrap this around him twice," Tim demanded, handing Hanna the metal cerclage cables.

The metal felt cold in her hands and the extra slack drooped down and touched the floor, dragging a little as she walked over to the side of the bed and began to wind the cables. Hanna tried to avoid doing so, but eventually she gave up and glanced downward at the unconscious young man on the surgical table. "How much longer will he be out for?"

Tim walked over and stood next to her. He put a finger between the cable and Isaac's skin to make sure it was tied tightly enough. "A while. I gave him a pretty strong dose. Can you pull some slack out? It's a tad loose around his waist."

Hanna tugged on the cables and heard them *zip* as metal slid against metal. "Why does it have to be so tight?" she asked, trying to shake the image of an anaconda coiling around its prey.

"We can't have him escape like Faith did. It wasn't tight enough last time." Tim took the cables from his wife's hands and gave them one last tug. Where the metal touched Isaac's skin, it had already caused bruising. "There," he announced. "That should be good enough."

Hanna nodded and sat down on the rolling stool beside the bed, her head swimming. She stared at the helpless young man bound to the bed. "Why him?" she asked.

"A few reasons. First, no one will come looking for him. Isaac made it abundantly clear that he has little contact with his family. Also, his eye color matches Twain's beautifully. And, above all, he's O negative. They all have that in common." Tim examined the cables a final time and continued: "I had to be sneakier with him. What I did out in the open with Brandy and the others was stupid."

Hanna looked at the floor. "I remember Brandy . . ."

"What was that?" Tim asked, the entirety of his attention focused on securing Isaac.

"Never mind," Hanna said with a sigh. "When will this all be over?"

Tim tightened a few more straps around Isaac's torso and legs and looked up. "When will what be over?"

"This . . . next procedure. Twain is getting anxious and, quite frankly, I am too." Her stomach was churning with disgust; when Hanna stood up, the stool was stained with her sweat. "I've been having these nightmares, Tim. Horrible dreams. I think we might be going to hell."

Tim stopped what he was doing and strolled over to his wife, wrapping his arms around her trembling body. "No, Han. You're wrong."

Hanna pushed Tim away. "How can you say that?" she said, a shaking finger pointed at Isaac. "Look what we're doing! This is insane, Tim. I thought when we did it for Sammi, that would be the end of it."

Tim placed his fingers on his forehead and started to massage, trying to eliminate the tension he felt. "You'll see. When this is over, you'll see."

"We're going to hell," Hanna said again, and not as a question.

Tim kissed her on the cheek. "No." He stood over a somnolent Isaac. "Just me."

Hanna wanted to go over and hug her husband, comfort him like he had her so many times before. But she couldn't. Deep down, she knew what he was saying was true and there was no counterargument.

As if reading her mind, Tim turned around and faced her. "It's okay. I can handle it. Here." He thrust a hand into his pants pocket and retrieved his wallet. "Take my card and order us some pizza. Twain has a big day tomorrow, so we should make tonight fun for him. Can you help me do that?"

Hanna smiled as she accepted his wallet. "Spend your money? I think I can make that happen."

"Good. I'll be down in a bit. Just need to make sure Isaac is . . ." Tim took a moment to think of an appropriate word. "Situated."

CHAPTER 22

SETTLERS OF CATAN

*H*anna gulped down her anxiety and plastered on a smile when she trudged down the stairs toward the family room, filing away her uncertainty in a mental drawer she hoped would never be opened again. She was lost in thought, the limited space in her head occupied by a battle of morals. *If this is right,* she thought, *then why does it feel so wrong? Is this my sacrifice to make my children happy?*

Her feet froze in place when they felt the marble floor of the family room. Her throat tightened and her stomach twisted, and an icy fear paralyzed her.

"M—Mom? Everything okay?"

Hanna glanced toward the source of the question and noticed Twain standing by the couch, his eye patch incapable of masking the worry on his face. Hanna stared at him without responding until an unexpected sense of ease swept through her muscles and allowed her feet to relax on the floor. They needed to go through with this, she realized. Good or bad, who cared? Her son was miserable; that was all that mattered.

"Everything is just fine, sweetie. I hope you and your sister want pizza for dinner."

Twain's face lit up and offered Hanna a snapshot of what could be. "Pizza! My favorite!"

Hanna smiled back. "Tell your sister to come downstairs for family game night and pizza. I'll go ahead and put the order in."

Twain grinned, then sprinted upstairs to get his sister. Hanna watched as he scurried away, making race-car sounds with his mouth.

The two cubes rattled in the palm of Hanna's hand. She looked at Twain on the couch to her left, then glanced at Sammi to her right, a smirk creeping over her lips.

Their eyes wide in fright, the kids grasped each other.

"Not a seven, *not a seven*!" Sammi squealed as she gripped the numerous cards in her hand.

Hanna shook the dice ferociously, then, for dramatic effect, kissed them both and threw them on the table. All three huddled around the thrown dice.

"What do they say?" Hanna said, squinting with all her might. "I'm not wearing my reading glasses."

"Jeez, you're getting old," Sammi said.

"Seriously, Mom," Twain chimed in. "I only have one eye and I can read that."

Hanna winced at Twain's comment and thought, *For now.*

"Ah!" Sammi screamed, throwing down her cards in anguish.

Hanna stood up, her primordial instincts kicking in. "What! What's the matter, hon?"

Sammi looked at Hanna, her eyes panic-stricken. "It's a seven!"

Twain jolted up and pointed mockingly at his sister. "Ha! Seven! Now give up half your cards to the bank, sis."

An expression of gloom befell Sammi's face as she returned every card to the bank. "That's not fair," she sniveled after putting back her last card.

"That's life for ya, Sammi girl," Hanna said to Sammi, whose arms were crossed in defeat.

"Don't forget to move the robber!" Tim yelled, descending the steps and plopping down next to his wife. "Settlers of Catan. My favorite. Bet y'all are glad I'm not playing, or this game would be over by now."

Hanna rolled her eyes. "Go bother someone else, why don't ya."

Tim poked his finger into Hanna's ribs, causing her to bounce on the couch cushion and giggle. "Oh, does someone not like that?" Tim mocked, his smile revealing white teeth.

Twain climbed on the couch and pointed at Hanna. "Attack Mommy!"

Sammi, Twain, and Tim all leapt up at once and overpowered Hanna.

"The ribs!" Tim yelled. "The ribs! Get her in the ribs!"

At first Hanna resisted, but eventually the tickling attack caused happy tears to roll down her cheeks as she giggled uncontrollably. "Stop it, stop it!" Hanna wheezed, trying to recapture all the breath she'd exhaled from laughing.

As if God heard her plea, the doorbell rang.

"Pizza!" Twain screamed, then scrambled off Hanna.

"That's my cue," Tim said as he hopped off the chair, the cushions springing back up in response to the absence of his weight.

When he opened the front door, a mouthwatering aroma of pepperoni and sausage and multicolored peppers wafted into the house.

This was what Hanna wanted, what she dreamed of: her kids playing happily with each other, food on the table, and fun on their minds. In this moment, things were perfect.

"That'll be $54.99," the delivery man said, holding out the receipt for Tim to sign.

Hanna's feeling of contentment dissipated when she saw Tim grab the pen and sign the receipt with his left hand.

"Thanks, and have a nice night," Tim replied, before turning around and winking at Hanna.

Half of the pizza was still on the table and the other half in the Hill family's bellies when the doorbell rang for a second time.

"I got it," Tim said as he leapt off the couch and dashed for the door while pizza crumbs fell from his lap to the floor.

Hanna eyed Tim with suspicion. "I didn't think we were expecting visitors on family game night . . ."

When Tim opened the door, Dr. Kevin Shung trudged in.

Hanna felt her body involuntarily tense as memories of the last time Tim's partner was over flooded her brain.

Shung stepped inside and took off his hat, hanging it on the mantle by the front door. He was holding a small briefcase. "Hi Han. How're you?" Shung asked, his voice flat and his dark hair disheveled. "Hi Twain, hi Sammi. Goodness gracious, you two have, erm . . ." Shung's eyes flickered toward Tim, who nodded back at him. "Grown up."

Hanna studied Shung, noticing how skinny he looked—not a healthy skinny, but a sickly or a malnourished skinny. His face was wan, but Hanna couldn't tell if it was from the moonlight coming through the windows or Shung's unease at being in the house.

"Hi Shung," she said, her response measured. "Everything is well with me. How's everything with you? It's been a long time since you have been here."

Shung started to respond, but Tim sliced his hand in front of his friend to interrupt the conversation.

"Oh, don't bother him, Han. I'm sure he's exhausted after a long day of work."

Placing a hand on Shung's shoulder, he asked, "Shall we?"

Shung gave a halfhearted smile and started to follow Tim up the stairs. "It was good seeing you, Hanna," he said. Looking over at the kids, who were sitting on the couch, he added, "And the kids, too."

"Shung!" Tim yelled from upstairs. "Get up here, man. We have work to do."

Shung nodded and headed for the stairs, the briefcase still firmly in his grip.

"Good night, Mommy," Twain said, releasing a large yawn as Hanna pulled the covers up to his chin.

"Goodnight, sweetie."

Hanna gently closed the bedroom door behind her, careful not to make a sound, and headed downstairs to the family room to clean up the game pieces and pizza. She placed the Settlers of Catan pieces back in the box, one by one, mindful of putting them in their appropriately colored sections. She tucked the game box away in the cabinet, then picked up all of the leftover pizza slices and wrapped them in tinfoil before putting them in the fridge.

Without warning, her mind once again wandered to the innocent person tied down upstairs. Heat, which originated in her toes, started to creep upward into her legs until it finally stopped in her head.

Hanna gasped at the heat stroke and opened the refrigerator door, dunking her head inside to feel the cold air wash over her face. She closed her eyes and let her emotions run their course, the ebb and flow of turmoil that swelled eventually receding. When she opened her eyes, the heat was gone and inner anguish was once again held at bay. Before she closed the fridge door, she made a mental note to save a slice of pizza for Isaac.

Moments later, she heard footsteps coming down the stairs. Hanna turned around to find Shung standing in the kitchen.

They stared at each other in silence, their words unnecessary.

After their understanding was reached, Shung grabbed his hat off the mantle and headed out the front door, the hand that once held the briefcase now empty.

TIM

CHAPTER 23

THE LINK

*E*ighteen years ago, when Tim was in high school, he would choose to read and study instead of hang out with friends or play sports. As a result, he excelled in all of his classes.

When his passion to become a doctor emerged, he decided he would attend Harvard Medical School in Boston, Massachusetts. It was in Boston that he would meet Hanna, his wife-to-be.

Hanna didn't go to college. Although she was raised in Boston, after high school she decided to go straight to earning money and not continue with her studies. She had always hated school. Hanna had dreamed of finding a well-established man who would take care of her.

And that's when she met Tim.

Hanna worked at a local restaurant near the university where she was constantly meeting future doctors and engineers, although none had seemed interested in her. Not to be deterred, Hanna continued to pursue her dream and was friendly and flirty with the students who walked in, hoping one of them would bite the hook attached to her lure.

It wasn't until a study-hungry Tim—who was at that time infatuated with prosthetics' potential to improve patients' lives and prepared to do his residency at Colorado State Orthotic University for Bioengineering—walked through the doors and sat at a table by himself that Hanna got a bite. She fluffed up her hair and smiled radiantly, then walked over to Tim's table, her high heels clacking against the floor. When her green eyes locked on his blue, the rest was history.

* * *

A hawk soared in the sky, homing its vision in on anything that moved. When the wind picked up in velocity, the predator spread its wings and soared higher. The hawk's feathers ruffled in the breeze that flowed easily through the oiled plumes lining its wing bones.

The hawk continued its flight, until a delicious movement on the ground caught its attention. Its wings tilted downward and the protective film lining its eyes guarded against debris as it dived, descending until the green scales on the lizard's body were distinct. Stretching its claws out in front and aiming its sharp talons at the lizard's torso, the hawk hoped to pierce the reptile's heart.

But hours of basking in the sun had made the lizard fast and allowed it to scurry out of harm's way in the nick of time—yet not without sacrifice.

While the lizard's chest had been spared, the hawk's talons dug deep into the tail and tore flesh and crushed bone. The hawk squeezed its claws and flapped its wings, elevating itself higher in the air to soar home and feed its eyases.

When the PowerPoint video clicked off and the auditorium lights flickered on, the class watching Tim Hill's presentation was illuminated. "But what the hawk forgot to do," Tim said as he adjusted the microphone attached to his collar, "is look down at its talons. If it had, the hawk would have realized those talons held just the tail of the lizard."

Tim pressed the clicker he held to move to the next slide. "Good thing for this guy, the hawk didn't."

On this slide was an image of the lizard scampering off into the bushes, dragging behind it the stump of its tail.

"This species is known as the Anolis carolinesis, also called the green anole, and they are prominent in the southeastern United States. I'm sure you've heard of them; they are known for their ability to regenerate their tail."

A hand shot up.

Tim pointed at the student. "Go ahead."

"How long does it take for the tail to grow back?"

Tim smiled at catching the attention of at least one fellow classmate. "About sixty days."

Another student raised her hand and began to wave it fiercely. "Have you discovered the gene correlated with the regeneration?"

"Yes and no," Tim said before starting to pace across the stage so as to ensure he gave everyone appropriate eye contact. "After several years of studying these little creatures, we have discovered that it's actually over three hundred different genes all working together to rebuild the tissue, cartilage, and bone."

Another student raised his hand, but Tim continued, "My hope is that one day we can utilize these genes for human benefit." The student lowered his hand. "My dream is to help amputees regrow their limbs. These simple lizards could be the cure for arthritis, scoliosis, and amputation."

The entire class stood up and applauded Tim, who would quickly rise in the Colorado School of Orthotics ranks.

He spent hours in the lab dissecting lizard after lizard, trying to determine their regeneration secret. The more time he spent in the lab, the more frustrated he became.

He hardly saw Hanna, who was upset by her new husband's attention being focused elsewhere. The man she knew and loved had become so obsessed with his lizard experiments that he was never home with her. She sat alone all day only to watch the sunrise turn to sunset and feel the darkness creep through the windows and enter her heart.

After a fourteen-hour day in the lab dissecting lizards and putting genetic samples on petri dishes,

Tim headed home. When he pulled up to his small brick house, he noticed the lights still on in the living room. The house was usually dark and quiet at this hour, the perfect time for pouring himself a scotch and then crawling into bed with his wife.

Tonight was different. The house wasn't dark, and it wasn't quiet.

"You're late," Hanna said from where she sat perched on the couch.

"I know, I'm sorry," Tim said. "I had to stay a couple minutes longer to finish up some extra work."

"A couple minutes? It's nearly midnight, Tim! I thought something happened to you. You never talk to me anymore."

"I'm sorry . . ."

Hanna pulled her wedding ring from her finger and tossed it at him. "Here, go put this on one of your little lizard friends, since you're practically married to them anyway."

Tim caught the ring in his hand and stared at its engraved *Always One*.

"You're always in that lab," Hanna mumbled. "I hope you figured out how to grow appendages, because I'm about ready to rip off one of yours."

Tim sat down next to his wife. He started to gently massage Hanna's back, working out some of the knots he knew he had caused. "I know my apologies won't make up for the time I have been gone, but I want to say I love you. I love you to the moon and back."

"I love you too, Tim," Hanna replied as she relaxed into his touch, "but I don't like you being gone all the time. I get worried that something happened to you. I love how you are trying to help people, but you're forgetting the one person who cares about you the most. Maybe it's time you help me."

Tim let her words sink in and nodded his genuine agreement. "Okay, you got it. I will make sure to spend more quality time with you." Tim paused, trying to think of something funny to say to lighten the mood. "These lizards are pretty cute, though."

Hanna swung her leg over Tim's lap, straddling him. "We can role-play, you know? I can go put on a green reptile suit and we can get weird." She slithered out her tongue, mimicking a snake.

They both laughed and Tim remembered why he loved his wife so much. Her presence was soothing after a long day of cutting lizards open and studying genetics. "Can I tell you a joke, hon?" Tim asked, thinking of one on the spot.

Hanna grinned and swung her body back, so she was sitting next to him. She grabbed his arm and put it around her. "I'd love that."

"Name three animals you'd never want to play poker with."

Hanna smirked. "Tell me."

"Lions because they're always lyin', cheetahs are always cheatin', and crabs are always acting crabby, so you wouldn't want to play with them either."

"And lizards, because they always steal my husband." Hanna sniggered.

Again, they both giggled, greatly enjoying each other's company. They sat on the couch for a few more minutes, then Hanna stood up and walked to the kitchen. When she returned, she held a half-empty bottle of wine and two glasses filled almost to the rim. Tim took a sip and, after the wine had slid down his throat, breathed out the taste of alcohol.

Hanna raised her glass and clinked it against his, then took a long gulp and sank back into the couch. "How are your experiments going, by the way? Have you made any progress with growing limbs?"

Tim stared into his wineglass, the red contents swirling and creating a maroon-hued whirlpool. "No, Han. I have not. I'm experiencing what you would call a science block."

Hanna stared at her husband before taking another sip. "Well, go on."

Tim polished off the rest of his wine and set his glass on the table. "I'm looking for the bridge, Hanna. The green anole lizard is the most closely related animal to us that can regenerate its cells. Humans and these lizards share the same toolbox of genes, yet I can't find the missing link that connects us."

Hanna pulled Tim's arm off where it rested on her, so she could look at him. She reached for the wine bottle and filled their glasses again. "We share the same genes with those creatures?"

"Yes, more than you would think," Tim replied, clinking his glass against Hanna's before taking another swig and swishing it in his mouth to bring out the full flavor. "But I can't find the bridge."

"You keep saying 'bridge' and 'connection.' What do you mean?"

Tim felt his cheeks warming and his head starting to swim from the Merlot. He crossed his legs and pushed his glasses up on his nose. "For instance, we even share the ones that allow them to regenerate tissue and bone. Why is it that they can do it, but we can't? It infuriates me that I can't figure it out. Every time I start to get close to an answer, it just slips away."

Hanna drank in both what Tim was saying and her wine, a red mustache forming on her upper lip. "What other animals do we share genes with?" she asked as she finished her second glass.

Tim laughed and chugged his second drink. He winced from its burn on the way down, then set the empty glass back on the table and looked at Hanna. "That's an easy one, babe." At this, he stood and waved his hands in the air like a circus ringmaster beckoning in the next wonder. "Evolution!"

Hanna rolled her eyes and snorted. "Did you just call me babe?"

Tim blushed. "I might be a tad tipsy."

"Oh, sit back down and stop being so dramatic," Hanna replied before slapping Tim's ass, her own tipsiness responsible for her interest in Tim's work.

"I'm talking about apes, the very animal we evolved from. We share 96 percent of our DNA with them, but just look at that critical 4 percent. It's the same with the lizards, Han. Our DNA is extremely similar to theirs, yet there's one thing we are missing."

"The link!" Hanna shouted, clapping with excitement.

"Yes, my love," Tim replied, "the link."

They both fell back on the couch, wine sloshing in their stomachs.

Hanna cupped Tim's face and stared into his eyes. "The link to a happy marriage is quality time together. Please remember that, Tim, next time you are with your lizard friends."

He stared back into her emerald eyes and realized how much he'd missed her. Promising himself he would spend more time with her and less time in the lab, he kissed her on the lips, snatched her up in his arms, and carried her to their bedroom.

CHAPTER 24

◆

THE DECISION

Several weeks had passed and Tim was spending less time in the lab. As his connection with his wife had improved, his inspiration to find the link between humans and the green anole lizard had dwindled.

Tim and Hanna were lying in bed, panting after a lovemaking session, when Tim flipped on his back and Hanna curled up beside him.

As her fingers played with the tufts of hair on his chest, Hanna leaned over and kissed Tim on the cheek, whispering in his ear, "I'm so glad I have my husband back."

Tim returned her kiss with one of his own. "Well, my dear, you are more attractive than any of the lizards I have ever worked with, so . . ."

Hanna giggled and Tim kissed her again on the cheek.

As he reached over to turn on the bedside lamp, the bulb flickered and flashed back on, causing shadowy figures to dance on the ceiling. He fluffed his pillow and leaned back against it so he was sitting upright. "I think I found the link, by the way."

Hanna was silent, nervous that Tim was going to leave her again for his studies. She puffed her own pillow and sat beside him. "Tell me," she said with obvious hesitation.

Tim chuckled and draped his arm around her. "It's not what you think, Han. I think the missing link is you."

Hanna naturally tilted her head when something made her curious, as if the mental weight of the question caused her head to lean.

"I don't understand," she said.

Tim felt emotion wash over him. "I've been spending so much time in the lab trying to find the cure for other people's problems that I didn't notice my own problems surfacing right in front of me. You, my loving wife, make me happy. I guess I didn't realize that simply being with you is enough for me.

To hell with those amphibians! I don't need 'em anymore."

Hanna paused and, before she knew it, felt tears streaming down her face. Tim reached out his finger and wiped away the tears on her face. He gave her a big bear hug and kissed her on the forehead, tasting the saltiness of her sweat mixed with her tears. They gazed into each other's eyes dreamily, gulping in every emotion pouring from their soul windows. It was at this moment that Tim and Hanna felt the most happiness they had ever experienced.

"I think we should have kids," Tim said, his voice low.

Hanna froze.

"Or we don't have to. Whenever you are ready, Han."

Without warning, Hanna jumped out from under the covers and straddled Tim, pushing her face against his and purring, "I would love to have kids." She kissed Tim softly on the nose and joked, seductively, "Maybe these lizards can help you regenerate an erection, Timmy."

Tim reached over and turned off the lamp and the shadows on the ceiling.

CHAPTER 25

THE SERUM

Several staff members surrounded Hanna's hospital bed: one nurse was putting in an IV, another was wiping the sweat from Hanna's brow, and the doctor was instructing her when to take deep breaths and when to push.

The most important job, however, was Tim's. More than ever before, he needed to comfort and re-assure his wife that all of her pain was going to be worth it when the baby arrived.

The doctor looked up at the monitor and eyed the heart rate ripples with suspicion. "I know you're tired, Ms. Hill," he said, "but you need to push with all of your might on the count of three. You ready?"

Hanna grabbed Tim's hand and they both nodded at the doctor, who snapped on his surgical gloves.

"One."

Tim looked at the worry brewing behind Hanna's eyes and asked himself, *Is she scared of the pain or worried about the baby?*

"Two.

Tim tried to settle his nervous expression into a soothing look, before giving Hanna's hand a gentle squeeze and communicating a go-ahead nod to the doctor.

The doctor returned the courtesy. "Three! Now, push!"

Hanna wailed in harmony with the beeping monitors. Then, the chorus ceased.

Tim looked up at the doctor, who was holding the baby. Whereas he had expected to see an expression of joy on the doctor's face, what Tim saw froze him to the core.

The doctor seemed to be studying the newborn. Then, like a light switch had been flipped, he turned pale.

The doctor looked at the nurse standing beside him. "Go grab a respirator."

The only sound came from the ticking clock anchored to the wall, its hands winding in circles and pointing the blame in all directions. Tim believed it was his fault, so he stood up and walked toward the infant, his eyes glued on the tiny lifeless body.

The doctor stepped toward him, but Tim raised his hand in protest.

"Can everyone give us a moment, please?" Tim asked, his voice surprisingly steady.

The doctor nodded and beckoned the staff out of the room to allow Tim and his wife time alone with their babe.

When the door closed, Tim picked his son up for the first time, cradling his tiny head.

After pushing her face deep into a pillow to muffle her cries, and unable to accept what was happening at the sound of Tim singing a lullaby, Hanna finally lifted her head from her now-wet pillow. "Can I hold him, too?"

"Of course, my love," Tim said as he eased over to Hanna and cautiously handed her the child. She took him softly in her arms and rocked him back and forth, gazing dreamily at the baby boy who would never wake from his perpetual slumber.

Her dreamy look quickly changed to a nightmarish expression, and she immediately handed the baby back to Tim. "Take it back, Tim. I can't . . . I can't look at it anymore."

Tim once again cradled the baby, and his eyes filled with a sudden determination. "Do you trust me, Hanna?"

Hanna glanced up from her pillow, her face a dark shade of pink and her eyes puffy. "Wh—what? Of course I do, Tim."

Tim kept his vision trained on his wife. What happened next would forever alter their lives.

The sound of knocking on the door interrupted their silent gaze. "Can I come in?" the doctor asked from the other side.

Tim glanced at the door, then back at Hanna's bed. He grabbed one of the blankets and wrapped it around his son, creating a chrysalis.

Hanna, her voice shaking, asked, "Tim, will you be okay?"

Without turning around, Tim answered: "I'm going to make this right. I'm going to fix this."

He tucked the wrapped child under his arm and rushed out the door.

The lights flashed on and illuminated the lab, causing Tim's pupils to constrict. The green anole lizards, awakened by the brightness, rustled in their cages. Tim walked over to the translucent part of the lab where he stored his dictations and test tubes, the automatic sensor robotically sliding the door open so Tim could enter and closing it smoothly behind him. He set the child down on the table and walked over to the command tablet on the wall next to the door. He turned off the automatic sensor and manually overrode the system, rendering himself the only person in control of the command tablet.

The clock read ten minutes past midnight, but Tim wasn't tired; in fact, he had never felt more alive. He walked back to the table and unwrapped the blankets mummifying his son. *What I'm doing is the right thing*, Tim reassured himself as pure adrenaline coursed through his bloodstream.

When the final fold of the blanket unraveled, he took a moment to really look at his son. The child had a full head of lustrous dark hair that stuck up in all directions from the static blanket. His skin had turned from pale to white, and his eyes were closed as if in a deep sleep. His fingers and toes possessed such potential for growth and development. Tim traced his finger along the child's face, drinking in his appearance.

The lizards on the other side of the glass were restless in their cages, confusing the bright lights with daytime, but Tim didn't hear them. He heard only his steady thoughts as he ambled over to the wire rack of various test tubes, each filled with a light orange serum, a white label and different date printed on each one. He grabbed the tube with the most recent date and filled a syringe with its contents. The orange liquid swirled into the syringe. Tim flicked the syringe a couple of times, then attached a needle on the delivery side.

A sudden chill fell on his glass lab workstation and the air inside thickened.

Tim stood beside the table and inhaled deeply before plunging the needle into his son's heart, pressing the back of the syringe so the sunset-colored liquid entered the infant's body. Tim turned on his phone's stopwatch application and set a timer for six minutes, calculating that the synthetic polymer he added to the regenesis lizard mixture would aid in breaking down the serum faster than the sixty days it took the lizards to process it. Tim wasn't sure why his son had died. Although he wasn't a religious man, he prayed to the heavens that the serum would transform into whatever cells his child needed.

Footsteps were bouncing off the empty lab's walls, and lights pierced through the glass walls of the cage. With flashlights gripped firmly, police officers barged out of the stairwell. After forming a straight line, they cocked their guns and pointed at the crystal enclosure. A few seconds later, the stairwell door opened and a lieutenant, pushing Hanna in a wheelchair in front of him, stepped out.

It looked as though a thousand years had passed since Tim left the hospital. Hanna's eyes were sunken sacks of tiredness, her exhaustion having leaked downward and now residing under the skin beneath her eyes.

The lieutenant raised his hand, signaling for the other officers to put down their weapons. He then placed his hands back on the handles of Hanna's wheelchair and rolled her to the edge of the glass, whispering something in her ear that was inaudible to Tim. Hanna nodded in response, a single tear sliding down her cheek, as the lieutenant stepped back to join the rest of his officers.

The police officers in the background faded as Tim focused his attention on Hanna, who raised a hand and placed it softly on the glass, her warmth causing a fog around her fingers.

Tim glided over and placed his hand on the opposite side of the clear wall.

"Let's go home, Timmy," Hanna said, her hand pressing against the glass.

Tim reached for his pocket and pulled out his phone to check the timer; only a few minutes remained. "Soon, my dear. Very soon," he whispered as his hand fell off the glass and he walked back to the table where their son still lay. Behind Tim, his foggy handprint rapidly dissipated.

Hanna felt a wave of anger shoot through her, and she dropped her own hand. "Tim, look at me when I'm talking to you!" she yelled, her nostrils flaring and heat pouring from her words. "What do you think you are doing? Our son is dead, but we can try again! The police said if you turn over the baby quietly and sign the documents, there will be no charges." Her hot words sliced through Tim like a dagger through butter. "I don't care if I go to jail, Hanna," he said in response. "I want my son back!" He stared down at his hands. "I can fix this!"

Feeling her strength return, Hanna pushed herself out of the chair. Wincing as she walked, she curled her hand into a fist and smashed it against Tim's crystal cocoon. "Even you can't cheat death, Tim! Please, don't do this to me. Don't do this to us!" She slammed her fist against the glass again, this time leaving a bloody smear. "I don't want to be alone again."

Tim glanced at the stopwatch and saw that only seconds remained. When he looked back up, the majority of the police officers held their guns raised. "You'll all see!"

A sinister smile crept across Tim's face. Hanna watched pure wickedness consume her husband, chewing up the good and spitting out something wretched.

The stopwatch alarm sounded, and the caged green anoles stopped their rustling. Everyone froze but Tim, who turned to face the table in eager anticipation of what was about to happen.

Hanna waited as seconds turned into minutes . . . and nothing happened.

Tim's wide-eyed expression dissolved when he realized the serum wasn't going to make his son's heart start to beat. He shuffled over to the wire rack and grabbed all of the vials, transferring their contents into additional syringes. Panicked, he ran back to the table with tears streaking down his face and plunged needle after needle into his son's sternum. The child's body jolted with every plunge in response to the shock waves of Tim's force.

Finally, Tim stopped and allowed the glass vials to slip from his fingers and shatter on the ground. The particles of breaking glass sounded like the green anoles' claws scratching the cages' metal floor.

Realizing at last that his son was gone and there was nothing he could do, Tim dropped to his knees. The wickedness was now gone, replaced with sorrow.

Even though her husband had committed a terrible act, Tim's brokenness filled Hanna's heart with the instinct to love him.

"I'm s—" Tim hid his face in his palms, his sobs interrupting his words. "I'm so sorry, Han."

Hanna turned around and looked at the officers, half of whom still pointed their weapons at Tim. "Will you give us some space, please?"

The lieutenant walked over to Hanna and put his hand on her shoulder. "You know we can't do that. He needs to come with us."

His hand felt firm on Hanna's shoulder, but she nevertheless shrugged it off and stared at him with a ferocity she didn't know existed in her. "Leave us. I'll get him out."

The lieutenant sighed and agreed, gathering the other cops and heading back upstairs to allow Hanna and Tim some time.

When Hanna turned back around to face Tim, he was already dialing in the code on the lock. There was a *swoosh* and the door slid open.

Hanna ran to her husband and threw her arms around him. She kissed him on the cheek and clung to him, his sweat-soaked T-shirt pressing into her.

Tim's shoulders bobbed up and down as another sobbing fit seized him. "I'm so sorry, Han." He pulled his face away from hers to reveal the river of snot and tears that flowed down it.

"Shh," Hanna said softly, breathing warm air into her husband's face. "You have always taken care of me, now it's time for me to take care of you."

Tim's eyes shifted back to the child, but Hanna quickly grabbed his face and forced him to look at her.

"What's going to happen now, Han?" he asked.

"We are going to say goodbye to our son and get out of here. I made an arrangement with law enforcement. If you come willingly, there will be no charges. They figure losing our son is punishment enough."

Before heading upstairs, Tim looked into Hanna's eyes and said, "I promise you, I will never let anything happen to our family again."

CHAPTER 26

DR. KEVIN SHUNG, PART 1: THE REVOLUTIONIST

*S*ammi was eleven and Twain had just celebrated his sixth birthday. He was in the first grade and the subject of his teachers' near-constant bragging. Twain was already able to read and write and was smarter than most students his age.

Sammi, on the other hand, no longer went to school and barely left the house. Tim was reluctant to let her stay at home, but when he saw her disdain and pure terror at going out in public, he let it go.

It was in the middle of November, when the trees were stripped bare from the cold, that Tim came home early from the clinic to be greeted by Hanna, whose kiss on his cheek was devoid of emotion. Soon after, he heard Sammi hobble down the stairs, mirror in hand and scars inscribed on her skin, to welcome him home.

The light reflected off Sammi's red locks. To Tim she looked like a female Hades, goddess of the underworld. When his daughter hugged him, he shook the notion out of his head.

Ever since she had stopped going to school, that mirror never left Sammi's hand. She had become obsessed with how she looked and carried the mirror with her into the shower, into her bed at night, and even to the table where the family ate dinner. Just like her scars, the mirror was a permanent part of her.

A few minutes later and right on cue, a large yellow school bus stopped in front of their house. Twain hopped off; his hands were covered with gloves and a bright red beanie shrouded his head from the light snowflakes, but nothing protected his face from the vortex of cold that swirled in the driveway.

Tim looked out the window and saw his red-faced son running up to the door. He threw the door open and permitted the frigid air to rush in like a burglar and steal the heat before Twain could reach his hands up to knock.

"Hello, father!" Twain yelled as he excitedly threw his arms around Tim's neck. In turn, Tim closed his eyes and let his son's love wash over him, calling to mind his promise to Hanna that he would never let anything happen to any of them ever again.

The entire weekend, Tim was upstairs in his study. He was pacing back and forth in pursuit of a solution for Sammi, one that would fix his family. It was time to put the green anole in the past and look toward the future.

Although Tim was a general surgeon, he knew many other doctors in different specialties. In the past couple of years, his clinic had grown in both size and operations. His surgery center now delivered babies and treated athletes, surrounding Tim with obstetricians and sports surgeons. Every day, he had conversations with them and would ask about the newest and coolest technology. Tim was fascinated with innovation, and new diagnostic treatments took his mind off his family turmoil. It wasn't until a few weeks later, when his practice hired a hotshot surgeon from California, that an idea germinated in Tim's mind.

Dr. Kevin Shung was a revolutionary sports surgeon who had graduated from medical school and finished his fellowship in North Korea before coming to the States. At first, people distrusted Dr. Shung's mysterious ways, but soon his results spoke for themselves. His methods didn't lie; he was getting the best patient outcomes nationwide, and everyone wanted to know his secret.

Tim played it cool and tried not to probe or act like a fangirl in front of Dr. Shung. But eventually, his hunger for answers took over and Tim invited Dr. Shung out to dinner.

On the night of the dinner, and after seeing his last patient, Tim packed his bag and headed straight to his car to meet with Shung for a couple of beers and some grub. To Tim, Shung's brain was a medical textbook that had never been opened; its secrets were just waiting to be gobbled up, and Tim was ravenous.

He parked the car and grabbed a pen and notebook before slamming the car door shut and heading into the pizza parlor. Heavy odors of garlic and cheese and spicy sausage wafted through the air, but Tim was only hungry for one thing.

Kevin Shung was already sitting in a booth near the back, a dark beer bubbling in the glass mug in front of him.

Tim sat down in the chair across from Shung, scooting up as close to the table as he physically could. "I didn't take you for an IPA kind of guy," he said, taking off his jacket and hanging it on the chair behind him.

Shung raised his glass. "Cheers, mate. The heavy beer keeps me warm on a cold night such as this one."

"Ain't that what wives are for?" Tim said with a wink, hoping his joke would stick.

And stick it did. Shung laughed and spat out some dark foam on the table. He then chugged the rest of its contents in one gulp and slammed the glass back down. "Opa! Well, at least I think that's how the Greeks say it."

When the waitress came over, Shung ordered them both a beer.

"Thank you for that, Shung!" Tim said. "I'll get the next round." He took a long sip from his dark beer, its nutty taste flowing with ease down his gullet. "I take it your move has gone well?"

"Extremely. The weather here may be bipolar, but the people aren't!" Shung said before drinking nearly half of the beer in a single chug.

"Right you are," Tim said. "People in Colorado are genuine and always down to offer a lending hand.

And that's exactly what I want to do." At this, Tim's face transformed from joking to serious. "If you ever need anything, I hope you feel able to ask me."

Shung smiled and raised his glass. "I appreciate that, Tim. Means a lot, and likewise." They clinked their glasses and proceeded to swallow the rest of the malt liquor.

When approximately two hours had passed and Shung got up to urinate for the third time in twenty minutes, it was clear the effects of high-altitude living were bearing down on the newcomer.

When Shung half-stumbled back to his chair, his face was bright red and a thin line of sweat was beginning to gather on his forehead.

Tim raised his finger and beckoned the waitress back over. "Two Left Hand Nitro Milk Stouts, and put them on my tab."

"Nitro milk what?" Shung asked. "What're you feeding me this time, Timmy boy?"

Tim slapped his hands together in excitement. "Oh, just a little magic trick. Since these beers are made with nitrous, you can pour them into the glass as fast as you can, and they won't ever foam out."

Shung's eyes widened. "You can't be serious." His head swayed back and forth, the alcohol inside him creating waves that felt like they smacked against the sides of his skull. "That goes against the laws of physics. Please, educate me!"

The greed that had been brewing inside Tim snarled at the prey dangling inches from his famished ego. Tim had Shung right where he wanted him, so his lips curled into a smile that invited Shung to spill his impressive insights.

"I'll tell you my secret, if you tell me yours," Tim said as he interlaced his fingers and set his hands down on the table.

Shung's brow scrunched in confusion and spread forehead wrinkles from left to right. "My secrets? What do you mean?"

Tim clicked his tongue in an attempt to hide his voracious appetite. "Shung, do you know the average success rate for rotator cuff surgery?"

"Hmm, about 75 percent?"

"Seventy-four." Tim reached behind his chair and pulled out the pen and notepad. "I've researched you, Dr. Kevin Shung. I always research my partners before we hire them. Do you know your own success rate for rotator cuff surgery?"

Shung blushed, his red face now turning violet. "A little higher, I suppose."

Tim gawked. "A *little*? No, your success rate is a whopping 97 percent!"

The waitress arrived back at the table carrying two icy mugs and two Nitro Milk Stouts. When she popped off the caps and set the beers down on the table, white frost emanated from the open tops.

Tim turned his beer perfectly vertical in the air, the bottle bottom sticking straight up toward the ceiling and the open top pointing downward at the empty glass. The thick, brown beer whisked out of the bottle and was funneled into the glass, stopping perfectly at the top with not even a single bubble barging over the rim.

Shung stood up, amused. "Impeccable! I have never seen anything like that before."

He reached for his own glass and bottle and reenacted Tim's pour, yielding the same result.

Tim grinned again at the amusement that had befallen Shung's face as he lowered his head to eye level with the rim and examined the lack of foam protruding from the top of the mug.

After allowing Shung a few more minutes of bewilderment, Tim's ego roared. "Back to our conversation, do you know the success rate for ACL reconstructions?"

Without looking up from his mug, Shung shrugged his shoulders.

Tim's eye twitched in mild agitation at Shung's curiosity switching from him to the nitrous beer. "Studies say that ACL recon surgery has a success rate of 80 to 90 percent, call it 85 percent. Again, you defy the laws of medicine with a success rate of 98 percent. Shung," he asked with evident agitation, "are you even listening?"

Shung's face shot up, beer dripping from his chin. "Yes, yes. Sorry. I'm listening."

Tim's eyes narrowed. He could barely keep from bursting out of his body and latching onto Shung's mind. "What's your secret, doc?" Tim asked casually, though his hand had moved underneath the table to grip his jeans. "I must know."

The moisture from the bubbles in Tim's untouched drink started to pop. Shung eyed Tim wearily, weighed down by being a mile above sea level. He spun his glass in a circle and sent the last remaining ounces of his beer whirlpooling.

"In Korea, they let us try things that we're not so proud of, Tim. The Eternal Chairman wanted us to find ways to heal our soldiers," Shung said in a low voice as he looked up and into Tim's eyes, "by any means necessary."

Tim pulled his chair as close to the table as he possibly could, his chest touching the hard wood. He grabbed his pen and flipped his notebook to a fresh page, then looked back up and matched Shung's gaze. "Go on."

"My grandfather, Wu Shung, was medical director during the Korean War, where millions of North Koreans and Chinese men died in battle. At first, North Korea had South Korea on the ropes, pushing them back and claiming their land. However, when the United States intervened, everything changed."

The waitress came back to their table after noticing Shung's nearly empty beer. When she asked if he wanted a refill, he simply raised a hand to decline her offer.

A few moments passed before Shung spoke again. "The US had trained troops and weaponized technology the likes of which Korea had never seen, and almost immediately they pressed us all the way back to China's border. My grandfather told us that no matter where you looked, dead bodies were strewn in the streets like confetti from a birthday balloon. The Eternal Chairman was furious and went to my grandfather for answers. You see, Tim, North Korea could not beat their opponents with better weaponized technology, but Wu believed we could beat them with medical technology."

"Like biological bombs and such?" Tim asked, his hunger finally getting a taste of what it desired.

Shung shook his head, the color beginning to drain from his face as his sobriety started to resurface. "Tell me, Tim," he asked. "How do you win a war?"

The question caught Tim off guard. He scratched his head while trying to figure out the puzzle, but eventually gave up. "I . . . I don't know. By having better weapons and more soldiers?"

Shung shook his head and waved his hand in the air to signal the waitress back over. After ordering a Moscow mule, he spoke gravely: "Nay, fear is what wins or loses wars, Tim. If you can conquer or instill enough fear in the opposing side, they will fall. And what is man afraid of most?"

Again, Tim shook his head.

"Death. Man is afraid of death."

Shung's words hung in the air until Tim absorbed them, the brown creaminess of his stout a welcome taste after the dark nature of their conversation. "So," he asked, "the more people you kill, the more fear you create?"

The waitress dropped the Moscow mule in front of Shung, who picked up the lime and squeezed, its guts popping and spraying sour juice into the brass mug below.

"Wrong," he said as he pressed the drink to his lips, wincing at the sting of the ginger. "If you take away the fear of death, people have nothing to fear."

The skin on Tim's ears perked up as an electrified shock wave rippled through his body. His hand automatically snatched the pen and pressed its inky tip to the blank notepad. This was what Tim had come for. This was what he wanted to learn.

"You can prevent people from dying?" he said incredulously.

Shung chuckled. "I'm not talking about immortality. I'll leave that one to the gods. I'm talking about rapid healing."

Tim scribbled *rapid healing* into his notebook, at last filling its empty pages with something worthy. Eagerly awaiting what would be said next, he glanced back up at Shung.

"Rapid healing, being able to heal someone completely before they lose too much blood or die from infection. If you can tell a soldier he will not die in battle and will be healed no matter the injury, he will do things other soldiers who fear death won't." Shung put the brass cup back down on the coaster and wiped his lips. "Or that's what Wu believed, I guess. The Americans swarmed and the war was over before he had time to use what he'd learned."

The pen in Tim's hand stopped moving when Shung finished speaking. "Is that it?" he said. "You still haven't told me anything except that fear wins damn wars."

Shung smiled. "Tim, sometimes things are better forgotten. Once you go down the rabbit hole, there's no turning back."

Tim slammed his fist on the table, causing several patrons to turn their heads at the commotion. Noticing the attention, Tim sat back down and hissed at Shung, "Go down the rabbit hole? I've been stuck down here for years, Shung. Ever since I injected my stillborn baby with damn lizard DNA, I've been lost." Tim wiped away a surprising tear before he continued. "I need an answer, Shung. Please help me."

Shung observed the whimpering man sitting across from him, not fully comprehending why he was so distraught. "Why do you want to know, Tim?"

"Because I want to help people more so than I do now. I want to make people perfect. I want to fix things."

Shung raised an eyebrow. "No matter the cost?"

Tim polished off the rest of his drink and slammed it on the table. "No matter the cost."

CHAPTER 27

DR. KEVIN SHUNG, PART 2: DEER HEAD

They each drank a bottle of water to cleanse their livers and sober them up before they hopped in their respective cars. Tim blasted the heat and switched the wipers to full power to eliminate the accumulated snow on the dash. The wipers crunched as they rubbed against the ice, making splintering sounds as the car awakened. As he waited, Tim blew warm air into his hands and rubbed them together.

Shung pulled out of his parking space and signaled for Tim to follow, then drove into the white abyss where everything but his car's headlights disappeared.

Tim threw his car in reverse, then shoved the clutch into forward, his tires spinning before gripping to the gravel below. He followed Shung for a few minutes on the highway, without the slightest idea of where they were headed. As Tim drove, the snowstorm worsened and wind roared through his AC vents and chilled the inside of the car. His headlight beams glowed against the falling snowflakes, reflecting light off them and casting a white light back in his face.

Finally, Shung took the exit ramp a couple of miles past their clinic. The eager predator inside stirred within Tim, and he licked his crusty lips at the thought of his forthcoming meal.

Shung's left blinker flashed and the car slowed as he took a left on a dirt road lined on both sides with pine trees. A metal gate blocked the path leading down the dirt road; Shung got out of his car and tossed his hoodie over his head as he strode over and opened the gate. After following Shung for another few minutes, a log cabin appeared as an outline amid the trees. The closer they got, the more the outline filled in until a hand-carved log house, gently tucked away in the pine-tree forest, stood before them.

Tim pulled his car next to Shung's and got out, winter's cold bite grazing his skin.

"Over here, Tim," Shung said, his face hidden behind the veil of his hood.

Tim carefully walked up the wooden steps that led to the front door, each stair creaking at his weight.

"Where the hell are we, Shung?" he asked, more than a little annoyed.

Shung shook the snow off his jacket then pulled out a pair of keys from his pocket. He jammed a key into the lock and turned his wrist, a *click* resounding through the forest as the door creaked open.

"Your Jekyll lived in your lab with the lizards," Shung said as he pushed on the wooden door to open it fully. "This is where mine lives."

At this, he stepped into a house where darkness welcomed them with a wide snarl.

Shung flicked on the light to illuminate the interior. Heads of deer and antelope and birds of prey, as well as cowboy hats and guns, hung on the walls.

Mouth agape, Tim looked around. "What is this place?" he asked as he rubbed the smooth wooden top of a table, admiring its craftmanship.

"My escape from the real world. All this belonged to my father and his father," Shung said with admiration as he considered his ancestors who were still very much alive in the getaway home. "Not all Asians like math, I guess."

A small laugh escaped from Tim. "Some of this belonged to your grandfather, Wu?"

"Everything you see here belonged to my father," Shung replied as he moved over to the deer head.

Tim followed and eyed the deer with suspicion.

Shung averted his eyes from the deer and looked at Tim. "When my father and I first moved here, he built this cottage just for us. He said it was for me to escape the hardships of the work world."

Tim kept his eyes glued to the deer when he asked, "Was he right? Is this place your escape from work?"

When Shung smiled, his white teeth contrasted against the dark wood interior. "No, it became my work."

"How so?"

"Promise me you won't tell a soul," Shung said. "It could mean the end of both of us."

Tim rolled his eyes. "I promise."

Shung shook his head. "Not good enough. I need you to swear it. Make it an oath."

Tim studied Shung until he realized the man was being serious. "Okay," Tim said as he raised his right hand in the air. "I swear."

Only the patter of the sleet outside could be heard before Shung broke the silence. "Do you want to see what Wu left me?"

The wind had started to calm down, and for the first time in a long time Tim felt afraid—afraid that if he stayed too long, he would discover all of the answers he desired. He wanted to grab his coat, run back to his car, and drive home to his wife, but his inner demon wouldn't allow his feet to move.

"Show me" were the only words Tim spoke.

"Very well," Shung said while pulling the mounted deer's left antler, which gave way too easily, and gently pushed to reveal the wall behind it that had swung open.

"What the—" Tim exclaimed, covering his mouth to prevent the dust from the penetrated vacuum entering.

"Follow me, Tim. And keep your mind open to all possibilities," Shung said as he stepped into the dark doorway before continuing. "I can sense," he muttered as his face disappeared, "your hunger."

Tim was about to act as if he had no idea what Kevin Shung was referring to, but there was no point. *I guess demons can sense other demons*, he thought as he proceeded after Shung into the passageway behind the deer head.

The mystery room was cold, but this was a cold that had some purpose. When Shung flicked on the lights, Tim couldn't hide his bewilderment.

It was a scene straight from *The Matrix*, with translucent sacks that contained differently hued red liquids that hung from the wall by flimsy wire that stretched the entire length of the hidden room. The room itself was actually more like a clean, well-organized hallway; the only decorations were the red bags, with little letters stuck to each that specified a particular type or order, although Tim couldn't be certain.

Shung closed the door, trapping the frigid air inside with them. When he spoke, white frost shot out with his every word. "You can look and ask anything, but please, no touching." He raised his hand and scratched the back of his neck. "Pretend it's a sterile field of sorts."

Tim's ravenous ego drank in the sight. He had no idea what was in those special bags that dangled from the wall, but he knew it was something special. His legs moved him forward, toward one of the red sacks, until his nose was mere inches from its contents. Since he couldn't touch, he took a deep breath in an attempt to distinguish any scent that might offer a clue; he smelled nothing.

He pressed his glasses back up his nose and stared at one of the bags with the letter *O* affixed to it. His eyes flicked to the next bag, which also featured a small *O* sticker. The more he shuffled along the row of bags, the more Tim noticed the letter *O* stuck or written on the bags. When he reached the opposite end of the room and tracked back to the beginning, he found more bags neatly lined up parallel to each other on the wall. The sacks' contents looked the same, but when Tim squinted his eyes, he noticed that this row of bags had the letter *A* embroidered into them.

Tim followed the row all the way down to the opposite end of the hallway-shaped space, acknowledging that they all featured the letter *A*. He repeated this process with the next few rows of red bags, the first row displaying the letter *B* and the next *AB*. Tim's mind churned as he searched for an answer as to what he was seeing.

Shung leaned against the wall and observed Tim's every move. "You want a hint?"

Tim released a puff of white frost into the air by laughing. "I think I know some of this riddle . . . I'm assuming the letters on the bags correspond to blood types?"

Shung clapped his hands and walked toward Tim. "Right you are with that one! Now, what do you think is in the bags on the right side of the room?"

In shock, Tim's eyes darted around the room. "I thought all these bags were filled with the same thing?"

"Then I am afraid your thought is wrong," Shung replied. "Maybe this is too much for you at once. We can go over this another time, when you . . ."

Tim threw his arms down in frustration. "No, Shung. I need to do this to fix my family. Please, show me the way."

Shung stood assessing the situation, trying to get a read on Tim. "For your family, eh? I have heard what happened to your daughter. I'm sorry to hear of it, Tim. Before my father brought me to the States, he always said family is the most important thing in life and to cherish it always."

There was a long pause as Tim stood rigidly at the exit door; he wanted to leave, but the demon inside him compelled him to stay.

Finally, Shung shattered the frozen walls between them by moving his hand up to gesture at the wall on the right. "On this wall we have blood plasma containing a vast amount of stem cells, the little letters indicate the donor blood type. O negative is the best choice in these circumstances because it is universal, and anyone can use it no matter their type. Plasma alone is great, but when it is mixed with stem cells the regenerative process is remarkable." Shung's face beamed with pride.

Tim ambled over to the bags. Light was reflected off them, so he could see better. They weren't fully red, he realized; there was a yellow tinge to them.

As if Shung read Tim's mind, he said, "The yellowish tint comes from the separation process. It contains the growth factors."

Tim nodded as his ego growled with delight. "And where do the stem cells come from?"

"We harvested them from bone marrow, concentrating on the donor's hip bone, the iliac crest. But you can also get stem cells from the top of the tibia and talus bones."

Tim looked up, confused. "We?"

"I told you how the leader of North Korea demanded that my grandfather find a way to save us in the war. Well, Wu didn't have time to discover it during the conflict, it was only when the fighting ended that he figured out the secret. As horrible as it sounds, he was given permission to use soldiers as test subjects for his experiments."

Despite the room's coldness, sweat ran down Tim's back. He had to ask the question, even though he assumed he already knew the answer: "And what happened to his subjects?"

Shung clasped his hands together and grinned. "Well, you're kind of looking at them!" He gestured around the room at all of the bags.

Tim was flabbergasted. He said nothing but eventually a roaring laughter exploded from him and caused him to drop to one knee. After a moment of hysteria, Tim took off his glasses and wiped his eyes. "What the actual fuck, Shung?" Where did you get . . ." He looked around at all the bags before completing his thought. "Where did you get all these bodies?"

Shung walked over to Tim and slapped him on the back. "Don't worry, Tim. I didn't hurt anybody.

Every bag in this room represents a patient from my grandfather's time. Before he passed, he gave me all of this to use as medication for my current patients. He didn't want anything to go to waste, so we shipped all the bags and kept them near frozen to preserve them."

"But a normal yield for platelet-rich plasma with stem cells is usually only a couple of CCs! How in the world did you fill whole bags with the stuff?" Tim asked, his interests peaked.

"Ah. Right you are, Timmy. That's because a normal blood draw for this, from the iliac crest, is about sixty CCs. These patients were dying anyway, and Wu convinced them to donate their bodies in their entirety, promising them they would ascend to Cheonguk, which is what you refer to as heaven. So instead of only harvesting sixty or so CCs of blood, he harvested their entire bodies."

Instead of feeling horror or disgust, Tim was intrigued. "That's actually brilliant," he said, his fiendish hunger finally getting a taste of the entree. "So, all this is just super-concentrated stem cells and platelets?"

"Correctamundo!" Shung exclaimed as he trudged over to the opposite side of the wall where more sacks of a darker red hue hung. "Complete body stem cell PRP treatment is only half the equation, though. What do you think these bags contain?"

Tim walked over to the sacks Shung pointed to and observed them, studying their Merlot color and the tiny flecks floating inside. He was puzzled, unsure of what he was looking at. "I'm not sure on this one, Shung. Educate me."

"The secret to all life starts at the beginning," Shung said from right beside Tim, as they admired the hanging bags. "You are familiar with amniotic fluid?"

"As in placentas?" Tim's eyes never left the red receptacles. "Not too much, no."

"I understand, it's new science. Not too much data to back it up." Shung walked back over to the hidden door that led out to the house's common area. "Let's chat out here, little less cold."

Tim followed Shung and watched as he gently closed the door, once again completely hiding the room behind the deer's neck. Shung headed straight toward the fridge and pulled out two Montucky Cold Snacks; he tossed one over to Tim. They popped the cans open and took a drink, washing away whatever trace of humility remained.

Shung sat down on one of the wooden chairs at the handcrafted oak table and beckoned Tim to do the same. He tipped his drink back one last time, then crinkled it into an aluminum ball and tossed it in the recycling bin.

Tim was only thirsty for answers to the ludicrousness going on in Shung's secret room, but he took a sip of his beer anyway. A burp escaped Tim's throat as he set the beer on the coaster, then crossed his legs in anticipation of what Shung was going to say. "Please go on, Shung. I'm truly fascinated by your work. Stem cells plus placenta, eh?"

"Hakuna matata." The chair creaked as Shung leaned back in it and rubbed the smooth surface of the table with his hands. "Amniotic liquid, Tim. Not placenta. We aren't savages."

"What's the difference?" Tim asked, noticing how dark it was getting outside. He needed to head on home soon or Hanna would worry.

"Amniotic liquid is the inside layer of the placenta, closest to the fetus. This thin membrane contains several incredible growth factors that help with the regeneration of cells."

Tim's eyes widened. "You say it helps with regrowth?"

"Helps? Ha! Tim, it completes the cycle. The stem cells in the bone marrow combined with amniotic tissue is the recipe for skin and tissue regeneration. The stem cells awaken the growth factors that signal tissue, bone, and skin to start growing, or regrowing in your daughter's case." Shung let the last words dangle in front of Tim.

Tim tried to bury his immediate excitement, forcing it down into a metal hole and throwing a latch over the top. He could feel it banging on the door and trying to get out. "If what you're saying is true, then why isn't every doctor doing it? Why haven't you published your work? You could be a hero, Shung."

"I've thought about that. And maybe one day I will release my work," Shung said as he looked down at his shoes. "This recipe only works if a patient donates their entire body, which is something not many people are willing to do. You see, for the stem cell plasma to work, we need far more than the standard blood draw, we need an entire body's worth to get the desired concentration."

"And where does the amniotic liquid come into play?" Tim asked almost unconsciously.

"Stem cells from the marrow alone work great for skin issues," Shung said as he rose from his seat. "The amniotic fluid is perfect for when you need a kick start."

Shung left the room and Tim could hear him pull the deer antler again. When Shung returned, he was holding a shoebox with frost escaping the lid.

Tim looked at the shoebox and the thought of an early Christmas gift washed over him. "What is this?"

Shung bowed. "A gift. I'll give you one bag of the special fetal liquid. Use it wisely."

Tim's demon screamed its greedy approval. "How do we get more?"

"We?" Shung shook his head. "There is no 'we' in this. You'll need to find your own methods. I told you what you needed to know to help your family because I can see the fire behind your eyes."

Shung must have sensed Tim's confusion. "Don't act like you don't know what I'm referring to. The eternal flame doesn't lie."

When Tim stood up, his hands were clenched into fists and anger coursed through his bones. He didn't know why he felt angry; Shung had given him what he needed to make his daughter whole again, to make her perfect.

Yet he stood there shaking with rage. "I don't know if I can, Shung. I'm weak. I'm not like your grandfather."

Shung's chair whizzed back and hit the bar as he stood up. "No, my friend. You are not like my grandfather." Shung ceased speaking for a few moments, allowing the weight to build with every second that passed. He lifted his hand and pointed to Tim's heart—and what he said next turned Tim to ice. "But he is."

Tim dwelled on what Shung had said, the notion disturbing him the entire car ride home. He pulled up the driveway and parked his car, careful to close his door gently so as not to wake his sleeping family and praying that his wife wouldn't be mad at his tardiness. The wolf's eyes gleamed in the moonlight when Tim pushed open the front door. He trudged through the family room into the kitchen, where he exited out the side door into the backyard.

The night was still and stars glimmered in the sky, shining their white light on the old shed.

Tim ambled over to the rusty shed, a shovel in his hands and evil on his mind.

CHAPTER 28

THE CALM BEFORE THE STORM

Tim walked for ages surrounded by darkness, until he saw a shimmer of light in the distance. He initially believed it to be false, but the light didn't fade.

His fear shifted to urgency and Tim dashed toward the light, his fingers reaching out to touch it and feel its glow on his skin, but he felt nothing. The light swirled ahead of him, transforming into vague objects he could barely recognize, until one shape emerged and held firm: a mirror.

Tim walked over and stood in front of it, looking at the crystal glass without seeing any reflection.

"Sammi?" Tim asked, turning around to search for his daughter. He found nothing.

When he turned back around to face the mirror, it reflected a man. The man looked just like Tim, but he wasn't Tim. Puzzled, Tim reached out his left hand to touch the glass; the man didn't mimic Tim, and instead just stood there staring back. Then he winked.

A jolt ran along Tim's spine, crawling from his lowest vertebrae right up to his brain stem. "Who . . . who are you?"

The words bounced off the glass and echoed through the void. They grew louder and fiercer and caused Tim to fall to his knees and clasp his ears with his hands. "Make it stop!" Tim screamed. "Make it stop!"

"If you want it to stop, then make it stop."

Tim stood up and faced the mirror once again. "Are you doing this?" he asked his reflection.

"No, technically you are," the man responded. "But I can if you need me to." The reflection winked at Tim again, a grin forming on its lips.

"Who are you?" Tim asked, even though the answer lurked right in front of him.

"I think you know the answer to that one, Timmy boy."

Tim took a step closer to the mirror, noticing its smoothness. He gazed at his own reflection and noticed how he had aged: baby wrinkles lined his once-smooth face, and the skin under his eyes sagged. But his eyes, those fierce blue eyes, were as sharp as ever. "I don't think I can do this anymore," he pleaded with the reflection.

"No, you can't. You are weak and always have been."

"Please, help me," Tim cried. He raised his left hand and placed it on the mirror, feeling its coldness seep into his fingertips and surge throughout the rest of his body.

The reflection studied Tim coolly. Then it raised its own hand and placed it on the glass as a mirror to Tim's.

When the two hands touched, the barrier between mirror and reality faded and two Tims stood together. A sense of ease washed over Tim; he closed his eyes and let the sensation flood his body.

"Too weak again?" his reflection asked.

Tim knew it wasn't a question. "Yes."

The hand on the other side of the mirror recoiled, then shot through the glass to grip Tim's arm.

Tim tried to pull back to no avail.

"Succumb to me," the reflection said, its hand clenching Tim's arm, pulverizing muscle and tissue as its fingernails dug into flesh.

Tim looked again at his reflection, the glass barrier that had once separated them now completely melted away. The reflection winked at Tim a final time, then pulled him through the mirror—to the other side.

Tim lurched awake, drenched in a cold sweat.

"That was one hell of a nap, Tim. Are you sure you're okay?" a concerned Hanna asked.

Tim wiped the perspiration from his brow and the heavy droplets flew across the room. "Yeah, I'm fine. Just a bad dream." He stood up from the love chair in the corner of the room and glanced at his clock. "It's almost time," he muttered.

They changed clothes as the sun began to set, waves of orange luminescence creeping through the windows and bathing the white carpet in a fiery glow. People typically change out of their work attire and settle into something comfortable, but not Tim Hill.

He put on his blue scrubs, systematically popping each button in its corresponding groove to secure his surgical jacket. His attire smelled clean, sterile. He looked over at his wife and caught her staring at the cane leaning against the wall. "You okay, Han?"

Hanna's eyes snapped away from the cane and on Tim. "Yes, I'm fine. I just hate acting."

"What do you mean?"

"Bad knees . . . C'mon, Tim. Ever since you and Shung injected me with that stuff, all the pain is gone. I feel great."

Tim smirked. "Isaac needed to think he was really helping us. That way, he would stay committed."

Hanna touched the soft patch of skin between her kneecap and shinbone. "I guess . . ."

"It worked, didn't it?" Tim asked rhetorically.

Hanna changed into her white robe and glanced at her husband. "Tim, are we doing the right thing?"

Tim sighed, then paused as he slipped the protective cloth shoes over his feet. "I think so, yes."

"You *think* so?" Hanna exclaimed.

Tim was lost in thought and unusually quiet.

"Tim?"

"Yes, I hear you, honey," he finally responded. "I asked Sammi the same thing, and we were right about that one." Tim flashed his smile, his teeth glimmering in the sunlight. "I have been preparing for this for so long, and the day is finally here. Today's the day I give my son his life back."

Hanna's voice was meek when she responded. "He has a life, though. A good one."

"You know what I mean, Han. Ever since Faith"—Tim looked down at the floor in disgust—"did that to our boy . . . I just want to give him the life he deserves." He sat on the side of the bed to massage his temples.

Hanna strode over and sat next to him. "Now, now, dear. Everything will be all right." She started to slowly rub his back, up and down, to make him comfortable. "Just remember that we are a team, babe. You don't have to do this alone."

Hanna leaned in closer to her husband, her lips mere millimeters from his ear. "Let me help, please. I want to do this."

Tim jolted to his feet. "No, I need to do this myself. I caused the accident, so let me finish it."

She didn't want to agree, but she nodded her head anyway, knowing deep down that he must do it alone.

ISAAC

CHAPTER 29

◆

IS, SHORT FOR ISAAC

*I*saac faded in and out of sleep, his consciousness pulled by the tide of the moon.

The doctor stared at the screen mounted on the wall, one hand clutching an arthroscopic grasper and the other the camera. "That's a good-sized tear we have on his rotator cuff." The end of the grasper pinched the torn tissue that had ripped off the top of the arm bone. "I'll take two anchors, Isaac."

"Do you want them loaded with tape or regular suture?" Isaac responded, angry that the medical sales rep hadn't made it to the shoulder surgery on time.

"Hmm, based on the size of the tear, what would you recommend?" the surgeon asked, testing him.

"Tape, 100 percent. Its wider width should secure the torn tendon better and cover more surface area than regular suture."

"Love it. I'll take two."

Isaac reached up and grabbed the appropriate white boxes from the cabinet that stored the room's medical supplies. "Expiration is 2024," Isaac read off the label. The surgical tech nodded, and Isaac sterilely handed him the two screws with tape.

Without looking back, the surgeon stuck his hand out toward the tech. "I need the punch for the anchor, please."

The tech grabbed the green-handled instrument and a mallet and handed both to the surgeon. With the help of his assistant and the arthroscopic scope, the doctor malleted the punch down to the corresponding laser line on top of the arm bone and pulled it out.

The surgeon inserted the two screws loaded with tape into the punched holes, the fluid inside the patient's shoulder turning light pink from the blood leaking out of the bone. "Perfect. I'll take the suture passer now."

Isaac watched the tech as he handed the surgeon the next instrument. The suture passer looked like a long grasper, but with a mouth at the end instead of pincers. The PA loaded the tails of the tape into the needle-tipped jaw of the passer, then the surgeon inserted it back inside the shoulder joint until it appeared on the screen. He maneuvered it around tissue and bone until the torn rotator cuff tissue lay in the jaw of the passer. His hand squeezed the instrument, firing the sharp needle through the jaw of the passer and cuff tendon, spitting the tails of the tape out the top side of the torn cuff tissue.

"Grasper again, please," the surgeon asked, dropping the passer on the mayo stand and sticking his hand out toward the surgical tech again.

He retrieved the suture tails from a small incision on top of the shoulder, docking them out of the way. "Two more anchors, please. Unloaded ones."

Isaac nodded, recited the expiration date, and opened the products, noticing how similar both the screws with tape and the unloaded ones were. The only difference being the unloaded ones had a small, plastic eyelet at the tip of the screw instead of the tape.

His eyes never leaving the screen, the doctor asked, "Can you tell me what tendon this is?"

Even though he never verbally directed the question toward anyone in particular, Isaac knew it was for him; everyone always picked on the young guy. "That's the supraspinatus."

Without acknowledging the correct answer, the surgeon made two more punch holes about fifteen millimeters further down the arm bone, then retrieved the tapes from his upper incision. He loaded the tapes from the first anchors into the eyelets of the unloaded ones, then screwed them into the last two holes, successfully folding the tapes over from the first two anchors and locking the tendon back down to its native position on the bone with the last two. "And that's a wrap!" the surgeon exclaimed, stepping away from the table and snapping off his bloodied gloves.

Isaac admired the repair on the screen and noticed small traces of yellow liquid float out of the final two bone holes the doctor made with the punch, until the saline fluid carried it away. "Guess what that yellow stuff is," the doctor asked, noticing Isaac observing the TV monitor.

Isaac stared at the screen, examining the different parts of the patient's inner shoulder. "I . . . I'm not sure."

"It's bone marrow."

Slowly, color filled Isaac's vision in dizzy swirls that contorted and shifted until sharp lines rendered objects distinct. His head swayed from the cocktail Tim had injected into him. As his nerves and muscles awoke from what felt like the worst hangover of his life, Isaac wiggled his fingers and toes, then let out a sigh of relief upon the realization that he wasn't paralyzed.

But the feeling of relief quickly dissipated and was replaced with terror when Isaac tried to move his arms and legs and discovered that nothing would budge.

Long, metal cerclage cables looped around his entire body like a python strangling its prey. Isaac was naked except for his boxers. The cold bite of the steel table gnawed at his bare skin, which had sprouted little goose bumps that resembled springtime mayflowers. He wanted to scream, bellow his rage, but the wet rag in his mouth absorbed the noise before it could reach the air. He forced himself to breathe through his nose, knowing he'd choke on the warm water-soaked rag. Panic set in like hardening and expanding cement in Isaac's gut. He couldn't move. He was trapped.

He rolled his eyes up to the ceiling and noticed huge surgical lights directly above him, the beaming-down spotlights reminiscent of those he'd seen on an Alcatraz tour. Isaac looked around the room and noticed its cleanliness; in fact, it looked sterile, and the horrible notion of what was about to happen to him solidified in his mind.

The room itself was quite large, with over one hundred square feet of mostly empty space. There was no furniture, except for a chair in front of a glass desk in the far corner and an empty mayo stand to the bottom left of the bed. Above the desk and on all of the walls were diagrams of the human body that mapped out every anatomical structure down to the last nerve.

His chest heaved up and down, the cerclage cables suffocating him. Isaac closed his eyes and recalled the last thing he remembered.

Glimpses of counting to ten, then searching for Twain, and finally the sting on the side of his neck . . .

I just had to play, Isaac thought to himself. "More like hide-and-go-die." He surprised himself, finding humor at such a horrific time.

Urgency flooded his system and Isaac realized he needed to somehow free himself. He began to shift his weight back and forth to rock the operating bed and determine if its structure would hold. At first nothing moved, but after his flailing he finally built up enough momentum to feel the wheels of the bed lift off the ground.

"Right, then left, then right again," Isaac repeated to himself. The sound of the wheels hitting the floor echoed in the room; with one loud *bang*, the bed toppled over.

This was when the cables holding him down would break from the impact of the bed slamming into the floor and Isaac could ungag himself and run out of the unlocked room to freedom. But none of that happened.

Instead, the action slammed his head to the ground and the resulting blood mucked up the sanitized floor. No cables broke or were loosened, and no door was magically unlocked. Blood soaked the gag rag and leaked from Isaac's mouth, filling the room with its metallic scent. Instead of a great heroic escape, Isaac choked on his own blood and was strangled by Tim's cables.

The crash from the surgical bed toppling over must have been louder than Isaac realized, because a few seconds later the door swung open and Tim stepped into the room.

But it wasn't the Tim Isaac was used to seeing. Instead of the quirky, nerdy little man who laughed at his own jokes, the Tim who entered was a shell of a man. Or maybe Tim had been the shell, and this was the real Tim in his true form.

Tim sighed and placed his coffee mug on the sole table in the room. He licked his hand and used the spit to straighten his jutting-out hairs, then walked over and squatted down next to Isaac.

"What a mess," he said, clicking his tongue. His fingers bounced off his chin as he thought and looked down at Isaac, his beady eyes squinting in frustration. "I'm going to remove your gag, and when I do you will not make a sound. If you scream, I will make sure my foot in your mouth is the last meal you ever have. Nod if you understand."

Isaac nodded in defeat.

Tim replied with a nod of his own and slowly untied the bloody gag before removing it from Isaac's mouth. The next few seconds included the sounds of Isaac gasping for delicious air, gulping it down and supplying his lungs with what could possibly be the last oxygen they ever received.

Grunting from the exertion, Tim grabbed the edge of the bed and flipped it back upright, the springs rattling as he did.

Tim stared at Isaac for a long time, as if trying to penetrate his mind. His once-warm eyes and crooked smile were gone, and Isaac wondered if this was even Tim any longer.

Tim's voice pierced the room when he spoke. "Do you want the good news or the bad news?"

Although Tim acted as if nothing was out of the ordinary, Isaac answered with silence.

"This could very well be the last decision you make on this earth. Do you really want me to make it for you?" Tim asked while slowly turning around.

Again, Isaac didn't respond.

"Isaac, please don't make this harder than it is and give me an answer!" Steam was practically sizzling out of Tim's ears and spiraling to the ceiling.

"Good news," Isaac croaked. "Give me the good news."

It turned out the good news wasn't such good news after all.

"The good news, Isaac, is that you will be the most important stepping-stone in medical history. Maybe the final step toward a miraculous clinical success!"

Doubt shrouded Isaac's question. "And the bad news?"

Tim smiled and pulled out a sterilely wrapped container; he broke the tape seal that kept its internal contents contaminant-free. When Tim flipped the container upside down, a waterfall of metallic sounds tumbled out.

Even though Tim's body was blocking his view, Isaac knew exactly what had been in the container.

At the beginning and end of every surgery was the all-important count. Towels, needles, knife blades, drills, everything had to match; if you started with ten blades, you needed to have ten blades at the end. The purpose of the count was to make sure nothing was accidently left behind in the patient's body.

On Tim's table, Isaac counted two needles, five blades, one hypo, and surgical gauze that was packaged in tens.

"Don't freak out, Isaac, I—"

"How am I not supposed to freak out, you piece of shit!" Isaac spat out.

Tim's eyes widened. "Of course, my fault. How stupid of me." He started to pack up the instruments, gingerly placing them back in the container. "I shouldn't have shown you these, not yet. Want to know why?"

"Because you're a madman?" Isaac said feebly.

Tim's tongue clicked in amusement, but the wheels in his mind churned as he tried to figure out what to say in response.

"Isaac, you're in the medical field. Remember our studies on glycogen? What does glycogen do?"

Robotically, Isaac replied, "It stores carbs in the body."

"Correct. Here's a riddle for you. If you answer correctly, I will free you from those binds. Answer incorrectly and . . . well, we can get to that later."

Isaac's lips curled into a snarl. His mind wandered back to Alabama and to how his mom would always say that "hate is a strong word"; in this instance, however, no other word would suffice.

"Why do scientists assert that more pleasant, humane slaughterhouses make for better meat?"

A smirk crept on Isaac's face, as memories of his hunting excursions flashed across his mind.

"C'mon Is, you want to be in the medical field, right? This is hunting 101. Glycogen is the answer. If an animal is stressed before it dies, it uses up its glycogen storage, turning the meat hard and distasteful. In an unstressed animal, that glycogen is stored and released as lactic acid upon death. The lactic acid keeps the meat pink, flavorful, and alive."

Isaac looked directly at Tim. "Are you planning to eat me, Tim?" He started to laugh at the notion. "I taste great with salt, you sick son of a bitch." He was hysterical now, hot tears streaming down his cheeks.

But Tim wasn't laughing.

"I answered correctly, Tim," Isaac said, somber once more. "Now be a man of your word and free me!"

Tim clicked his tongue again. "I said I'd free you from those binds, which I will . . . eventually."

Isaac wasn't surprised at Tim's response. He hadn't actually thought Tim would free him if he got the answer correct, but the taste of hope lingered and he was hungry for more. "You're a coward, Tim."

Tim sighed and looked down at Isaac, his eyes empty and dull. "I am many things, Isaac, but a coward is not one of them."

He patted the bed's metal railing, then turned around and headed out the door, leaving Isaac to be tormented by thoughts of the lurking unknown.

CHAPTER 30

————————◆————————

THE LAST SUPPER

*D*ark blue bruises had formed around Isaac's wrists and snaked their way up his arms to where the cables were wrapped. Pain pounded behind his eyes from his head smacking the floor, the throbbing blurring his vision.

The gash inside his mouth had reopened and blood trickled down Isaac's neck to pool on the floor beneath him. However, none of the aches and pains compared to the gnawing hunger that was eating away at his stomach and chewing on his liver and intestines.

Isaac was also parched; he could start a fire with his sandpaper lips. The IV in his arm was pumping a light brown liquid into his vein: the anti-fear serum that was keeping his terror at bay.

Part of Isaac wanted to lie forever in his dreamless slumber. The table felt softer, the metal more malleable. The cables seemed looser and a warm current filled the room. The piano chords of Beethoven's *Für Elise, WoO 59* serenaded him, his eyes flickering, then shuttering as the light faded away.

"Is he awake, Daddy? Does he feel any pain?"

Isaac jolted awake at the sound of Twain's voice. Thanks to the medicinal cocktail hangover, Isaac's head still swirled and made it difficult to open his eyes. Eventually, light poured in through his pupils and distinct colors began to take shape. There was Tim, with one arm around Twain's shoulder as the boy observed the human experiment on the table.

"Twain," Isaac gasped, making every effort to warp vibration to sound. "Help me . . . please. I need water."

Twain pulled a glass from the waiter's tray he had carried from downstairs. The cup was filled with a light blue liquid. Twain grasped it and walked over to the side of the bed. He held the cup out gingerly, the lip of the rim inches from Isaac's mouth.

Isaac scowled at father and son, using the last of his energy to raise his voice. "Y'all think I'm stupid?

I'm not drinking that. It's probably liquid Xanax or something to knock me back out."

"It's Gatorade, Isaac, you need the electrolytes," Tim said calmly, in a steady voice.

"Bullshit."

"Language," Twain whispered, looking down.

Tim rolled his eyes and grabbed the glass. He put it to his lips and took a long sip. "Ahh, Arctic Freeze. My favorite. Hanna always argues that orange is the best, but nothing ever satisfies like Arctic Freeze after a long, hot day of yard work. Let's try this again."

Tim handed the glass back to Twain, who refilled it. Twain looked at the swirling Gatorade, then slowly walked back to the side of the bed. He held the glass back up to Isaac's lips.

"For you," Twain said meekly. "Please drink it."

Isaac nodded and took a little sip. He paused, half smiling, as memories of post-soccer game Gatorade-chugging contests flashed across his mind. He quickly shook off the nostalgia and pressed his face into the glass. Twain tipped the cup at a higher angle, opening the floodgate for the Gatorade to pass down Isaac's throat.

Tim was right. Arctic Freeze was the best, but Isaac would rather die than admit it to him. *Better not say that out loud or my wish may be granted sooner than I thought*, Isaac thought.

"I'll send Twain back later with some food I'd suggest you eat. We start the procedure in sixteen hours," Tim said while rustling Twain's hair. "Twain, go back downstairs, Daddy wants to say a couple words to Isaac in private."

Twain nodded and grabbed the tray holding the cups and empty Gatorade bottle, then scurried back down the stairs. Isaac could hear the thumping of Twain's feet as they hopped down the steps; he closed his eyes and imagined it was him running down those stairs to freedom.

This dream dissolved quickly when Tim asked, "What do you want to eat, Is?"

"Why do you all of a sudden give a damn?" Isaac responded.

Tim reached out with one hand and grabbed Isaac's face, scrunching up his cheeks and squeezing, until Isaac's face started to turn different shades of purple. Isaac tried to yell, but Tim clenched his hand around Isaac's throat and cut off his air and any sound he tried to make.

"Listen to me, you, and you listen good. This will probably be the last meal you ever have, so make it count. You can either die hungry tomorrow, with your blood being the last thing you taste, or . . ." Tim released his hand from Isaac's throat and for a moment watched him gasp.

He then exhaled and continued. "Or . . . you can eat. I'm sure you're hungry." He started to pace at the foot of Isaac's bed, his index finger tapping his chin as he thought. "I'm trying to make things right, Isaac. For me and my family. I know it probably doesn't mean anything to you, but I do hope you get some food in your stomach. You deserve that."

Isaac kept his mouth shut, but his growling stomach answered on his behalf.

CHAPTER 31

———◆———

HANNA'S OFFERING

The door cracked open a final time and Tim trudged into the room carrying a paper towel–covered plate. Isaac's nostrils gulped in the smells of oregano and cheese when Tim set the plate on the table at Isaac's bedside. "Hanna made me give this to you. It's the rest of our pizza from last night."

Tim pulled away the paper towels like a magician and two slices of pizza appeared in front of Isaac, whose mouth salivated to the point that he had to drink his drool to keep it from overflowing. "Thanks" was all he could muster.

"I'm going to loosen one of the straps to free an arm," Tim said. "I want you to promise you won't do anything stupid, okay?"

Isaac glared at Tim, the fire of his resentment scorching hot. But he swallowed his ego and nodded in agreement.

"Good. Now hold still for a second."

When Isaac felt one of the cables around his right arm loosen, he gratefully thrust out his arm and stretched his confined muscles to restart a healthy blood flow.

Tim kept the plate far from Isaac but dropped the two pizza slices and a napkin near enough that Isaac could grab them.

The cheese sizzled and the hot sausage popped meaty juices in Isaac's mouth when he took his first bite. The first morsel slid down his gullet and into his stomach, which welcomed the pizza by absorbing the nutrients and delivering them to different parts of his body. The last bite eaten, Isaac closed his eyes and felt warmth enter his body for the last time. Tears secreted out and he sobbed silently, for he knew his end was near.

Tim stood up from his chair, retightened the metal straps, and cleaned off the crumbs. He grabbed another paper towel and gently dabbled the excess sauce and grease from Isaac's chin. Once the table was free of trash, he threw everything in a paper bag and headed to the door. Isaac's crying felt like an emotional gut punch to Tim, and guilt stopped him when he reached the door. "Did you like the food?"

Isaac was unable to look Tim in the eyes. "What's going to happen to me?"

"You're going to make my son a very happy boy, Isaac. And I, and my family, will be forever grateful. I know it's not what you want, but you can't escape the inevitable."

HANNA

CHAPTER 32

◆

THE ODD DAY

The door to Twain's room was cracked when Hanna went upstairs. She was about to push it open when her vision managed to squeeze through the seams between door and wall to see Twain, his eye patch off, looking at himself in the mirror.

Hanna stood still as she watched him observe his reflection. His fingers traced the scars wrapping around his eye, spiraling around the phantom epicenter. He grabbed a small washcloth and dabbed his disfigured skin, prepping himself for his own surgery. His good eye glowed blue, desperately seeking a companion.

Hanna reached up and tapped on the door, startling him. Twain immediately dropped the washcloth and quickly pulled his eye patch back on, feeling the need to hide his embarrassment from his own mother.

"Okay, you can come in," Twain responded.

The pit in Hanna's stomach hardened into guilt that consolidated in her gut. "How're you feeling, tough guy? You ready to get this over with?"

She sat on the side of his bed and held out her arms. Twain glanced at the mirror again, then felt his mother's love beckoning him into an embrace.

He jumped up on Hanna's lap, letting her hold him. "I don't know if I'm ready, Mom."

Hanna weaved her fingers through his hazel hair, parting it to the side. "You're getting a haircut after all this is said and done, mister. You've gone too long without one."

"Why? I don't want to end up like Dad."

Hanna giggled. "That's something your dad would say."

"I bet he would be a bald eagle if he was an animal," Twain said, turning around in Hanna's lap to laugh with her. "Ya know, because he's bald."

"Oh jeez. Are you sure Daddy hasn't given you any medicine yet?" Hanna replied, happy for her son's jokes at a time like this.

"Yuck. I hate medicine."

Hanna stroked the top of Twain's head, then rested her chin there. "Twain, I hope you know you don't have to wear the patch in front of me. I want whatever you want, and I'll love you no matter what."

Twain's warmth vanished and he got up from her lap. "But Mom, after today I will never have to wear the patch again!" He grinned wide, reminding Hanna that this was what he wanted—what he needed.

The guilt in her stomach loosened and she returned Twain's grin with one of her own.

"Okay, guys. I'm ready!" Tim yelled from down the hall.

"One second!" Hanna replied. She turned and faced her son. "Are you ready?"

Twain looked out his window into the distance, where the sun was setting below the mountains. "What's the room like, Mom?" he asked suddenly.

Puzzled, Hanna responded. "What room?"

"Dad's secret study. I've never been in there. He told Sammi and me to never go in there. Have you ever been inside?"

"Only once," Hanna said flatly.

"What was it like?"

Hanna's mind drifted back to a day she hadn't thought about for some time.

* * *

Hanna opened the door and welcomed a jovial Kevin Shung into their home.

"My, oh my, this is a nice new house you two have," Shung exclaimed while observing the artistic details of the Hills' new mansion.

Hanna clasped her hands. "I know!" she said excitedly. "It's marvelous! We are so happy to finally be in a new home." She looked around to make sure no one else could hear her. "Tim says y'all are on the verge of some medical treatment?"

Shung rolled his eyes, then moved in front of one the statues and saluted it. "Tim and his big mouth." He walked over and gave Hanna a hug. "It really is great to see you, Han. It's been a minute."

"Hiya, Dr. Shung!" Twain yelled as he ran down the stairs.

"Twain! Boy, you have gotten big since I last saw you. Come here and let me take a look at ya."

Twain sprinted toward Shung's outstretched arms and leapt at him, holding on for dear life as Shung spun him around like a helicopter.

After putting Twain back on the ground, he knelt beside the boy and ruffled his hair.

He looked back up at Hanna. "He has his father's eyes, that's for sure."

"And his mother's nose," Hanna chimed in. "Can I get you anything to drink, Kev?"

"Thank you, but I'm all set. Where's Sammi girl?"

A dull feeling crawled into Hanna at the mention of her daughter. "She's upstairs in her room."

"Still doesn't want to come out?" Shung whispered so that Twain couldn't hear.

Hanna nodded. "It's been like that for months."

Shung cursed under his breath. "I'm sorry, Han." He stood silent for a moment, trying to determine what to say next. "Where's the birthday boy? Is Timmy upstairs?" he asked, standing back up and grabbing his briefcase.

"Always," Hanna replied. "Go easy on the birthday boy, Kev!" she yelled as Dr. Shung hopped up the stairs and disappeared into Tim's study.

Hours passed and Hanna remained downstairs watching *The Bachelor*. When she heard a rumbling sound coming from upstairs, she ignored it; when more commotion was followed by a series of shouts and a loud *bang*, her interest was well and truly piqued.

Boys will be boys, she thought as she ascended the stairs.

Reaching out and knocking on the door, she asked, "Is everything all right in there?"

After a moment with no response, she again lifted her hand. Her knuckles were inches from the study door when it suddenly flew open and a pale-faced Shung walked out, quickly closing the door behind him.

Hanna eyed him suspiciously. "Shung, what's going on in there?"

Shung jumped at the sound of her voice. "Oh, um. Nothing. Look at the time. I really must be going."

Shung made to walk down the hallway, but Hanna shot an arm up and blocked his path.

"I heard noises. Are y'all okay? Is Tim?"

Shung's face glistened with sweat; his skin was ghostly white. "Hanna . . ."

"Shung, what is—"

The door to Tim's study opened without warning and Tim poked his head out, straightening his crooked glasses. "Everything is fine, Hanna. Nothing to worry about!"

While Hanna was distracted talking to her husband, whose face was dripping with sweat, Shung ducked under her arm and ran out the front door.

"What the . . . Shung, where are you going!" Hanna yelled at him. But Kevin Shung was already out the door and in his car, the engine sputtering, then roaring to life as he sped down the driveway.

Hanna turned back to face Tim, fuming at the unanswered questions. "What was that all about?" She took a step toward the door. "Tim, are you okay?"

Beads of sweat were now splashing near Tim's bare feet. "We're fine," he replied. "Just fell out of my chair is all."

He let loose a magnificent smile, then slammed the door behind him.

CHAPTER 33

◆

CHRIS HARRISON

"It's just like any other room, my son. Nothing to be afraid of, all right?" Hanna said as she patted Twain on the top of his head. "Your father is waiting for you. Best go ahead and change into your gown, and I'll roll the cot to your room."

"Sounds good, Mommy. I'll be ready in a second."

Hanna walked out of Twain's room and closed the door behind her. She strolled over to Tim's study where a cot was waiting. The metal bed's railing felt cold against her hands as she strolled it toward Twain's door, trying to reenact what would happen in an actual hospital. "Twain. Are you ready?"

"Yes ma'am." Twain opened the door and walked out, leaving his eye patch lying on top of his bed. The paper-thin blue gown stopped at his knees and tiny goose bumps sprinkled his skin.

"Are you cold?" Hanna asked. "Here, hop in this bed and let me get you some blankets."

Twain crawled up into the bed and let his mother smother him in wool cloth.

"Better?" Hanna asked.

Twain, exuding nervous excitement, nodded.

Hanna nodded in return and started to push the cot down the hallway.

"Wait!" a voice screamed from the opposite end of the hall. Sammi popped out of her room, her blond hair flowing behind her. "Good luck, baby brother! I love you." She ran to the side of Twain's bed and gave him a hug and a kiss on his cheek. "See you on the other side." She grinned and punched him on the shoulder before returning to her room.

Hanna rolled the cot until it was outside Tim's study—an offering for the devil himself. She gazed down at her son, studying his appearance without the patch: the scars and disfigured tissue that surrounded the empty socket. She then reflected on when she did the same routine with Sammi a few years ago. The whole spectrum of emotions hit Hanna like a train, and she bit her lip in an attempt to fight off her tears and remember the good times.

Twain noticed his mother's hesitation. "What're you thinking about, Mommy?" he asked innocently.

* * *

Tim walked over to the Mr. Coffee machine, where the ground coffee beans were emitting a chocolatey scent throughout the kitchen. He grabbed two mugs and filled them to the rim; he and Hanna both preferred their coffee black.

Hanna sat on the couch watching television as Tim walked back carrying the steaming cups of joe.

"Did some fine fox order a cup of coffee, black?" Tim asked cheekily.

But his voice caused Hanna to flinch when it jolted her away from the reality show.

Ever since that night at the hospital—and their stillborn son—Hanna hadn't been the same. At first she had played it cool to help Tim get over his mistake, but after he bounced back, she had slid down the dark side of their seesaw of emotion. It wasn't that she no longer loved Tim; it was that his wicked grin was etched into the back of her mind and consumed her thoughts.

She managed to avoid eye contact when she grabbed the mug and pressed it to her lips. "Mmm, thanks, Tim."

Apart from the television, it was so quiet in the room that Tim could hear Hanna's throat muscles working to press the coffee down and into her stomach.

He leaned over and kissed his wife on her forehead, then sat down beside her on the couch.

When he put one arm around her, he felt her lean reluctantly into him. "Want to know the secret ingredient to this coffee?" he asked as he pressed his own coffee to his lips and gave it a slurp.

He couldn't see it, but he knew that Hanna rolled her eyes.

"What?" she asked, without taking her eyes off the TV screen.

"I made it with love, *baby*."

Hanna's shoulders started to shrug up and down, bouncing Tim's arm like a basketball. She let out a small laugh, then covered it to pretend it never happened.

"Was that a laugh I just heard?" Tim asked. "I haven't heard one of those from you in a while."

Hanna jerked her head back toward the screen, still trying to mask her reaction.

Tim poked her in the ribs, well aware it was her ticklish spot. "Let's hear you laugh, woman! It turns me on!"

Hanna tried to resist, but eventually she was cackling like she hadn't done in years. When she turned to look at Tim, her eyes had a glow that he hadn't seen since that dreadful night. When they had finally gotten home afterward, Hanna made Tim swear he wouldn't pursue anything like that again if he wanted her to continue being his wife.

Seeing the glow back in his wife's eyes brought a cheeriness to Tim. Husband and wife sat snuggling, drinking their coffee, and watching *The Bachelor*.

Tim set his coffee down on the table, and a look of bewilderment enveloped his face. "So, you're telling me all these women are competing to marry this douchebag?"

Hanna slammed her own mug down on the table and glared at Tim. "First off, you're a douchebag. And second, that bachelor is the most amazing human being to walk this earth!" Hanna shrugged his arm off her and scooted to the opposite end of the couch.

Tim chuckled. "Please explain. How is *he* the most amazing man to grace this planet?"

Hanna returned Tim's chuckle with a fake laugh of her own. "Because he rides horses . . ." Hanna twiddled her thumbs as if they were Ferris wheels, blushing. "And he has pretty eyes."

Even though this wasn't the exact conversation Tim had envisioned, at least they were talking. It had been a long time since they'd had anything to talk about. The last few years they spent most of their time verbalizing to each other but not actually having real conversations. This was at least a step in the right direction.

Tim swung off his glasses and, with the most sex appeal he could muster, looked at Hanna. "Sexier than this, babe?"

Hanna's eyes drunk in the sight of her husband: glasses off, premature balding, and hair connecting his chest to his neck. Her pinched lips quivered, then the laughter erupted.

Tim smiled. "Score one for the good guys," he said, returning the glasses to his nose.

They both sat on the couch, Hanna googly-eyed over the bachelor and Tim doubting all the female participants' motives, when the show finally cut to a commercial break.

On that break, however, Hanna whipped out her new smartphone to browse the Internet, which irked Tim. He wanted her to pay more attention to him, to browse *his* thoughts and ideas.

He scooted over closer to his wife, until he could feel the warmth of her shoulder pressing against his. "Han, can I ask you something important?"

"Hmm? Did you say something?" Hanna mumbled, not bothering to look up from her screen.

Tim sighed and reached for her phone, clicking the button on the side to turn the screen black so all she could see was her reflection. "Can we try again?"

The heat from Hanna's shoulder shuddered, then shut off, and Tim could see from her reflection in the screen that her eyes were wide.

"T— Try what?" she asked, despite knowing precisely what he meant.

"Being a family . . . a whole family."

The commercial break ended with Chris Harrison's voice interrupting their silence.

Tim stared at the TV, but there was now no sound, as Hanna was pressing her finger firmly on the remote's mute button.

The remote was shaking ever so slightly. "What're you saying, Tim?"

Tim didn't know if Hanna's shaking was from fear or excitement, though he prayed it was the latter. "I want to try to have another kid. I want to be a father, and for you to be a mother." He put his hand on Hanna's shoulder and squeezed. "And I want all of us to be a family."

Hanna's eyes shimmered with tears. "Are you sure, Timmy? What if what happened last time . . . happens again?"

"It won't."

Hanna shook her head and her tears flew out as if from a sprinkler. "How can you know, Tim?"

"Because I have you as my anchor. You made me promise not to go down that road again, and I intend to keep that promise." He kissed Hanna's shoulder and felt her skin's warmth grace his mouth.

Tim looked back at the TV and at Chris Harrison's soundlessly moving lips. "If it's a boy," he said, "we can name him Chris Harrison Hill."

Hanna grinned and wiped away her tears. "I'd like that."

Tim gleamed. "Ditto."

"Just to clarify, I'd like to have a kid, but I don't want to name him Chris," Hanna said as she laughed and picked up her coffee mug for another sip. "I think I'd rather have a daughter. A daughter sounds pleasant."

Tim let her words sink in as he thought about a life with kids. "A daughter sounds marvelous, but I hope we have a son."

* * *

Tim opened his study door and grabbed the railing on Twain's metal cot, pulling his son into the mysterious room. "Say goodbye to Mommy," Tim said coolly.

"Goodbye, Mommy!"

Hanna placed her hands over her heart. "I love you, Twain. I love you both!"

Tim responded with a barely perceptible nod, before closing the door and leaving Hanna in the hallway with only her thoughts of broken promises.

TIM

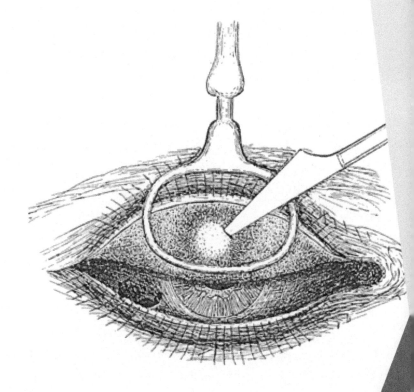

CHAPTER 34

———— ◆ ————

THE OPTIC NERVE

Tim watched the splotch of blood spread across the gauze's woven white threads.

"Ouch! I thought you said this wouldn't hurt, Dad?" a pale-faced Twain said.

"I know, I know. That's the most painful part, I promise," Tim replied, dabbing the trickle of blood caused by the needle that he'd stuck into his son's forearm. Twain was lying down on the surgical bed next to Isaac's. Tim had decided it would be best to knock out Isaac with the strong anesthetic before wheeling Twain into the room.

Twain, his one good eye shrouded from the medicine, glanced over at Isaac. "Is he going to be okay?" he asked, shuffling further under the sheets as he pulled the blankets up tight to his chin. "It's cold in here."

Tim patted Twain on the shoulder and took one last long look at the boy before he went under. Studying his son's eye, and the horrible zigzagging scar around where the eyeball should have been, Tim recognized how gruesome a sight it was. He would never admit it to Twain, of course, but the sight of it made him antsy to get the procedure over with. "Isaac will be fine, my son. He will barely feel a thing, I'll make sure of that. And sorry for it being so cold. I can give you another blanket, if you want?"

Twain shook his head, his hair bouncing from side to side over his eyebrows. "No, I'll tough it out. Why *does* it have to be so cold?"

Tim pointed at the large overhead surgical lights. "You see these lights? When they are fully on, they produce a lot of heat. That, combined with wearing this surgical gown, can make me feel pretty hot."

"It looks like you're wearing a blue dress!" Twain laughed at his own words, the drugs beginning to kick in. "I feel sleepy, Dad. I think I'm going to take a nap."

Twain closed his eye and in no time his chest was rising steadily and matching the beeping from the monitor set on the bedside table.

As the only conscious person in the room, Tim stood up and walked over to the table next to the sink and turned on his speaker. The approval *beep* sounded as it connected to his iPhone. Tim scrolled through his playlist until he got to his preferred classical music, the list comprised of everyone from Bach to Beethoven and Mozart to Bizet. His eyes closed as the opening string instruments of Mozart's *Symphony No.25* reverberated, bouncing off the walls and into his ears where they would penetrate the very depths of his soul; even the demon inside him would be quieted by its beauty.

After ambling over to the sink, Tim turned the hot water faucet and was comforted by the warm water washing over his hands, sterilizing his most prized tools. After patting them dry, he snapped on his surgical gloves and sat on the rolling stool between the two beds.

The beams of light from the overheads reflected off the stainless-steel instruments placed neatly on the table. He counted all of his blades, needles, and gauze that had been organized in rows on the mayo, taking extra precaution to note the location of the blades. Tim lifted one and attached it to the knife handle, admiring its sharp gleam as he twisted it in the air.

The stool wheels glided smoothly as Tim moved back to Isaac's bed, careful not to roll over any of the tubes. He grabbed the light handle to focus its beam on Isaac's face. The knife sliced through the air as Tim brought it down near Isaac's eye, but right before making an incision he paused. A wave of sick washed over him as doubt rushed through his mind. He stared at the innocent young man sprawled out on the bed beside him, and said, "I'm so sorry for this" before sticking the blade into the soft skin just underneath Isaac's eye.

The BARD-PARKER logo engraved into the razor edge of the knife quickly disappeared as blood pooled around the tip. Isaac's skin spread like two lovers parting ways, allowing the knife to invade the subfascia. A spurt of blood shot out from where Tim nicked a vein; he reached for the cauterizer to stop the bleeding from turning into a flood.

Gracefully moving the knife around the eye socket, Tim carved out a perfect circle. Next he removed the innards, using the sterile gauze to dab the blood that oozed out of the incision. Tim was focused only on two things at this moment: the glorious music coming out of his speaker and cutting with precision so as to not damage the precious optic nerve.

His foot tapped to the beat of the song as he finished the circle, folding the skin over itself so he could see the muscles beneath Isaac's skin and around his eye. The flesh was pulsating, eerily matching the tapping of Tim's foot.

He reached for the eye retractor and placed it on top of the folded skin, holding it in place as an extra pair of hands yet wishing he had an assistant. The coagulator did its job, though, clotting the blood around the eye and emitting wisps of smoke that smelled like burned flesh. Tim wrinkled his nose at the scent but pressed on with the surgery.

The bones surrounding Isaac's eye socket crunched as Tim shattered them with a small mallet, loosening the joint for eye extraction. Tim held the metal clamp calmly and lowered it, reminding him of the claw game he used to play as a kid. The clamp moved down steadily until it was in line with Isaac's blankly staring eye, capillaries wriggling on the ball. He gently pressed the handle, wary not to damage the vitreous body as the clamp squeezed onto the ball.

Once secure, Tim slowly pulled the eyeball up until the precious optic nerve came into view. A wide grin formed under Tim's mask. *It's beautiful*, he thought. The bloody, noodle-like nerve inched up in the air as Tim pulled; its tiny branching blood vessels wrapped tightly around and feeding the nerve nutrients as they too pulsated.

Drops of sweat tumbled down Tim's back from the overhead lamps' heat, illuminating every minuscule anatomical detail. Very carefully, Tim used his surgical scissors to cut away the tissue holding the optic nerve in its place in the socket, slowly releasing the nerve from Isaac's socket until Tim saw its full length of five centimeters snaking out of his body. He reached for the mayo table and grabbed a sterile basin already filled with the half stem cell plasma, half amniotic tissue liquid Shung had graciously gifted him with all those years ago.

Tim gingerly placed the eyeball in the restorative bath within the basin. He was careful, safely preserving the precious nerve still traveling from the back of the eye and into Isaac's head. The viscous ball floated in the healing pool, its blue iris rotating lazily within the liquid as it watched Tim finish his work.

Tim reached toward the mayo table and dropped the bloody clamp on top in exchange for the blade. He traced the optic nerve back into the empty socket, then worked to slowly dissect and release the remnant tissue still connected, until the whole nerve except for its attachment site to the visual cortex in the back of the brain was free.

He had to work fast while the majority of the nerve and eye were outside the body, waiting for contaminants to hop on and damage the tissue. After wrapping sterile gauze around the external nerve and eye to keep them safe, Tim rolled his chair until he was behind Isaac's head.

The music faded as Tim focused on the most excruciating part of the procedure: the removal of the base stem from the back of the brain. He grabbed the lever controlling the bed and pressed the up arrow, causing half of the bed to bend until Isaac was sitting upright instead of lying supine. A small hole was cut in the padding behind Isaac's head, which allowed Tim easy access to the posterior aspect of the skull. After shaving off the hair on the back of Isaac's head, he took the knife and made the incision before promptly scraping away the flesh until white bone was visible.

His hands trembled as he placed the bloody knife back on the instrument table—there was no turning back now. Tim picked up the small powered saw and pressed the forward button. The serrated titanium blade came to life, spinning forward and screaming over the classical music. He took a deep breath and eased the blade into the back of Isaac's skull.

Blade touching bone shrieked as the saw ate away the back of Isaac's skull, sending occipital bone bits flying across the room and smearing Tim's mask and glasses with skull debris and flesh. He worked systematically, cutting perfect angles until an even block of skull was outlined. He pulled the saw back and switched it off, the screaming from the spinning blade diminishing as Beethoven's symphony took its rightful place as the dominant sound. Blood streamed from the cut site, splashing red drops on the floor in rhythmic patterns.

Tim cauterized the flow of blood, then grabbed a small osteotome and mallet. Wielding the hammer and bouncing its blunt metal tip off the back of the osteotome, Tim slowly peeled away the cut outline on the bone until it was fully loosened. The amount of blood on the floor was matched by the used instruments on the table as time passed. One of the few remaining clean instruments was a dental pick with a sharp hook on the end. Tim used the pick to leverage the cutout bone and pry it off, opening a bloody canal to the back of Isaac's brain: the visual cortex.

The pink brain pulsated, expanding and contracting like ocean waves in a storm. When Tim poked it with a large, hollow needle, a purple substance oozed out and sloshed on the floor between his feet. He reached for a second hollow needle and placed it parallel to the first, so as to be perfectly adjacent. In the hollow hole of the first needle, he stuck a tiny surgical camera to view the nerve attachment site. Once he found the base of the stem on the camera screen sitting atop the table, Tim stuck a nanoscopic blade down the hollowness of the second needle. The blade eventually appeared on the arthroscopic screen. Tim slowly started releasing the base from the visual cortex, cautious not to damage the brain and, more importantly, the optic nerve.

The *BARD-PARKER* embroidered edge sliced through the only remaining fibers of the left eye's optic stem. As pressure was released, a small *pop* sounded. Black blood bubbled where the base of the nerve had been and filled the brain like a geyser.

Keeping the camera in place in needle number one, Tim removed the blade from the second needle and inserted a tiny cauterizer to halt the bleeding. Once the bleeding stopped and the clot was secure, Tim backed out with both instruments and pulled out the needles. He grabbed the square block of bone that had been removed earlier and placed it back in the empty crevice where it had once resided. He shot two screws across the block and native skull to hold the pieces together for healing, then quickly sutured the back of Isaac's scalp to close off the open wound.

Tim's sweat-drenched scrubs clung to his skin as he pulled the bed lever back down and brought Isaac into a supine position once again. He rolled his stool and the instrument table back to the side of the bed and changed his gloves.

The new gloves snapped on his sweaty hands after he wriggled his fingers into position. Tim looked down at Isaac; his right eye was closed in a dreamless slumber while his left eye socket was stuffed with gauze. A ligamentous nerve jutted out until it ended with the eyeball soaking in the restorative juices in the basin, everything wrapped in sterile bandages to prevent bacteria from attaching.

For a second, Tim felt nauseated as he looked at Isaac's motionless body. The young man had been nothing but helpful and kind to Tim's family but was now fileted on his operating table. These feelings inside him bubbled up to the surface and a single tear formed, gaining mass until its heaviness caused it to fall. But as quickly as the emotions came, they left— Tim's ego awakening and consuming the sorrow.

He closed his eyes and when he opened them, he recognized his inner demon—void of any emotion— gazing down on the body.

Tim approached Isaac's face, the clamp he'd used before pinched between his fingers. His eyes followed the wrapped optic nerve until it entered the socket and disappeared somewhere within the depths of Isaac's brain. He lowered the clamp and pincered the nerve as close to the empty eye socket as possible, then pulled the remainder of the nerve out of Isaac's head. At first, Tim felt resistance as the snakelike fibers resisted his pulling, but eventually they gave way and the entire nerve slid out of Isaac's head, dripping dark red blood from roots once connected to the back brain cortex.

Isaac shuddered as the nerve exited his body, his unconscious self somehow aware of the horrible sensations crawling through him.

Tim placed the whole nerve and eyeball in the bowl filled with the prized stem cells and amniotic liquid and let it soak before suturing Isaac's eye closed and cleaning the wound to prevent infection. Once that was done, he turned toward his sleeping son.

Tim experienced an array of feelings as he looked at Twain. He was nervous about what he was about to do and anxious that the experimental procedure wouldn't work, but the elation of finally being able to make his son whole again and fixing his family so they were perfect superseded everything else.

He placed a hand on Twain's cheek and smiled down at him, drinking up the precious moments with his son before he started the procedure. The classical playlist ended and silence filled the room, until Max Romeo's reggae voice introduced the next song and Tim went back to work.

"Chase the Devil" played from the speaker as he changed out of his scrubs, face mask, and gloves to prevent cross-contamination. Once he had finished putting on new surgical clothes, he slid the stool behind Twain's head and raised the bed so that the boy was sitting upright. Similar to Isaac's, the cushion behind Twain's head had a hole for easy access to the part of the brain that contained the visual cortex. Tim shaved the hair until there was only skin, then made the same six-inch-long incision and retracted the skin to hold the cut open. He took the blade and cut away all of the soft tissue and flesh until the knife scraped against the back of his skull. Tim grabbed the power saw and exchanged its blade for a new one; he turned it on and pressed the blade against his son's skull.

The vibrations screeched once again and Twain's body spasmed as the saw's torque ripped through his bone, outlining another perfect square in the skull. With another osteotome and a dental pick, Tim removed the bone fragment until Twain's visual cortex was in view. He placed two brand-new hollow needles parallel to each other inside the cortex and stuck the micro camera up one of the needles to view the inside of Twain's brain. Through the second needle, Tim inserted a long, skinny wire with a nitinol loop at the end.

Tim's eyes were glued to the camera screen as he watched the wire with the loop insert in the brain right at Twain's withered left optic nerve stem. Once the wire was in the correct position, he slowly pushed the wire farther into the brain, careful to avoid any important structures, until the looped portion pushed against the underside of the scarred-over skin of Twain's bad eye.

Tim positioned himself in front of his son's face and pulled out a fresh knife blade, puncturing the scarred prominence created by the wire pushing from underneath. All Tim heard was the ticking of his clock as he ran to the other table and unraveled the optic nerve from its stem cell–soaked bandages, the eye staring blankly at him as he carried it over to Twain's bed.

Grabbing a tiny suture and weaving it at the base of the optic nerve, Tim pulled the sutures' tails into the loop of the long skinny wire going through Twain's brain. With one hand holding the eyeball and the other on the wire coming out of the back of Twain's skull, he shuttled the sutures and the nerve stump into Twain's brain by pulling the wire backward. Once the eyeball was seated in Twain's socket, he rolled his stool behind his son's head one last time.

The overhead lights' heat was scorching, but Tim continued to work meticulously, sticking the tiny camera back into needle number one to observe the location of the transplanted optic nerve stump. When Tim was satisfied with the positioning of Twain's new optic nerve, he tied the sutures woven through the base of the stump to anchor everything in place.

Waves of hot energy were emitted by Tim's shoulders as he filled the remainder of the restorative juices from the basin into a syringe, injecting half into Twain's visual cortex to jump-start the healing process; the other half, he injected into his son's new eye and socket.

Satisfied with his work, Tim let out a deep breath of relief, then disinfected and closed the surgical sites. He stitched up the incisions and wrapped Twain's new eye in clean bandages, then supplied more anti-inflammatory and pain meds through the IV in the boy's forearm.

Tim stood and slowly walked around the room

as he lifted each bloodied instrument for disposal. Outside, thunder blasted through the skies in apparent applause for Tim. He switched off the music speaker and sat in silence, mulling over the procedure and making sure all of his counts were correct and his strategies precise.

The weather went from thunderous to windy before finally calming down as the storm passed over the surrounding woods. Fresh raindrops clung to the leaves, but another hour would pass before the animals came out of hiding and scurried along the dirt to drink the fresh water. Tim closed his eyes and listened to the sweet sounds of nature, praying that his son could soon join them in their lively chorus. Tim heard the blankets on the bed stir, believing that maybe just this once his prayers would be answered.

"D— Dad? Is it over?" Twain asked weakly as he attempted to sit up, though his head still wavered from the weight of the drugs in his system.

Now a single entity, Tim and his ego smiled in unison. "Yes, my son. It's over."

CHAPTER 35

───────◆───────

THE EYE OF THE STORM

Tim rolled his son to his room to rest and heal, then went back to his office to clean. When he opened the door and beheld the mess that lay before him, the warm scent of blood wafted into his nostrils. He forced himself to continue down the path, to ride out the adventure to its end. Puddles of semi-clotted blood littered the once-sterile floor in a pattern reminiscent of dalmatian fur. The overhead lights still hummed their perpetual tune.

Tim walked across the room, trying to avoid the puddles of blood, his feet sticking to the ground and causing him to wonder if walking across the suction cups of an octopus would feel similar. Besides the humming lights, the only thing Tim could hear was his awkward breath coming out in bursts, as if two people were sharing one set of lungs.

Isaac was still on his bed. The dripping of his meds had ceased, and his one good eye remained shut. The smeared blood from the procedure had colored his drained complexion a pinkish tone. Isaac's body was nearly motionless; if it wasn't for his chest moving as he slowly breathed, he could have been presumed dead.

Tim had expected a sense of isolation more powerful than anything he had ever felt would drown his soul at the knowledge he had gone to *that place* and back to fix his family, but something else waited in the shadows and sent away any unease that would knock at Tim's front gate. When he looked down at his hands, he was surprised to see that they were perfectly steady. Where a sense of regret should have been was elated pride—his void was now filled.

Laughter, harder than he had ever experienced, caused Tim to bend over and expel spittle from his mouth. He placed a hand on the ground to steady himself. Tears streamed madly down his face and dripped off the end of his nose, splashing onto the floor and combining with Isaac's and Twain's blood in a gory trifecta.

When the laughter subsided, Tim stood up and grabbed the mop. After dipping it in the water and wiping the floor, he watched the blood turn the surface into a crimson swamp. Maroon bubbles formed on the tiles as the applied triclosan killed the bacteria, eating away at the hardened clots.

Once all of the gore, bone, and flesh were wiped clean, Tim put the used instruments into a biohazard bag and zipped it up. Cleaning it up felt to him like a metaphor.

Without warning, the chains on the bed jingled.

Isaac was awake.

He tried sitting up, but the chains still restrained him, though loosening and tightening a little as he moved his body. His one eye flickered open, its iris dilating and constricting while trying to adjust to the light in the room.

Tim shut off the light to dim the surroundings and make it easier for Isaac to adjust. He walked back next to Isaac and unlocked the wheels on the bed. Isaac moaned as Tim rolled him out of his office and into the hallway, careful to avoid bumps. When they reached the basement, Tim placed a hand on Isaac's legs. "Thank you, Isaac."

In response, Isaac emitted another pained moan.

TWAIN

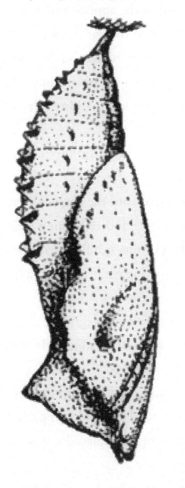

CHAPTER 36

METAMORPHOSIS

*T*wain used to stare at his feet when he walked, but now his eyes were directed upward and guided his feet where *he* wanted them to go.

Twain gazed into the mirror in his room, his fingers wiggling with excitement as they took off the surgical gauze for the first time. Dimples formed in his cheeks, and his smile magnified until he couldn't control his giggling.

Emotions Twain hadn't felt in a long time—ambition, admiration, confidence—surged. He scrunched up the bloody gauze and tossed it all in the trash. His new eye, beautiful as it was, still felt sensitive. Years of living with a phantom eye had tricked his ocular synapses, and Twain's brain was still having some difficulty registering the new one. It was an odd sense, and he kept thinking of Gandhi's famous quote and how eerily it related to him. Fresh hand towels were folded on his bed next to the hydrogen peroxide. He poured a little on the towel and placed it on his eye, hearing the sizzle of the peroxide as it eliminated harmful contaminants. When he removed the towel, white foam bubbled from his eye where his father had incised, but there was no visible scarring.

Twain, ecstatic about finally going out into the world, beamed. He wanted to play with friends, meet new people, fall in love, and excel in school, but his former disfigurement had halted his dreams and ambitions and paralyzed him inside the house. Now, he felt free.

After wiping his eye clean, he grabbed another cloth and dabbed it into the peroxide, making sure to also disinfect the wound on the back of his head. He tossed a handful of bloody bandages and towels into the filled trash bag, then stared back into the mirror.

"Now do you understand?" Sammi asked, surprising Twain.

"Jesus, you scared me." Twain turned around and faced his sister. He glanced at the mirror, then back at her. "I think I do understand."

"You look great, baby bro," she said, giving her full attention to him and not her mirror, for the first time.

"I wish you'd stop calling me that."

Sammi ushered herself into his room and put an arm around Twain. "You will always be my baby brother." She kissed the top of his head. "Nothing will ever change that."

It felt nice, being normal—at least outwardly. Twain knew his family was messed up, but he hoped his peers would only witness the surface. "You really think I look good?" he asked.

"I mean, not as good as me," Sammi said, punching him in the arm. "But still marvelous."

The siblings stared in the mirror for the first time—together—admiring their father's impeccable work.

ISAAC

CHAPTER 37

A VISIT FROM TWAIN

A river of pain ebbed and flowed, and Isaac teetered on the brink of consciousness. The hole where his eye used to be burned, causing tears to flow out of his other eye in the hope that it could douse the flames—but the blaze didn't go out. Now that the chains around his arms were loose, Isaac could move his hands up to his face to touch the fresh bandages covering his left eye. The white bandage felt wet when he touched it; when he looked down at his fingers, he noticed bloody residue on the tips.

His head swam from the procedure and time no longer seemed to exist; Isaac couldn't tell if minutes, hours, or days had passed since Tim had done what he did. He wondered if his coworkers were looking for him . . . if *anyone* was looking for him. It had been almost a year since he'd last communicated with his family, and he doubted if any of them were searching for him.

Feeling defeated and slouching his head, Isaac started to think about how paying overpriced rent and medical insurance no longer seemed that bad. Sobbing for the first time after the surgery was a strange sensation: his phantom eye tried to shed tears, but no liquid droplets came. The empty socket vibrated, confused nerve endings having nowhere to go and no outlet to plug into. When Isaac heard the basement door swing open, he realized that his depth perception was affected; he couldn't tell if the door was inches away or several feet from him.

Nevertheless, he heard footsteps approach, and closed his single eye to pray that no more pain would befall him.

"Go away!" Isaac screamed, his helpless body shaking.

Yet the footsteps continued and he heard a familiar voice. "Isaac, it's me. My father doesn't know I'm here, and I'd like to keep it that way."

When Isaac looked up, he was stunned to recognize Twain, but not as the little boy he had known. Where Twain's eye patch used to be was Isaac's own eye, and this realization sliced deeper than Tim's knife.

The eye's blue iris stared back at Isaac mockingly and provoked his queasiness to crest. "What do you want, Twain."

"I . . . I don't know exactly. I just wanted to see you. Can I get you anything?" Twain asked, more confident than he had ever sounded.

"Get out," Isaac said, his words barely audible when he turned his back.

Twain took a step closer. His hands were clasped as if in prayer, and his eyes were brimming with the desire for forgiveness. "Isaac—"

His anger swelling, Isaac screamed, "Get out, Twain!"

The words echoed in the room, growing ever fainter with each bounce off the walls until they dulled to nothing. Twain stood his ground against Isaac's scream and took another step closer. He reached out with one hand and touched Isaac's face, his fingertips brushing against Isaac's cheek.

"Isaac, look at me. Please," Twain said.

Although Isaac initially recoiled at Twain's touch, he slowly moved his head until he faced the boy. A dizzying motion sickness crept into Isaac's stomach as his one good eye attempted to focus. Eventually, after tilting his head at several awkward angles, his eye adjusted and he could make out Twain in detail.

The first thing Isaac noticed about Twain was how remarkably he had healed. The skin on his face was barely swollen, and there were no surgical scars to be seen. And the eye, the beautiful ocean-colored eye that had once belonged to Isaac, sat naturally in Twain's socket; it moved left and right and up and down with ease, the vitreous juices assisting its glide.

"Twain, I know it was your father who did this, but, please, help me," Isaac urged.

Twain took a step back and Isaac noticed that the boy seemed lost in thought. The kid was feeling normal for the first time in years yet couldn't share his happiness with Isaac—his friend.

"You know," Twain said, "you were the only person besides my family who talked to me. The only one who treated me like I was normal and didn't judge based on my appearance. Even my dad's friend treated me like I was a disease that needed a vaccine, a cure." Twain lifted a hand to his left cheek, feeling sensation there for the first time in a long while. "You're the only one who played with me, Isaac, and showed me music and actually spent time with me."

Isaac didn't know what to say. Twain's words were heartfelt, but Tim may have also stolen Isaac's emotions; the words rebounded off him like sunrays hitting ice and reflecting back into the sky. "What's going to happen to me?" Isaac asked solemnly.

Twain paced back and forth, one hand still on his cheek. Isaac thought it almost looked as if Twain was trying to hide his eye.

Acting as if he hadn't heard the question Isaac had just asked him, Twain rambled on. "You have no idea how sorry I am for this. When Daddy said he could fix me, I didn't think it would be like this!" Twain turned to Isaac. "And Daddy has been acting even more weird recently, too." Twain's voice rose to a shrill pitch. "He keeps talking about putting you with the others and inviting his dear friend Dr. Shung over to celebrate. Is he nuts? Shung's gone. He didn't say to where, but last time he left I knew he wasn't coming back. Something evil has happened, I just can't pinpoint what."

Isaac's eye widened as terror seeped in. "Wait, Twain. *Twain!* Stop moving and look at me."

Twain finally halted and rubbed the snot from his nose.

Even though Isaac only had one eye, fear leached out of it. "What do you mean . . . others."

Twain looked immediately down at his feet and twisted his ankle in recognizably nervous circles. "Well, when Daddy fixed Sammi, he had to move her somewhere. He called it a better place for her to be."

It took more than a few moments for Isaac to connect the dots. Memories of listening to music in the kitchen with Twain flashed into his brain, and he recalled seeing missing person reports on the news while they danced to The Eagles.

"Twain, you weren't talking about moving Sammi, were you . . ."

Twain averted his eyes and bit his lip. When he moved, it was only to take a couple of steps backward. At that, the wooden planks from the floor above creaked and a voice from upstairs sounded. "Twain?" It was Tim. "Come up here. It's almost time for dinner!"

"Coming, Dad!" Twain replied, running back to the door. He gripped the knob and paused for a moment, much like his father once had, and glanced back at Isaac.

"I'll be back. I promise," Twain whispered as he turned the knob, then exited the room, leaving Isaac alone with his daunting thoughts.

CHAPTER 38

————————◆————————

THE GUIDE

Tim never visited the post-operative room where Isaac was held.

For Isaac, it felt like a millennium had passed since he had been able to walk around freely. Although he was still strapped down, he daydreamed about breaking from the chains' grasp, running outside to his truck, and driving far away from Tim's glass house. He'd often wake up in the middle of an REM cycle, only to feel the cold bite of steel against his blistered skin. His muscles had atrophied so much that the chains were now looser, allowing the slightest bit of wiggle room for him to stretch. Every day, he would push his stretching to the limit, until the *clink* of metal hitting the back of the bed rang throughout the room.

Of all life's luxuries, there was only one thing Isaac truly missed: music. Even while bound, rhythm and melody provided a mental escape almost freedom enough for Isaac.

He lay wrapped in chains in another deep slumber, when the door opened.

"Psst, Isaac! Wake up!" Twain whispered urgently.

Isaac's eye focused on a blurry Twain and the blood rushed to his head, thumping like a drum behind his lids. "Go away, Twain. I was having such a good . . ."

That was when he heard the magical jangle. And saw the light reflect off the metal in Twain's fingers.

"Isaac, we have to hurry! Dad left a few minutes ago, and I don't know when he will be back. He's been acting really strange."

"Twain, you idiot!" Isaac hissed. "I'm strapped down and can barely move. How am I supposed to hurry if you don't unlock me?"

Clearly embarrassed, Twain backed away. "Gosh, I'm sorry. You're—"

Isaac shook his head, taking deep breaths to calm his excited nerves. "Apologize later!" He looked at Twain with his only working eye and urged, "Please, get me out of here!"

Twain nodded and stepped toward Isaac. He studied the chains crossing over him and located the padlock behind the bed. Twain took a deep breath, then pressed the gold key into the lock.

Isaac lay with muscles tensed in anticipation until he felt the metal cables release their callous hold of him. He pushed the cables off and started to unwrap the ones on his legs. "Twain! You fucking did it! My man!"

"I hope you don't kiss your mom with that mouth," Twain said, beaming from ear to ear as he dropped an imaginary mic.

Despite atrophic muscles and heavily bruised skin—and absent an eye—Isaac returned the smile. "You are such a nerd. Let's get out of here."

"Like Houdini?" Twain joked.

Isaac kicked himself off the bed and staggered as his feet found the ground. Blood rushed to his brain and his vision was foggy until he adjusted to the vertigo.

Twain moved to Isaac's side and looped an arm around his waist to steady him.

Isaac looked down at Twain as he shifted his weight. "Thank you," he said, his appreciation palpable to the boy.

"Well, I did owe you one," Twain said, tapping a finger to his new eye before opening the door leading up the stairs.

A chuckle emerged from Isaac. "That you did."

"Oh, I almost forgot." Twain reached into his pocket and pulled out his old eye patch, a blue eye drawn on its surface. "I want you to have this."

"That's disgusting." Isaac grabbed the patch from Twain's hand. "Help me put it on."

Twain guided Isaac through the underground maze, as they weaved through the numerous passageways.

Isaac looked around nervously. "Where are we?"

"Underneath the house."

"Jesus," Isaac said as he looked at the candles lining the murky walls. "How do you not get lost down here?"

Twain laughed. "Sammi and I used to play hide-and-seek down here. I always won. The dark freaked her out too much."

The stairwell finally appeared, and Twain wrapped his arm around Isaac once again. He hummed Led Zeppelin's "Stairway to Heaven" as they ascended, but when they reached the top of the stairs, a large door stopped them and his humming ended.

Isaac's muscles regained strength enough that he could stand without Twain's assistance. "Wait, I know where this is. This is the door that Tim said to never worry about because it leads to the basement."

Twain nodded, then reached out a finger and held it to Isaac's lips so as to silence him. "Listen, Is, we don't have much time, so we have to move quickly and quietly. Sammi and my mom are upstairs, and my dad left a little while ago. Just follow my lead. Got it?"

Isaac nodded, although he knew that trying to control his emotions was likely to prove as difficult as the great escape itself. Memories of playing outside and hiking through the mountains sprang to his mind as Twain cautiously reached for the doorknob.

The door creaked ajar and sun-filled light penetrated the darkness that led downstairs. The glass windows ahead of Isaac and Twain exponentially brightened the light filtering in and the tree limbs that were dripping with melting snow. A vacuum of fresh air rushed into Isaac's nostrils, filling his lungs with a crispness when he breathed in deeply.

Isaac took a few careful steps out of the dungeon into the living room, where he immediately heard birds singing their springtime songs as if in response to his return to life. He gazed desperately out the windows, but it wasn't until his sight fell on the front door leading to freedom that the cocooned butterflies inside his chest awakened. "Is my car still here?"

Twain frowned. "No, my dad got rid of it a while ago."

But Isaac didn't care, he could smell the freedom leaking out from behind the front door.

His heart lurched with exhilaration and he took a few unsteady steps toward the door. Twain, his head on a swivel to look for signs of trouble, carefully led Isaac. They were mere inches from the door when Isaac stretched his fingers to grasp the knob. He could almost hear the wolf knocker on the other side howling in delight.

Until another sound echoed throughout the woods. Car tires.

"Daddy's home!" Sammi shouted from upstairs, mirroring Isaac's and Twain's recognition of the tires rolling on gravel.

The color drained from Twain's face and an expression of horror reflected off the windows' glass. Isaac looked at Twain, the blood in his veins turning to ice. He had always believed that hell would be hot, but now he knew it would actually be a frozen wasteland of anguish and sorrow. When Twain didn't move, Isaac grabbed the boy by his shoulders and shook him until he responded. Just as they heard the car door slam shut, Twain grabbed Isaac's hand and sprinted toward the kitchen. Meanwhile, Sammi was coming down the stairs.

Twain led Isaac through the kitchen until they reached the door leading out back. He threw the door open and dashed out, pulling Isaac along with him. They reached the center of the fenced-in yard and Twain stopped to assess the situation. The fence surrounding the yard was too tall to climb, but if they went back inside they would be caught.

They looked in unison at the shed, its wooden frame gesturing for them to come inside. Twain found another key on the keychain and thrust it into the padlock. The lock fell to the mud and the door swung open. Twain shut the shed door, closing off the light and enveloping them in darkness once again.

CHAPTER 39

THE SHED, PART 2

*H*eavy breathing was the only source of sound as Isaac and Twain peeked through the cracks in the wood to see what was going on inside the house. The windows shimmered from the sunlight, and shadowed bodies moved behind the glass.

Tim walked in through the front door and kissed Sammi nonchalantly on the top of her head before giving Hanna a quick hug. Afterward he went directly to the master bedroom, leaving Sammi and Hanna alone in the family room looking at his back as he strode away.

Clearly disgruntled, Hanna put her trembling hand to her face. Isaac and Twain saw her mouth something to Sammi before she followed Tim into their bedroom. Sammi shrugged and ran back upstairs, the mirror glued to her hand.

Isaac and Twain stayed in the shed, trying to figure out a plan. They sat cross-legged on the dusty floor, staring at each other, as they considered solutions for securing Isaac's freedom. In a matter of minutes, dusk turned to night and the sun settled behind the mountains.

Isaac shifted his weight to prevent his leg from falling asleep. "Twain, you should go inside before they realize you aren't there." He stood up and placed his eye against a crack in the wooden wall but didn't see anything stir inside the house.

Twain studied Isaac for a minute, then stood up and walked over to Isaac's side; he squinted his old eye and peeped through the cracks with his new one. "I can't just leave you in here alone, Is. We need to figure something out, and fast. It's almost dinnertime."

As if on cue, Hanna strolled out of the hallway leading from the master bedroom and appeared in the kitchen. She went directly to the freezer and pulled out two frozen pizzas, popping them in the oven. She cupped her hands around her mouth to amplify her voice, no doubt calling everyone—including Twain—down for dinner.

"Shit," Twain mumbled, sweat stains forming on the back of his shirt and under his pits.

Isaac turned to Twain. "I hope you don't kiss Hanna with that mouth."

"Balls," Twain responded, still peering through the cracks.

Isaac rolled his one eye. "Oh, never mind. If you end up saving me, I don't give a damn about your language. Now get inside, quick. Before someone notices you're gone."

"I know, but if they see me coming from the shed, they'll know something is up. Dad told us we aren't allowed in here." Twain pulled away from the cracked wall and started to pace, leaving dusty footprints on the ground under him.

"Is there anywhere in the house where you *are* allowed?" Isaac responded.

There was, however, no mistaking the room in which Hanna wanted Twain to make an appearance. Neither Isaac nor Twain needed to hear Hanna say Twain's name to know that she was yelling at him to come to the kitchen.

Twain froze on the spot. The clock was ticking, and they still didn't have a plan.

"Shit!" Isaac whispered, keeping his eye glued to the crack as he watched Sammi, Tim, and Hanna pull silverware out for dinner.

Too afraid to respond to Isaac's cussword, Twain stopped pacing and placed his ear against the crack.

Hanna looked to be getting agitated at Twain's absence. She clearly yelled something and in confusion glanced at Sammi.

Without looking away from the mirror, Sammi shrugged.

Hanna walked over to Sammi and snatched the mirror out from her hands before giving her what was without doubt an order.

Sammi ran up the stairs, undoubtedly to check Twain's room. As quickly as she disappeared upstairs, her feet reappeared on her way back down.

Sammi was scratching the back of her head when Hanna, who by now looked panicked, asked her a question.

Sammi shrugged.

Hanna said something else, and Sammi threw down her hands and stormed out. When she returned, she also looked concerned.

The three family members remained still until Tim calmly stood up. Without saying a word, he crossed through the kitchen and opened the door leading to his downstairs post-op prison room.

"Oh no," Twain gasped, mimicking what Isaac was thinking.

Seconds later, Tim sprinted up from the floor below and slammed the door. His roar sent the family scattering in all directions, leaving the kitchen empty.

Isaac and Twain looked knowingly at each other. The time to plan was gone—it was now time to act. Without a word, Twain slipped out of the shed and headed inside.

Isaac watched as Twain shuffled across the yard and into the kitchen, gently shutting the door behind him.

The rest of the family ran instantly into the kitchen, nearly bumping into each other. Hanna hugged her son fiercely, before checking him for cuts and bruises.

Tim strode forward, eyeing Twain suspiciously. He placed a firm hand on Twain's shoulder and, pointing toward the freshly cut grass, said something that Twain responded to.

Tim looked through the wall of windows and stared into the backyard as he scanned the area. He looked like he was saying something when his eyes stopped on the padlock lying on the ground in front of the shed. He dropped his hand from Twain's shoulder and opened the door into the backyard.

Isaac flipped the bar down into its groove to hold the door shut from the inside, but he knew it would only stop Tim for so long. Every step Tim took toward the shed, Isaac took a step back, until he felt cold wood pressing against his back. In a matter of seconds, Tim would burst through the doorway and capture him . . . again.

Adrenaline zoomed through Isaac's body; he let out a silent prayer, hoping it would flutter on the wind up to God's ears. He dropped to his hands and knees and scrambled for a shovel, stick, rake—anything to use to fend off Tim—but he felt nothing but dirt.

As Tim got closer, Isaac continued to search. He was about to give up, horror filling every sinew in his body, when his fingers felt a misplaced metal loop sticking out of the ground. With a groan, he tugged the loop as hard as he could and opened a door hidden below. Isaac coughed as the dust rose around him and irritated his only eye. He powered through the pain and agitation, forcing himself to see the contents under the door. Tim was now banging on the shed, cracking the wood with every pound of his fist. The dust finally settled, and Isaac saw a small passageway leading to a dark oblivion. With nowhere else to go, he dropped into the abyss.

CHAPTER 40

THE HIDDEN CELLAR

Isaac closed the door hatch above him, which drowned out the sound of Tim's fists slamming against the shed. A single string dangled in front of Isaac, who reached up and pulled it. A series of lightbulbs turned on and brightly illuminated the interior of the underground cellar.

Cold brick lined the walls of the small room and extended upward to the concrete ceiling. The floor was dusty, and a musky smell seemed to have moved in permanently, causing Isaac's nose to scrunch in disgust. His ears picked up on a low but continuous vibrating sound that seemed to come from nowhere, but then flies swarmed out of the dark and on the swaying lightbulbs, causing shadows to flicker across the walls and reminding Isaac of Peter Pan trying to catch his shadow.

He took a couple of steps forward, searching for an escape route or at least a weapon. He tried to bat away the insects that came to life as he proceeded through the room. With every step he took, the musky scent more closely resembled that of rot and seared Isaac's eye until it teared up.

"Ugh, what the . . ." Isaac whispered, covering his nose and mouth as he gagged from the overpowering smell.

The buzzing continued and the scent festered, but Isaac moved his feet. He followed the single row of dangling lightbulbs, batting away the wings that fluttered right in front of his face. One by one the insects fell to the floor, their exoskeletons shattering from the impact of Isaac's swatting.

Eventually, Isaac saw the fourth brick wall come into view. At the cellar's end, a single light switch was embedded in the mudbrick. Isaac reached out his trembling hand and flipped the switch. Nothing happened. Then he felt a dull tremble. As the walls shook more vigorously, dirt started to fall from the ceiling and splattered into Isaac's hair and caused him to cough.

A high-pitched *zip* sounded and the hanging lights shot back up into the ceiling to be replaced by powerful overhead lights that sparked on immediately. The brick walls flipped backward and turned 180 degrees until their opposite sides appeared.

The cellar now looked entirely different. Instead of brick walls and old-school hanging bulbs, the walls were now smooth concrete and brightened by fluorescent tube lights. The insects also disappeared and their buzzing was replaced by the humming lights.

Isaac held his breath as he took in his new surroundings.

Drip . . . drip

He turned around, trying to find the source of the sound that bounced around inside the room and rattled his brain.

Drip . . . drip . . .

The noise grew louder, and the liquid started to splash on the concrete floor.

Drip . . . drip

Isaac closed his eye and allowed the sound to wash over him and settle inside his body where it stilled his blood. Since half of his vision was gone, he needed his hearing to counteract his loss of sight. Slowly, his eardrums picked out the sound and were able to determine its location. When he opened his eye and turned in the direction of the source, what he saw sent a shock of terror through his spine.

Rotten food and broken plates littered the floor. The organic components were in a state of decay, the bacteria eating away the old in order to shit out the new.

But this wasn't the sole cause of the putrid smell.

Still swaying from the momentum of the walls' recent turning, several bodies were hanging by their feet. Stained red tubes that had once been translucent protruded from the bodies and wound and snaked all the way down until they reached their appropriate container—one container per body. Isaac observed the hanging figures, his legs rooted to the ground. Nearly all of the bodies were female, and the one at the end had a scarred gash across her neck and circular scars on her shoulder. Time slowed to a standstill until the swaying bodies were once again unmoving, like their hearts.

Isaac took a few steps forward to observe the corpses. Their skin was as pale as the moon and leathery, shriveled like dried fruit. Six tubes jutted out of each body and drained into the body's personal receptacle. On each corpse, a pair of tubes were inserted into the hip bones, shinbones, and ankles, all funneling into one large tube that transported the substance into the appropriate storage vessel. Another clear tube connected each vessel to a centrifuge, where a single empty syringe jutted out of every machine, except the last, where emptiness filled the void of the last centrifuge.

Isaac bent down to observe the vessels, noticing that each had an attached dust-covered label. He wiped away the dirt and unveiled different names, the first label reading BRANDY – O NEGATIVE.

A once-seeded fear had now grown into a forest inside Isaac. He moved to the next label and wiped away the dirt: SARA – O NEGATIVE. He moved to the next label, then the next, wiping the labels and reading the names of the corpses that dangled before him. He reached the final label, licked his finger, then wiped it clean: FAITH – O NEGATIVE.

A wave of déjà vu snuck in as Isaac stared at the names. He had seen these names before, but he couldn't pinpoint their origin. Isaac's brain bulb flickered, but then shined brightly when he realized where he had seen them: the first time was right before his interview with Tim, and the second was when Tim and Hanna went skiing and left him alone with the kids; they were watching the Colorado news when the missing person report flashed on the screen.

Isaac knew some of these names were on the list of missing persons.

Then, he heard a ragged voice, barely louder than a whisper. "Who's there?"

Isaac jumped and turned around, focusing his diminished vision on the source of the voice.

The tube lights above pierced the dark cellar, but one corner of the room was still cast in black shade and indistinguishable to the human eye.

Isaac stood his ground, his fear morphing into courage. "Show yourself!"

Chain links clinked against each other and feet scraped the ground. Isaac could see a contoured silhouette moving, and what he saw next would give his nightmares their own nightmares. A pair of blue eyes sprung open, then an emaciated man appeared from the depths of the unknown. The air in Isaac's lungs escaped his body in disbelief at what he was seeing.

For it was Tim Hill who stepped out of the shadows.

CHAPTER 41

THE SECRET OF THE GREEN ANOLE

His beard was gray with dirt and grime, which had caused the overgrown hairs protruding from his chin to clump. The skin on his face was sunken into his skull and Isaac could count all twenty-four ribs jutting out of his torso. Isaac could see the muscles contorting as they worked to help the weak body stand.

Isaac took a step back, still not quite believing what he was seeing. But when those eyes, those distinct blue eyes, fell on him, Isaac knew it could only be one person.

"T—Tim?"

The man stood swaying, until his eyes locked on the eye patch and gauze that covered the surgical site.

He opened his mouth, his chapped lips peeling from the exertion. "He got you, too?"

Isaac's hand automatically touched the bandage covering his left eye, his brain trying to register what his one eye was seeing. "Is this a trick?" He took another step back, almost slipping on the rotten food.

"No, your eyes . . ." Tim shook his head. "Your *eye* doesn't deceive you. I'm the real Tim Hill. Who are you?"

"I'm . . . Isaac. But if you're Tim, then who the hell is that?" Isaac shrieked as he pointed to the ceiling, which the other Tim was still trying to break through.

Tim Hill mustered the necessary strength to kick the metal bucket on the ground next to him, its contents sloshing. "An abomination."

"No, no, no, no!" Isaac pressed his hands to his face, squeezing his cheeks in disbelief. "Am I going crazy? How is this even possible? How can I know that you're the real Tim?"

"How is this possible? I can answer that. How do you know if you can trust me? Well, that's something you'll just have to decide on your own." Tim sat back down and leaned against the wall. "Let me take you back to the day he was born."

* * *

"Did you bring it? Did you bring it!" Tim asked enthusiastically, bouncing up and down on his toes like an excited child on Christmas morning.

Shung, grinning from ear to ear, lifted the briefcase. "Right here, Timmy boy. Happy birthday, by the way."

"Thank you. Now, quick! Close the door and let's get started." Tim cleared his office table of everything except a picture of Sammi, while Shung closed the door behind them.

Tim's eyes never left the briefcase in Shung's hand; they grew wide when he plopped it on the table before them. Shung had to slap Tim's greedy hand away when he reached for the briefcase.

"Hold your horses, Tim. Before we begin, let us take a moment to thank our donors." Shung rubbed the leather of the briefcase.

Tim pulled his hand back. "You're right. I'm sorry." He took a moment to appreciate the dead. "Thank you, donors."

Shung chuckled. "That's more like it." He unzipped the briefcase and pulled out two plastic bags, one filled with a light pink substance, the other darker. "You still have the one I gave you, right?"

"Yes. I'm saving it for a special day." Tim's stomach rumbled, growling from his hunger for knowledge. "Explain to me what these bags are again."

Shung poked the first bag. "This one contains extremely concentrated levels of platelet-rich plasma, derived from a person's entirety of blood and bone marrow, a thousand times the potency you'll find in your average platelet injection for common sports surgeries. Since some of the blood comes from bone marrow, it is also rich in stem cells, which facilitate the regrowth of tissue, cartilage, et cetera. It's also worth noting that all DNA from the donors is gone, which is good for us."

Tim was confused at what Shung was saying. "The DNA is dead?"

"Yes, I added an enzyme that kills DNA. We wouldn't want to introduce new DNA to someone's body. It could cause inflammation."

Tim sucked in his drool before it could dribble from his mouth. "And bag number two?"

"Ah, the good stuff, and the gift I gave you when you came to my house. This is viscous amniotic tissue, rich in stem cells, growth factors, and other regenerative proteins such as cytokines."

"How did you get this?" Tim observed the small bag sitting on his table, watching the liquid swirl beneath the plastic.

"Remember, my grandfather, Wu, left me everything in his will. As for his retrieval methods, I don't know. And I'm not sure I want to know. What I do know is that this was harvested from the inner wall of the placenta."

Memories of that night with Shung returned to Tim. "I guess we had been drinking." "And we certainly shouldn't have been driving!" Shung replied.

Tim looked at his friend and beamed. "You truly are amazing, Shung."

"For most of my surgeries, and for Sammi's condition, the stem cell platelets are enough. I only use the combo when it's an emergency. Just make sure to match the blood type with your patient." Shung pointed to the little labels on the side of the bags.

"Of course."

Shung reached back into his briefcase and pulled out some test tubes and a petri dish. "Shall we get started?"

Tim looked Shung in the eyes. "Absolutely."

Shung grabbed two test tubes and set them on the table. "It is important you do this right. We pour the stem cell platelets in the first test tube and the amniotic tissue in the second. If it's a surgery where you need to mix the two, I suggest letting them marinate together for a while, but for today's lab I'll add a polymer that rapidly binds the two."

"How are we going to test this?" Tim poured the liquid amniotic tissue into the test tube, cautious not to spill a single drop.

"Ah, I thought you'd ask that." Shung pulled a small army knife from his briefcase and tossed it to Tim. "When everything is ready, give yourself a small cut on your finger, then we will pour our mixture over your cut and watch the magic happen."

Tim clapped his hands together. "Best birthday ever."

The surgeons worked diligently, carefully pouring the respective liquids into their proper tubes. Shung pulled out the fast-binding polymer and poured the dusty substance into the petri dish. He then grabbed the two test tubes and poured them into the petri dish to mix with the polymer. "Hand me that instrument," he said as he pointed to a small rod sitting at the table's edge.

Tim handed Shung the rod and watched as he mixed the three substances together.

"And just to be safe, since we are doing this quickly, hand me that last vial in my briefcase. That's our enzyme."

Tim took the enzyme vial from the bag and handed it to Shung, who poured a couple of drops into the dish. "Good." He glanced at his watch. "We will wait five minutes, then it'll be time to prick yourself."

Tim glanced at his own watch. *Three hundred seconds until I find out how to fix my baby girl.*

A minute passed, followed by another, then another, until only seconds remained. "Wait. I have an idea," Tim said.

Shung looked up, curious. "What's that?"

Tim walked over to his desk and opened one of the drawers. "A long time ago, I tried to find the secret of the green anole regenerative phenomenon, but I could never determine the link."

Shung squinted his eyes. "I'm aware of your study, Tim. But lizards are lizards and humans are humans. Sometimes, there just isn't a link."

Both of their watches beeped: five minutes were up.

Tim reached into his drawer and pulled out a vial filled with an orange substance. "I've been saving this for a long time." He flicked the vial and watched the salmon-colored liquid dance.

Shung stood up, a grave expression on his face. "Tim, what are you doing?"

But Tim ignored Shung and grabbed the knife. After he cut his hand open, fresh DNA-filled drops plummeted to the floor. Tim then dropped the knife and strolled over to the petri dish, holding the orange anole serum over it.

Shung clapped his hands angrily. "Tim! Snap out of it, man."

But it was too late.

Tim tipped his bloody hand and poured the serum into the petri dish to bind with the stem cells and growth factors; his own blood also dribbled off his fingertips into the dish. Blood, serum, and cells intermingled, which Tim then smeared on his bleeding cut. Neither surgeon moved as they awaited what would happen.

"Ouch!" Tim yelled, shaking his hand and sending the mixture flying onto the floor.

"Ha! What did you expect?" Shung asked. "I'm sure that lizard serum stung!" He was laughing and shaking his head. "How's your hand?"

Tim grimaced from the pain, which rapidly diminished as the healing triad started to take effect. Opening his hand to look at his palm, Tim studied the gash.

The cut looked normal, his skin sliced in two and blood bubbling up to the surface, but then something happened. The bleeding ceased, and the cut diminished in size. Skin tissue was visibly growing and latching onto the opposite side of the cut, effectively closing the wound. When the cut was fully sealed, there was no scar and no sign of a gash having ever existed at all.

"Amazing, isn't it?" Shung said as he glanced down at Tim's hand.

Before Tim could respond, a noise emanated from somewhere near Tim's desk.

Tim and Shung looked at each other questioningly, then walked over to determine the source of the noise.

At first, they didn't see anything. Then, they did.

The mixture that Tim had flicked off his hand now lay bubbling and sizzling on the floor near the desk. The mixture contorted, bending and growing. It increased from a few drops to a small puddle, then grew upward toward the ceiling. The liquid blob formed tissue, then bone, followed by cartilage— transforming into a single distinct shape.

Shung's and Tim's eyes were wide in horror when they realized what they were witnessing. The thing was gasping and writhing on the floor, its immature limbs flailing and knocking over the chair and kicking the desk.

It lay on the floor panting and moaning, naked in its first moment in the world. A hand shot up and grabbed the top of the desk, using it as leverage to assume a standing position. When it turned around to face them, Shung turned pale and Tim screamed.

What they were looking at was an exact replica of Tim Hill.

The replica Tim stared at Shung, clearly confused. When it looked upon Tim, however, it sneered and leapt in the air toward him.

Shung backed away as he watched the two Tims wrestle on the ground. The replica Tim grabbed the picture of Sammi from atop the desk and smashed it into Tim's face, knocking him out cold. Then the replica Tim stood, panting, as it hovered over the real Tim's motionless body.

A knock on the door snapped it to attention. "Is everything okay in there?" Hanna asked from the other side.

Shung moved toward the door but stopped in his tracks when replica Tim spoke for the first time. "Wait," it wheezed, shocking Shung to his core.

Replica Tim began undressing the real Tim and then slipped into his clothing.

Shung snapped out of his fear and fled the room, leaving the two Tims alone.

The replica Tim stared down at the real Tim, whose unconscious body was completely nude except for the glasses still on his face.

The replica bent down and plucked the glasses off the real Tim's nose, before answering the door to start its new life.

* * *

Isaac stared at the real Tim. "So, none of this . . ."—he pointed to his eye, then to the swinging corpses—"was you?"

Tim looked down at his dirty feet. "Yes and no. You see, we share the same memories and thoughts and sometimes emotions. I can feel when he's angry or confused, and my thoughts are his and his are mine. The only difference is our actions."

Tim picked up a piece of bread from the ground and flicked it across the room. "The other Tim can't understand what's going on, for he is not natural. He feels emotions but can't understand what they mean, which leads him to do ridiculous things, as you well know. It's also why he keeps me alive."

"This is absolutely nuts," Isaac stammered.

"The worst things are. He visits me from time to time, asks me things. Tells me what has happened. He's like me. He inherited the innate need to help and believes his role on this earth is to save his family."

Isaac studied the real Tim, slowly starting to believe his story. "But it's not his family."

Tim's eyes sank further into his skull, his bony prominences revealing more. "The line separating what is and isn't, what can and can't, and what's his and what's mine has faded away. Maybe it is his family now."

"Would you do the things he's done?" Isaac asked, noticing that the pounding from above had ceased.

"There was a time when I thought I could." Tim looked at the bodies hanging upside down on the other side of the room. "But after seeing the things he's done to people, never." He spat on the floor in disgust. "We're both toxic, but he's the venomous one."

"And what does that make you?"

"Simply poisonous," Tim responded.

Suddenly, the cellar hatch opened and light beamed down from above. Isaac retreated to the back of the room and flipped the main light switch, shutting the overhead light tubes off, while keeping his eye glued to the open hatch.

A veiny hand shot out from above and grasped the wood, the strength of its grip causing it to crack. Isaac turned around to run, but there was nowhere to go. He backtracked diagonally until he felt the cold skin of one of the corpses hanging on the wall, which caused his hairs to stand erect. A heinous laughter filled the room as the replica Tim dropped to the cellar floor, its few strands of hair sticking up straight thanks to the maniacal energy coursing through its body. In its bear-sized hands was a shotgun, with only one intention loaded in the chamber.

Cornering its prey, the replica Tim's voice cackled with delight. "Ready or not, *HERE I COME.*"

CHAPTER 42

THE TALE OF TWO TIMS

*I*saac had to act fast, for he was staring into the jaws of despair.

After he turned the lights off, he dashed behind one of the suspended bodies, his own swaying body keeping time in order to remain hidden. When replica Tim's feet hit the cellar floor, the force detonated a circle of dust.

Both of the replica's hands were splintered and dripping with blood from beating on the shed door and had stained the shotgun's barrel a cranberry red. Its breathing was ragged and its chest heaved with every forceful breath. Spittle shot out of its mouth when it cackled in delight. The hunt was almost over for replica Tim.

Isaac held his breath, but the corpses' horrible stench was stinging his eye. Sweat started to slide down his fingertips, before dripping like the blood drops falling from the replica Tim's hands.

More footsteps from above rattled the ceiling and dislodged the dirt and dust falling on the Tims and Isaac below.

"Tim! What's down there? You're scaring us!" Hanna yelled from overhead.

Sammi's voice followed, matching her mother's in concern. "Daddy! Are you okay?"

Replica Tim raised the gun to its hip and cocked it. "I'm fine, girls. Don't come down here. Go back inside."

Chains rattled on the floor as the real Tim stood up and cupped his hands over his mouth to amplify his voice. "Hanna! Sammi! My girls, I'm down here!"

But it was too late—they had already retreated far enough away that his voice couldn't reach them.

Another set of footsteps echoed across the floor and two more feet slammed against the cellar floor. The replica turned around and pointed the gun, but when it realized that it was aiming at Twain, it moved the barrel away. "Jesus, son. Don't scare me like that!"

Twain's eyes were wide with fright at the sight of his maniacal father. He raised both hands and slowly backed away. "Dad . . . what's going on? Why do you have a gun? What is this place?" he asked. "And what's that horrid smell?"

The replica Tim pulled the gun back and faced in the opposite direction, searching for anything that would give away Isaac's presence. "Isaac is gone, son. And we need to find him before he hurts us."

Twain raised his hands in astonishment. "He's not trying to hurt us, Dad! We're the ones who hurt him!" Twain put his hands down and took a step toward his father. "Dad! Look at me! You're acting crazy again, please just look at me!"

Isaac peered out from behind the body and saw the real Tim hidden in his corner. The replica Tim turned around but didn't drop the gun. Instead, it squinted its beady eyes at Twain, as if trying to determine the right thing to say. The cellar went quiet as fake father stared at real Tim's son. Finally, the replica's wild expression disappeared. It smoothed its few ruffled hairs back over its balding head and lowered the gun.

Twain ran to the clone and they embraced, causing the replica to hold the gun with one hand instead of two.

It was now or never. Isaac slipped between the corpses and dashed over to the light switch, flipping it on and revealing the replica Tim's secrets to Twain. The flies immediately came out of hiding and buzzed around the room, their wings' vibration forming a deafening cacophony.

The replica Tim pushed Twain back and spun around to point the gun directly at Isaac. "I've got you now, you little . . . Get on your fucking knees!"

Isaac dropped to one knee, not bothering to swat the flies landing on him. With an expression of desperation, he looked directly at Twain.

But Twain wasn't looking back at Isaac; he was looking at the corpses hanging from the walls. "D— Dad. Who are they?" he asked, his voice trembling in anticipation of the answer. "Oh no . . . Is that Faith?" Twain collapsed to his knees, anguish rushing into the sacks under his eyes.

With an eye still trained on Isaac, the replica Tim responded, its voice filled with confidence. "I did it for you, son. I did this for our family."

"You're a monster!" Twain shrieked.

A fiery anger burned through the replica Tim, scorching its beady eyes. The surrounding air grew wavy as heat poured out of its skin and into the cold cellar. "Twain, who was it that saved your sister and cured her from her burns? Who was it that gave you your sight back, so you could go out into the real world and not always be stuck at home with Mommy?"

Twain's voice boomed in response to his fear. "I didn't ask for this. *They* didn't ask for any of this!" He pointed his finger at the bodies dangling by their feet. "I don't even know who you are anymore, Tim!"

The replica's facial expression changed when it heard Twain use the name it had assumed and not "Dad." It turned around to face Twain, the blood on its hands beginning to dry, and its shoulders hunched as the inner monster evaporated and left behind only a shell of a man.

And that's when the real Tim revealed himself.

"That's my son!" the real Tim screamed, stepping out of the shadows and tossing the contents of his bathroom bucket at the replica.

Urine and liquid feces soared through the air and landed on the replica Tim's face, the bile burning its eyes and causing a howl of disgust—and the gun to fire in the direction of the real Tim.

Isaac roared, his anger the fuel. Even the flies scattered when he lurched at the clone, tackling it with infernal emotion.

He clawed and scraped and bit the replica Tim until all he smelled and tasted was blood. The replica screamed and dropped the gun, the metal clanging against the dusty floor. Isaac closed his eye and ripped at anything he could touch, shoving the replica Tim on to its back.

The clone's eyes popped out of its cranium from the impact of hitting the ground. As it gasped for breath, the replica Tim felt its ribs crunch as Isaac dropped his full weight on them, splintering the organic calcium phosphate. Isaac then raised his fists and let out another bloodcurdling scream, pummeling them against the replica Tim's face. Skin ripped apart and teeth flew into the air as the brawl continued, the once-frigid cellar now a battle sauna.

After being tied down for so long, it didn't take much for Isaac's strength to dwindle. The real Tim noticed his foe weakening and shoved Isaac out of the way.

"Stop!" Twain bellowed.

The three of them stood in a triangle, the shotgun lying in the center. Isaac's eye shifted from the replica Tim to the shotgun, one final spark of hope surging through his body.

They all dived for the shotgun at once, and a musical symphony of pain and hurt orchestrated in the cellar. Then, a body fell limply to the floor.

CHAPTER 43

❖

TIM

The replica writhed on the ground, the spasms causing blood to gurgle in its mouth. The crude body bent and twitched in its fight to stay alive.

Eventually, however, death won.

The replica Tim's chest ceased its rhythmic rise and fall, and Twain tried to crawl to the clone he believed to be his father.

"Move!" Twain yelled in panic at Isaac, who was blocking his path.

Isaac didn't know how to say it; maybe there was no good way. "That's not your father, Twain."

A raspy voice echoed from the far cellar corner. "Twain, my son."

Twain stood up, confused, then trudged over to the source of the sound.

All of the lights were on and all of the secrets now revealed. The real Tim was sprawled on the floor, a steady stream of blood trickling from his chest.

"Who . . . who are you?" Twain stammered, though somewhere within himself he already knew the answer.

Tim used the last of his remaining strength to prop himself up against the wall. Grunting in pain as his efforts strained the pellet holes penetrating his stomach, he managed to say, "Come closer, my son."

Twain knelt next to his dying father and placed a hand on his cheek so as to turn Tim's head. As they faced each other, Tim's chest gave one last heave and exhaled for a final time. Blue eyes stared into blue eyes, then one pair closed forever.

Twain held his father for the first time in years and rocked back and forth.

Isaac thought it odd how both Tims were shot by the same gun in almost identical locations, but then it seemed right. One soul cannot occupy two bodies, and the war for it had torn them both apart.

Without saying a word, Twain gently released his father and stood up. He walked over to the replica

Tim and squatted down, placing his hand over the replica Tim's eyes in order to shut them eternally.

Emotions bubbled to the surface, even as Isaac tried to force them down. "Twain . . ."

"Leave," Twain said softly without turning to face Isaac.

"I'm so sorry, Twain."

Twain swung around and angry tears flooded out of his two eyes. "Leave!"

Isaac flinched from the sting of Twain's anger, but he knew it wasn't his fault. When he stood fully upright, he couldn't help but grimace at the cuts and bruises covering his body. The flesh beneath the gauze was throbbing and rattling his head, but he couldn't stop now.

Without a word, Isaac lumbered past Twain and the two Tims as he exited the cellar.

CHAPTER 44

POSTMORTEM

*R*ed and blue lights tangoed through the forest as police cars flooded the driveway, the lights then bouncing off the glass walls and pirouetting into the night sky. The lieutenant got out of his car and walked to the house's main entrance.

Upon entering the family room, his radio sprang to life: ". . . shots fired . . ." resounded as the lieutenant walked past his fellow cops and toward the kitchen.

The grass crunched under his feet as he strolled toward the commotion at the shed, where several officers held flashlights that whirred beams of light and pierced the bleak night. Yellow tape lined the perimeter of the wooden hut, stopping anyone without a badge from breaching it. A young officer stood guard, but when he approached the shed entrance, she tipped her hat.

The lieutenant scrunched his nose at the penetrating stench, which felt like it was searing the hairs in his nose. "What in God's name is that smell?" he asked.

The officer stopped when she reached the hatch leading to the cellar. "Sir, if you think this is bad, you might not want to continue farther."

"Give me the rundown," he said.

"We have several bodies, and they're . . ." The officer paused and shook her head in dismay. "They're the likes of which we have never seen before."

The lieutenant raised his eyebrows. "What do you mean?"

"Sir, you're just going to have to see for yourself," she said as she looked down at the ground.

The lieutenant placed a hand on her shoulder, trying to comfort the disturbed officer. "Hey, you're doing great. Take a deep breath."

The officer inhaled, then exhaled carbon dioxide and felt the color return to her face.

"Good, now do we have any leads?" the lieutenant asked gently.

"Well, it's strange. We have the wife in handcuffs in the back of the patrol car, but she's not in good mental shape. She keeps muttering about finding a Dr. Kevin Shung. But when we checked, we found that he left the country a couple weeks ago."

"And the kids?"

"They're being taken to a foster care home, for now. Neither will speak," the clearly concerned officer replied.

"A man who disappeared, and a whole lot of dead bodies. Can this night get any weirder?" he muttered.

The police officer paused. "That's the thing, though. It *does* get weirder. Two of the bodies are identical, but there are no records of them being twins."

The lieutenant blinked and scratched the back of his head. "I'll need to see this for myself."

The wind picked up and whistled through the shed. The lieutenant nodded, then pressed on his flashlight and descended into the abyss.

He landed softly on the ground and immediately swatted at his face to keep the flies at bay. "Dear God!" he muttered, cupping his hand over his nose to prevent breathing in any more of the horrid stench.

His eyes watered but he pursued deeper in the cellar, even as the flies tried to latch onto his eyes for a quick drink of their liquid.

The lieutenant's heart sank when the lights illuminated the corpses. More flies and insects swarmed and attached themselves to the light fixtures, dimming the cellar light.

The air was strong with the musty odors of blood and sweat. The lieutenant counted the bodies hanging from the wall: eight. Goose bumps popped up on his skin as he continued to study the dangling corpses—which somehow continued to sway in the stagnant air. He slid on his gloves and took a closer look. After pulling out his notepad, he wrote down the names etched on the vessels for later DNA matching.

More insects buzzed on the pad as he wrote, causing him to drop the notebook. When he bent down to pick it up, he noticed the disturbed dust on the floor that signaled a massive struggle. Metal pellets covered the floor like the innards of a pinata, but it was when he saw the last two bodies lying in a puddle of dried blood that his vision stalled.

He took a couple of steps toward the first body, the force from his steps causing hundreds of flies to take flight away from their feeding oasis. The smell of death was at its epitome when the lieutenant knelt down beside the corpse.

His eyes widened as he grabbed his radio to signal his findings. He flipped the on switch and static jolted out of the mouthpiece. "We have several bodies hanging from the wall, they seemed to be part of some sort of experiment. Two male bodies were found on the floor, where cause of death for both seems to be gunshot. Both males are balding and have several shotgun wounds entering the chest and exiting the midback. Signs of a struggle are present." He pulled out his handkerchief and used it to cover his nose and mouth as he observed the last body leaning against the wall in the corner.

The lieutenant gasped and his skin drained of color when he saw the person's face. He picked up his radio and reported his new findings. "Male seems to be in his late fifties and, from simple observation, looks identical to the other male body."

CHAPTER 45

―――――――◆―――――――

THE INTERROGATION

*M*akeup-filled teardrops splashed off the metal table and formed perfect residue circles. The skin under Hanna's eyes was puffy and swollen, but every time she tried to wipe away her tears, the jingle of her handcuffs served as prevention.

"What's the meaning of this? Where are my kids? Where is my husband?" Hanna shrieked as panic set in.

The unwavering officer looked directly at her. "Ma'am, please stop yelling." He pulled out an unopened manila folder and placed it in front of him.

"I'll stop yelling as soon as you give me some answers! Where is my husband? Where are Twain and Sammi?" Red sores had spread like a disease from the cuffs rubbing her skin, but Hanna ignored the rawness.

The officer sighed in response to the events of the long night now bearing down on him. "Your kids are safe, Ms. Hill, I can promise you that. The sooner you start cooperating, the sooner you can see them."

Hanna's shoulders hunched as she thought through the practicality of the situation. She was alone, something she had become accustomed to over the years. "Okay" was all she could muster in response.

The officer nodded. "Okay, then." He flipped over the manila folder and spread official-looking documents across the table. "Let's get started."

Hanna looked away from the table—away from the images of the dead that had long haunted her, but had now finally gotten the last laugh.

"Do any of these people look familiar to you?" the officer asked as he slid the photos toward Hanna.

Hanna's lip quivered as Faith, Brandy, and all of the other victims mocked her in response. "No."

The officer stared at Hanna for a moment, trying to decide the best way to circumnavigate her mental defenses. He pushed the photos closer again. "Were you aware of your husband's . . . circumstances?"

Hanna, puzzled by the question, stared into the bottom corner of the room. "What circumstances?"

"Ms. Hill, did you know about the 'other' Tim?"

Hanna's eyes darted from the corner of the room to the officer, her initial interest quickly transforming into rage. "What do you mean 'other' Tim? There is only one Tim, my beloved husband! Let me speak to him!"

"I'm sorry, Ms. Hill, but your husband is deceased."

Hanna stared in disbelief at the officer, though part of her knew what he was saying was true. She fumbled for her words and only nonsense slipped out. She put her hands on the table and gave the officer her full attention.

"Do you know the types of experiments he was conducting underneath your shed?"

Hanna looked back to the corner of the room, where in its void she found safety. "It's not my shed."

The officer rolled his eyes, agitated at her uncooperative attitude. "Do you know what he did to the victims in these photos?"

Hanna dived into the contents her mind, searching for an answer that would get her out of this mess, but she found nothing. "No."

With narrowed eyes, the officer pushed on. "Are you sure, Ms. Hill? Are you positive you have no idea what your husband was doing?"

"I'm positive."

"Okay, then." The officer stuck his hand into the manila folder and pulled out a final photograph. "This was recently—and anonymously—emailed to us. I think you should take a look." He slid the photo toward Hanna.

Hanna glanced down and felt her heart stop, for she was looking at the photo of herself, Tim, and the two kids. In it, Tim, prematurely balding, was leaning against his golf club. Sammi's hair was still her natural red, and she had horrible scars tracing her lower body.

"Ms. Hill, explain how your daughter went from this"—the officer touched the photo that lay before her—"to this." He pulled out another photo of Sammi, taken just after the previous night's events.

Hanna glowered at the officer, her hate for him sizzling to the surface only to once again be doused by her handcuffs. "I want to speak to my lawyer."

EPILOGUE

*T*wain sat in the front seat of the police car, relieved that the flashing lights were finally turned off. "Where are you taking me?" he asked the officer driving.

"I have to take you to a foster home until all this gets resolved," the gloomy officer replied.

"Where's my sister?"

"Don't worry, she's in the car behind us. We're taking you both to the same place. You'll see her soon."

Twain adjusted the AC vent, angling the cold air away from him. "When can I talk to my mom?"

"Soon. She just needs to answer a few questions back at the station, then y'all can be together again."

Twain sat in silence for the rest of the ride, as thoughts of what he'd witnessed in his father's cellar festered in his mind. He rolled down the window, hoping the fresh air would dissipate the image of his dirty, malnourished father. And of course, the man he had believed was his father: the monster.

The next thing Twain's mind flickered to was Isaac, picturing a one-eyed Isaac sprinting through the woods at the base of the Rocky Mountains. *I hope he's okay*, Twain thought. *At least he has my patch.*

The police car finally stopped in front of an old Victorian-style home. Twain shut the car door behind him and stood in front of the house, which was daunting at this time of night. Of course, it also occurred to Twain that it was the terrible events from earlier that were casting shadows on the house.

"Twain!"

Sammi ran across the yard and hugged her brother with all her might, tears leaking from her eyes. "What's going on? Where are Mom and Dad?"

Twain realized that no one had told his sister what happened. Maybe it was for the best. He thought about telling her about the two Tims but decided to wait for another day—one less gruesome and traumatic. Twain wrapped his arms around his sister, remorse hitting and the shock subsiding.

"I'm not sure. They aren't telling me anything," he replied. It wasn't exactly a lie, but it also wasn't the entire truth: probably something he had learned from the replica Tim, he guessed.

The officers escorted Sammi and Twain inside the home and showed them to their rooms, making sure the kids were accounted for before they left.

Sammi eyed her room with suspicion. "I wish we were back home with Mom and Dad."

"I know," Twain responded. "Me too."

Sammi hugged her brother and shut the door. "I'll see you tomorrow."

Twain walked across the hall to his own room, before passing it for the bathroom.

He closed the bathroom door behind him and flipped on the light. After turning on the water faucet and taking off his glasses, he washed the dirt and confusion from his face. When the brown water droplets stopped dripping into the white sink, he patted his face dry with the hand towel.

Twain looked in the mirror. Although his reflection gazed back at him, thoughts of his family, Isaac, and Shung raced through his mind. The sudden urge to correct his father's mistakes jolted him. *Where are you, Shung*, he asked his reflection, which only returned his stare.

Twain put his glasses back on and watched his appearance in the glass. In the mirror, he saw a boy who had been forced to grow up too quickly. His blue eyes flashed while he observed himself.

When his reflection winked, a wicked grin spread across Twain's face.

Made in the USA
Coppell, TX
23 October 2020